BETTER THE BLOOD

MICHAEL BENNETT

**SIMON &
SCHUSTER**

London · New York · Sydney · Toronto · New Delhi

First published in Great Britain by Simon & Schuster UK Ltd, 2022

This paperback edition published in 2023

Copyright © Michael Bennett, 2022

Story and characters developed by Michael Bennett and Jane Holland
'Brown and Screaming' lyrics by Matariki Star Holland Bennett © 2021
Original Māori illustration by Māhina Rose Holland Bennett

Supported by Creative New Zealand.

ARTS COUNCIL
NEW ZEALAND TOI AOTEAROA
creative nz

The right of Michael Bennett to be identified as author
of this work has been asserted in accordance with the
Copyright, Designs and Patents Act, 1988.

1 3 5 7 9 10 8 6 4 2

Simon & Schuster UK Ltd
1st Floor
222 Gray's Inn Road
London WC1X 8HB

Simon & Schuster Australia, Sydney
Simon & Schuster India, New Delhi

www.simonandschuster.co.uk
www.simonandschuster.com.au
www.simonandschuster.co.in

A CIP catalogue record for this book is available from the British Library

Paperback ISBN: 978-1-3985-1224-5
eBook ISBN: 978-1-3985-1223-8
Audio ISBN: 978-1-3985-1506-2

Typeset in the UK by M Rules
Printed and Bound in the UK using 100% Renewable
Electricity at CPI Group (UK) Ltd

MIX
Paper | Supporting
responsible forestry
FSC
www.fsc.org   FSC® C171272

For Jane, Tīhema, Māhina and
Matariki. Arohanui always.

Kia whakatōmuri te haere whakamua

*I walk backwards into the future
with my eyes fixed on my past*

Māori whakataukī (proverb)

1

A SMUDGE ON THE PAGE OF HISTORY

5 October 1863.

His hands move quickly as he polishes the sheet of silver-plated copper to a perfect mirror finish. He is well practised at this. On a good day, say on a day where he has been engaged to create portraits of a number of members of a wealthy London merchant family, he could easily craft thirty daguerreotypes, perhaps more. In this godforsaken place on the other side of the world, though, it is far more difficult. Engaged by the Queen's army to make permanent records of the colonial campaign, he finds himself again and again practising his art in the field where he has no permanent studio, no light-safe room where he can prepare the materials.

It is a challenge. To say the least. But he prides himself on his professionalism.

Under cover of a black cloth, the daguerreotypist places

the highly polished plate in a sensitizing box containing iodine crystals. He waits patiently for the fumes to react with the silver.

Others there are not so patient.

'We haven't got all day for this,' says the captain of the troop. 'Hurry up, man.'

The captain is quite drunk and has been so for hours, ever since his men successfully apprehended the captive. If truth be told, he is inebriated far more often than he is sober, a fact his men know well, attested to by the ongoing lack of rum in their evening rations, and while none would dare make a complaint about the situation, the captain's appetite for the bottle has made him no friends amongst his subordinates.

Under the black cloth, the daguerreotypist quietly counts the seconds for the chemical reaction to take hold sufficiently. Twenty-five elderflower, twenty-six elderflower ...

'What are you up to under that damn sheet?' the captain demands, impatient to get back to his tent. His bottle is only half finished and there's little left of the day.

In the darkness under the sheet, the daguerreotypist sighs. Thirty-five elderflower, thirty-six elderflower ... For a while, he entertained grander plans for his life. He once had dreams of studying at the Royal Academy Schools, imagining a life as a painter who might reinvigorate and modernize the Flemish style for an adoring British art world. But as the son of a long line of blacksmiths, there was scant hope of either being accepted into the Academy Schools, or being able to afford the extraordinary tuition fees. Faced with the horror of carrying on the family trade of horseshoes and iron gates, he settled instead on this new art form, the imprinting of the light spectrum onto silver plates. Preserving frozen images of life not in oil or watercolour but in copper and mercury and silver. A way for him to make a shilling while using his considerable skills in the play of light on the landscape or on the human form.

It's not painting. But it will do. Forty-five elderflower.

He emerges from the black cloth. 'About fucking time,' says the captain.

The daguerreotypist goes amongst the soldiers, carefully moving and repositioning each of them to most advantageously address the stark New Zealand light as it falls through the branches of the towering tree they stand beneath. 'This is modern-day alchemy,' he enthuses, aware that for those unfamiliar with this new technology, the process of creating a daguerreotype can be disarming. 'A little piece of magic. Your images are captured for all time; this moment will remain long after your bones are dust.'

'Get a move on,' slurs the captain. 'I need a shit.'

'Rum does that to a man's bowels,' one of the soldiers says, being sure it is not loud enough for the captain to hear.

The daguerreotypist returns to his box apparatus, irritated by the captain's drunken disregard for his art. 'This is called the lens,' he explains, indicating the small protrusion that emerges from the middle of the wooden box. 'When I remove the cap, you must stay perfectly still. *Perfectly* still. The slightest movement and you will be but a smudge on the page of history.'

Apart from the captain's rum breath and flushed face, the soldiers have approached this process with gravity, polishing their uniform buttons, cleaning their tall dress boots to a shine.

'How are we meant to look?' one of them asks. 'Do we smile?'

'Was Christ smiling in *The Last Supper*?' snaps the daguerreotypist.

'He was about to have bloody great nails hammered through his hands,' the youngest soldier points out. 'No wonder he wasn't bloody smiling.'

Ignoring the laughter, the daguerreotypist perseveres. 'Did Michelangelo carve a fool's grin onto David's face? Smiling makes a man an idiot,' he insists. 'Smiling is for simpletons. Don't smile.'

He positions himself by the lens.

'Ready,' he warns. 'Quite still, please. And ... *hold*.' He removes the cap.

Instantly the exposed image ricochets between a series of mirrors within the body of the wooden box, the light finally falling upside down against the polished silver plate. The photochemical reaction begins to capture the moment.

The six members of the troop, the inebriated captain and his five men, are gathered under a towering pūriri tree on the crest of a volcanic cone overlooking Auckland harbour. As the reaction develops, it is plain that, despite not attending the Royal Academy Schools, the daguerreotypist has an instinctive grasp of the rule of thirds. The image has a sense of proportion that is almost classical.

Below the tree, the six soldiers face the lens in an aesthetically pleasing curving semicircle. Suspended above them, a few yards over their heads, secured to one of the lower branches of the great tree by a length of twelve-strand British Army rope noosed tight around his throat, a seventh person forms the apex of this carefully considered composition.

The dead man is naked, the captive stripped and humiliated before he was executed, retribution for having evaded the pursuing troop for a quite embarrassingly long period. As well as the rope around his neck, his hands are tied in front of his torso, his feet bound at the ankle. The man is Māori, and the tā moko* tattooed on his face and body show the markings of a high-born leader. He is silver-haired, in his fifties, and the swirls and lines gouged deep into his skin tell a tale of his lineage, his status, the knowledge he carries, the whakapapa† passed down to him across generations.

A rangatira, a chief of great stature.

'How much longer?' the captain slurs.

'Do not speak,' the daguerreotypist barks. 'You will be a smudge on the page of history!'

After the necessary sixty seconds, the cap goes back on the lens.

---

* Tā moko – traditional form of Māori tattooing, signifying status or social standing
† Whakapapa – genealogy, line of descent

2

HANA

One hundred and sixty years later.

Hana's hands are in the earth. Where she likes them to be. The soil in her garden is ridiculously fertile. Auckland is the first major city built on an active volcanic field since Pompeii, and millennia of violent eruptions have left the gardens of the central suburbs productive and lush. The downside is that a new fissure may form any day without warning; whole neighbourhoods could disappear in hours under an onslaught of lava and ash. Hasn't happened for a thousand years, but for a pessimist that's more a reason for worry than assurance. The upside is that inner-city Auckland is a really good place to grow things.

The back yard is an oasis, a retreat to a simpler world than the one Hana walks in every day. Not so much garden as mini rainforest. Cabbage trees, flax, a repurposed goldfish pond bursting with water lilies and cress. There's a native palm, a towering seven-metre nikau near the edge of the property that the neighbours on that side periodically leave pissed-off messages about, notes that Hana reads, folds up and tosses in the wheelie bin. The nikau is eighty years old, probably more. It's been resident longer than anyone in this suburb. No way is Hana trimming it or cutting it down just because the recently arrived accountants or architects or whoever they are want a better view.

There's a buzzing from her phone, in the pocket of the old jeans she wears to garden. She ignores it, instead stands, stretches, wipes her hands on her jeans.

Hana's eyes are dark, a shade so deep that in some lights it's hard to know if they are brown or black. The smudges of soil left behind are almost as dark as her eyes. Almost. A creeper vine has tangled its way through the branches of a flourishing stand of kawakawa.* She'll need to deal with that. She breaks off a kawakawa leaf, one with lots of holes in it. She remembers in the village she grew up in, far from Auckland, an elder from her tribe taking a group of young kids into the bush, teaching them about the plants of the forest. 'The caterpillars know which leaves have the most goodness,' the elder said, in te reo Māori.†

That was a long time ago.

A lifetime ago.

Hana bites the leaf she's found, the one shot through with caterpillar holes. The leaf has a familiar peppery

---

* Kawakawa – small native New Zealand tree, the leaves used traditionally and today for medicinal purposes
† Te reo Māori – the Māori language, also referred to more simply as 'te reo'

tang. It's good. Really good. She chews as she reaches into her pocket and retrieves the phone. She opens the new text.

Have you found the papers?

She looks at the words. Hana is a problem-solver, someone who faces the most difficult issue head-on and without hesitation. But this question she doesn't want to answer. She puts the phone back in her pocket.

At the back door, Hana kicks off her muddy shoes.

Her home is utilitarian. Stripped-back and minimalist, the opposite of her jungle-like garden, a place for a woman in her late thirties living happily alone, a woman who values space and order. Upstairs, the spare room is set up as a studio. It's full of light, and it's the one room in the house that's full of stuff. Rolled-up canvases on the floor. Boxes of paints and pencils.

On the walls, pencil sketches. The drawings are accomplished. Careful, precise, skilled. A series of images of a girl, tracking her progress from very young child to a teenager. In the earlier pictures, when the girl is a baby, there are some group sketches – a woman, a man, the child. Then as she becomes a toddler and older, something changes. The images now are just of the girl, or the girl and her mother.

In her room downstairs, Hana retrieves a box from under the bed. She digs through a pile of bills and takes out a legal document from the bottom.

Application for Order Dissolving a Marriage or Civil Union.

She holds the document for a long moment. Then she puts it back under the electricity bills and slides the box back beneath her bed.

There's a particular spot Hana tries to sit in during a trial. The defendant's family and friends always take the seats closest to the defendant's box. Not the most comfortable place for a cop, especially the arresting officer in charge of the investigation. But there's a sweet place, a few metres distant from the supporters of the accused, where you can see the defendant's face in profile – it's surprising how much you can read from the angle of the jaw, the tilt of the head, whether the eyes rise or stay fixed to the floor – at the same time as being able to watch the defence lawyers and the judge.

'Saved you the good seat, D Senior,' Stan says, as Hana takes her place next to him. Hana has all the time in the world for the gangly and often awkward detective constable. Stan graduated top of his cohort, but Hana is far more impressed that he knows police college isn't the real world and marks on a grade sheet are worth less than nothing. He's smart, a fast learner who actually wants to learn.

The defendant hasn't been called to the dock yet, but his family are already seated. Like Hana, they're waiting, the ridiculously expensive QC they've employed talking with them quietly. The door of the public gallery opens and a large group enters, quiet and respectful. A young woman, Ria, accompanied by her parents, a middle-aged man and woman, all of them Māori. A dozen or so members of their extended family are there in support. Hana smiles warmly at Ria and her parents as they sit on the opposite side to the defendant's family. For these three, the complainant and her mother and father, the worst is over and Hana is glad. At the trial, the mother and father watched their daughter give evidence, the young woman bravely refusing the chance to testify by video link, determined that the defendant should see her face as she told the court what he did to her.

Hana assured the parents that it would be hard. It would be awful for Ria. 'But it will make a difference.' And it did.

On the stand, Ria was composed. Strong. She told the jury how she responded to the young man's profile on a dating site, having a good feeling with the back-and-forth messages. He was final year at law school, a representative rugby player, but he didn't seem arrogant or a dick; he could laugh at himself. She met him at the bar in a fancy hotel, what seemed a safe meeting place. Straight away, she knew she'd made a mistake. The greeting air kiss on the cheek that became an unwelcome real kiss on the lips. He sat beside her, right by her, leg to leg. No sense of personal space. A certain smile on his face that felt less like warmth, more like entitlement. The young woman told the jury she felt like because she swiped right, in his mind there was no question sex was going to happen. But no matter how uncomfortable she felt, and she felt uncomfortable, she has a rule: even if there's zero chemistry, you have a polite drink. Etiquette. 'Guys have feelings too,' she told the court. 'Least you can do is have one drink. Just a drink.'

One drink was enough. The blood tests later showed the presence of a fast-acting sedative that had made its way into her mojito. It was like an out-of-body experience, she said, it came on fast; she tried to go to the bathroom, but she was struggling to stand. The law student helped her to the elevator, promising he'd take her down to the lobby, order her an Uber, get her to hospital. But when the elevator doors closed, he didn't hit the down button. He hit up. Up to the room he'd booked in readiness. By the time the elevator door opened again, she couldn't talk. She could barely walk. He was a good thirty kilograms heavier than her, the big-boned muscles of a blindside flanker; he didn't break a sweat as he carried her from the elevator to his room. If she'd been able to scratch or punch, it would have made no difference. By the time they reached the door of the room, and he swiped his access card with that same smile on his face, she couldn't even lift her arm to try . . .

Hana had watched Ria's mother and father listening in silence during the trial. Restrained, dignified. The only glimpse of what they were feeling in the tightness with which they clasped each other's hands. She wondered, if she had been in the same position – if it was her daughter on the stand, if it was Addison giving evidence, telling a room of strangers about how she had been drugged, humiliated, raped – would she be as calm? As dignified as these two? Could she each morning come to a courtroom

11

and nod politely to the blood kin of the man who had done these things, as Ria's mother and father did, every day of the trial?

That was two months before. It took the jury three quarters of an hour to return a guilty verdict. For Ria and her whānau,* the worst of it is done. Now it's the formality, the full stop. The vindication of formal sentencing.

A stirring in the courtroom; various court officials ready themselves, the QC representing the law student takes his position, the crown prosecutor acknowledges Hana. Hana feels a buzzing in her pocket, an incoming email. There's still no sign of the judge, so she takes the opportunity to check her phone. She opens the email, noticing that the sent-by address is just a series of numbers, an anonymous address. And there's no message in the body of the email. But there's a video attached.

She toggles her phone volume to silent. She opens the video.

On her phone screen, video footage plays. It's hand-held, unprofessional, shot at night, one continuous shot of a derelict apartment building that Hana is familiar with, long-since condemned, taken over in recent years by the homeless and addicted. The locals ironically refer to the place as the Palace. She watches as the image zooms in slowly on the decaying building, finally settling on one particular flat, the last flat on the second level.

'All rise,' the court registrar suddenly says. Hana pauses the video.

---

* Whānau – extended family

The judge enters. The defendant is called; he takes his seat, acknowledging the supportive smiles of his family. For a moment he turns and looks straight at Hana. There's a coldness in his eyes she has seen before. The same coldness as when she came to his family home to arrest him. It's not pleasant. But Hana is well used to not pleasant, and she's certainly not letting this guy intimidate her.

Finally the law student turns back towards the judge.

Hana glances again at the strange, stilled image on the video. The Palace. She pockets her phone. She'll deal with whatever it is later.

'Patrick Jonathan Thompson, the jury found you guilty of sexual assault,' says the judge. 'Stupefaction. Your actions are a cowardly and heinous betrayal of a young woman and her right to engage in a simple social interaction without fear.'

As the judge speaks, Hana notices again how so many of the occupants of a courtroom seem pressed from the same cookie cutter. With police, it's different. All shades and sizes make their way into the cops, for their own reasons, washing up from all kinds of backgrounds. Like Hana and Stan, sitting here on this bench – Hana, Māori, late thirties, originally from ten kilometres south of nowhere, who came to the big city when her small town started to feel just too small. Stan, mid twenties, freckled blonde and blue-eyed, from a determinedly middle-class big-city family. But the QC and the judge are mirror images, both silver-haired, both cut from the same cloth. From legal dynasties, carrying on the family tradition, looking like they not only went to the same law school, they probably went to the same kindergarten.

'This court condemns your actions, Mr Thompson,' says the judge, 'in the strongest possible terms. However . . .'

Hana stiffens. However? Until that word, this was an entirely expected preamble. 'However' shifts things in a way she can't fathom. It's an open-and-shut case, date rape where the offender used a powerful drug to subdue the victim before he sexually violated her – how is there a 'however'?

'However,' the judge continues, 'in sentencing you, this court takes into account various submissions presented by your counsel. We note the compelling commendations from your law school professors. The great promise for your future career in the legal fraternity. Your considerable prospects as a national representative rugby player.'

Hana can feel to one side the victim's mother and father, their bewilderment, *where is this going?* To the other side, a confident smile growing on the law student's face. 'You're fucking kidding me,' Stan says under his breath.

'I am persuaded it would be manifestly unjust to impose a period of incarceration that would most certainly destroy both your legal and your sporting careers,' the judge says. 'You are sentenced to twelve months home detention, with permanent name suppression in all forms of media.'

Hana watches as the student's family celebrate.

Thompson's father takes his son in his arms, a bear hug. And she sees something else.

For a moment, Thompson's mother looks towards the victim and her family; her eyes meet Ria's eyes, registering the younger woman's confusion, her bewilderment, the sentencing a whole new pain and trauma to add to what has gone before. She looks at Ria for a long moment, with what seems to be something like an apology in her eyes.

Then she turns away and embraces her son.

The crown prosecutor comes to Hana in the gallery. 'This isn't happening.'

But it is. It has.

Afterwards, the crown prosecutor and Hana take Ria and her family to a conference room within the court building, the prosecutor doing her best to console them, telling them she will appeal the ridiculous leniency of the sentence, she won't let this go. As they have throughout a legal process they can take no active part in, but which has had such a profound effect on their lives, the mother and father sit in silence, Ria's mother holding her daughter's hand, some of the family around them crying quietly. The muffins and take-away coffees that Stan had fetched sit untouched on the table.

Hana says, quietly, 'It's wrong. So wrong. I can't believe it.'

Looks pass between the family members. Ria's mother turns to Hana. 'If it was the other way around,' she says. 'If it was a Māori man who did this, not some privileged rich white kid. If the victim was a Pākehā* girl. You think that scumbag would be going home? *I* believe it. My daughter, she's been raped a second time.'

Hana stays silent. There are no words that can help this family deal with the injustice of what just happened. Ria's mother stands, her family gathering around her. 'People like us, we get through.' She straightens her cardigan. Holding her dignity. She takes her daughter by the arm, leading her from the room.

At the door, Ria turns to look at Hana.

'You said it would make a difference,' she says.

Hana walks through the underground car park that adjoins the high court, towards where they left their car, as Stan waits patiently in line to validate the parking ticket. It's a few hours later, but Hana's disbelief at the verdict hasn't faded. The car park is all concrete walls and floors and pillars, Hana's steps echo off the cold, hard surfaces. As she walks, she becomes aware of another set of footsteps. Then a figure steps out from between two vehicles.

'Detective Senior Sergeant Westerman.'

It's Patrick Thompson. The law student.

Hana glances across the intervening rows of parked cars. Under a pool of cold white fluorescent light, Stan has reached the front of the queue, slipping the ticket into the

---

* Pākehā – New Zealander of European descent

machine. He is completely unaware of what is happening on the far side of the car park.

She turns to face Thompson. 'What do you want?'

He smiles. A smile Hana knows well now, the smile Ria described as he carried her to the hotel room, the smile Hana saw in the defendant's box as Thompson listened to the verdict. A bitter acid taste comes to her mouth.

'Just thought you should know,' says Thompson, 'she enjoyed herself. She fucking loved every moment.'

Hana would love to lash out. She doesn't. 'Stay away from me, Mr Thompson.' With an effort of will, she continues towards the car. But he follows her.

'I've seen your daughter,' he tells her. 'I follow her on Instagram, the hot rapper chick.'

With the mention of Addison, Hana stops.

On the far side of the car park, Stan retrieves the validated ticket. He checks his pockets for his keys, still completely unaware that anything is amiss. Thompson stops beside a concrete pillar, facing Hana. 'Might DM her some time,' he taunts. 'Looks like she could be my type.'

The bitter taste in Hana's mouth is nearing unbearable, and before she knows what she's doing, her hand balls into a fist around the guy's shirt, and she shoves him hard against the pillar. 'You piece of shit.' Catching herself, she lets him go, though she'd sorely love to do more. 'Stay away from my daughter, stay away from me.'

Thompson smiles again. 'You wanted to send me to prison. You tried to fuck up my life. Guess what? I'm gonna fuck up yours.'

Before Hana knows what's happening, *slam*, Thompson

smashes his face into the pillar. Blood pours from his nose. The sound of approaching footsteps. Stan comes from around a row of parked cars and sees the law student, blood now covering the front of his shirt.

'She's fucking crazy, man,' says Thompson to Stan. 'She's out of control. She should be fucking arrested.'

The unmarked police car drives away from the car park. Stan didn't see what happened. He believes what Hana told him, of course, without question. But he didn't witness it with his own eyes. Hana knows it's her word against Thompson's. Just how he wanted it.

Her hand is still shaky as she looks at her phone. The stilled video that was anonymously sent to her is still there. She looks for a moment at the strange image of the dilapidated doss house, the Palace. Then she closes the video.

As Stan drives, Hana looks out at the passing streets. Wondering about the ways this mess with the law student could play out.

None of the scenarios are great.

3

BROWN AND SCREAMING

An international flight takes off from the airport in Māngere, the jet roar reverberating across south Auckland, the residents in the suburbs below so accustomed to the huge planes lumbering skywards that the sound doesn't even register. The south side of Auckland has its own unique flavour, a stir-fry of races and religions, the kind of place where you get on a train or a bus and hear five different languages from five different continents. Newly arrived refugees welcomed from trouble zones around the world; Pasifika families who moved from the islands of Tonga or Sāmoa or Niue and are now fourth- or fifth-generation New Zealanders; immigrants from the subcontinent and beyond; and the other kind of migrants, wannabe-home-buyer Aucklanders shut out by rocketing house prices in other suburbs who come in search of a first home in the vibrant, colourful south of the city.

Tonight, in one particular cul-de-sac, the jet engines compete with another sound. Amplified music. A driving bass line. Excited voices. Turntables scratching. One voice rises above everything else.

'Fighting's in my blood / Called the minority / Saying we're half of everything / You don't know us / We're more than both!'

At the end of the cul-de-sac there's a house with a big back yard. The yard is a writhing sea of tattoos and piercings and joints and pills; fires burn in drums, strings of coloured lights hang above. The back deck of the house has been converted into a makeshift stage with strobe lighting. A stack of amplifiers tremble with each booming bass beat, a pair of DJs compete on twin turntables.

A young woman is the ground zero of everything. With good reason. She's seventeen years old, brown and proud; she's alive with energy and joy, a perpetual motion machine. She doesn't move, she bounces, part gazelle, part bungee, part high-tension springs. She raps, a flaming song about identity and individuality, a polished and distinctive style, segueing effortlessly from English to te reo Māori and back.

'We were born brown and screaming / Won't survive in silence! / Te hā o ngā tūpuna / The breath of our ancestors / Anei mātou! / Here we are!'

Her voice is achingly beautiful, weaving smart, angry lines about equality and standing up for who you are, whoever you are, whatever your gender or your sexuality or your race. Addison has the same dark eyes as her mother. In the sketches on the walls of Hana's studio, her hair is long, black and wild, but here on stage under the strobing lights, her clean-shaven head shines like a glorious full moon.

She soars with the chorus of the song. '*Who got the power to fight the power?*'

The crowd sings back at her. '*I got the power to fight the power!*'

Addison beams. '*Who got the body to rock the party?*'

The crowd mimics her every move. '*I got the body to rock the party!*'

Capturing it all on video is PLUS 1, Addison's age, gender non-binary, long dreadlocks wound up in a crazy wild beehive over khaki and camo pants and boots and bling. On the screen of PLUS 1's phone, Addison is beatific, her smile brighter than the lights illuminating her performance.

At the other end of the cul-de-sac, there's another gathering. It's not in the least joyous. A dozen men and women in police uniform, adjusting their forage caps, pulling on hi-vis reflector vests. Containers of pepper spray are distributed, tasers readied. Two team policing vans block the end of the cul-de-sac, responding to a call from a neighbour who thought a visit from the cops was the best chance she'd have of watching telly that evening without the inconvenience of loud music. To make sure the authorities responded in a timely manner (as in, before the late-evening news), the neighbour used considerable poetic licence. 'I heard windows being smashed,' she told the 111 operator. 'Swearing, offensive

21

MICHAEL BENNETT

behaviour. Bottles being thrown.' She was very worried.
A riot waiting to explode. Her call had the hoped-for
result. The officers fan out to form a skirmish line, each
figure an arm-length from the next.

In the back yard, there are no bottles being thrown,
no windows being smashed. Nothing remotely resem-
bling a riot. Just Addison, young and transcendent, and
the audience swaying with her, in love with Addison,
in love with each other, in love with love. She takes the
phone from PLUS 1's hands and kisses her best friend.
'Love you, PLUS 1.' The crowd cheers, but then PLUS 1
glimpses something, out on the street.

The skirmish line advances in unison down the cul-de-
sac, headed for the house, the sergeant at the rear calling
time, move-move-move.

PLUS 1 snatches the microphone from Addison,
screaming, '*Pigs!*'

Without a moment's thought, PLUS 1 grabs a mic
stand, jumps the fence out onto the street. Facing off
against the approaching cops, swinging the mic stand
like a taiaha.* Meanwhile, in the back yard, mayhem.
Some partygoers run off through neighbouring gardens,
tossing away plastic bags of pills and weed as they go.
But others charge onto the street to join PLUS 1, fuelled
by outrage and adrenaline and other miscellaneous
chemicals. The line of police officers closes on them.

Move-move-move.

Addison watches. Alone on stage now. Dismayed. The

* Taiaha – wooden spear, usually carved

joyful celebration about to turn into something very different. Knowing she can't do anything to stop it.

Central Police Station is twelve storeys high, an unattractive and unspectacular grey concrete building in the middle of downtown Auckland. The interview rooms are buried in the floors well below street level. The rooms are claustrophobic and uncomfortable. Which pretty accurately describes how Addison is feeling right now.

'What? We're just gonna sit here?' she says.

On the opposite side of the table, Hana has a printed copy of Addison's offence report in her hands. Next to Addison is Jaye Hamilton. Early forties, warm blue eyes, no airs and graces despite being one of the most senior cops in the Tāmaki Makaurau* policing region, a detective inspector. But that's not the reason he's in this interview room.

Jaye is Hana's boss. He's also her ex. And he's Addison's dad.

Beside Jaye is Marissa, his partner of several years. Clear-eyed and earnest, Marissa is itching to step in and offer succour to Addison. She's a born care-giver and comforter of birds with broken wings. Literally. She's a veterinarian. But she manages to stay quiet. Addison, after all, is Hana and Jaye's daughter, not hers.

The heavy silence in the room makes Addison want

---

* Tāmaki Makaurau – Auckland

to turn the table upside down. 'You can't put me in the naughty chair and ignore me,' she complains, in a tone of voice not unlike a child put in a naughty chair and ignored. Maddeningly, still no response. At last she can bear it no longer. 'We weren't breaking any laws,' she says, talking fast, trying to brush off what's happened. 'I mean, this is exactly what I sing about on stage! It's not a crime to have a nose ring or be brown. To be queer or Māori or non-binary or whatever. But they treat us like we're kicking in shop windows and stealing TVs! PLUS 1, they got tasered, whacked in the face when they were dragged into the van. Might've broke a cheekbone.'

Hana watches her daughter, observing the steady build of momentum, a sled picking up velocity as it careens downhill.

'That's who should be arrested,' Addison continues. 'Those bastards, the racist fucking homophobic pigs—'

'Addison, that's enough,' Jaye snaps. It takes a lot for Jaye to talk like this to his daughter. She's gone too far, Addison knows, feeling the skin on her throat burning in a way she wishes was far less visible. Meanwhile, Hana sits opposite in complete silence, straightening the creases of the offence report.

Jaye has Marissa on one side, Hana across the table. He measures his words with tightrope-walking care. 'No permit for a public performance. Disorderly behaviour. Resisting arrest. A chemist shop worth of pills found thrown away around the neighbourhood. Your friend, PLUS 1? She ... uh ... he—'

'They,' Addison corrects impatiently.

'*They*.' Jaye nods. 'They attacked the police with an offensive weapon.'

'It was my mic stand!'

'Was he using it to sing?'

'Jesus, Dad! THEY!'

Hana still hasn't spoken. More than anything in this awful confrontation, it is her mother not confronting her that is freaking Addison out.

'You absolutely broke the law,' Jaye tells his daughter. 'You broke so many laws.'

'Of course you stick up for the cops,' Addison complains.

'We *are* the cops.'

'Exactly! Both of you! You're part of the whole fucked-up system!' Addison gets to her feet. Deciding to fight fire with fire, she grabs the offence report from her mother's hands, waving it to emphasize her words, as if they need emphasizing. 'I mean, no surprises with you, Dad, you're white, you're a man! You got it made. They even made you Mum's boss! But Mum. Jesus! A brown woman. How do you look in the fucking mirror—'

'Okay.'

Two syllables. Quiet. Emotionless. But the effect of Hana at last speaking is a bomb exploding. Marissa's eyes dart. Jaye blinks. Addison swallows.

Hana holds out her hand for the offence report. Addison meekly gives it back. 'Sit down, please,' Hana says, and despite the politeness of *please*, it's not a request. Addison sits; tears spring to her eyes. She has no idea what's coming, no one does. Hana walks to her daughter's side of the table. And ...

She leans down and kisses Addison on the forehead, she holds her daughter's head to her breast. Addison immediately dissolves into silent tears, clinging to her mother.

Marissa puts her hand gently on Addison's. 'Addy, sweetheart, it's going to be all right—'

'Oh, fuck off, Marissa.' Addison swats Marissa's hand away. 'I fucking hate being called Addy. Can't you just go fix a rabbit or something.'

As Marissa struggles determinedly not to take this personally, Hana looks towards her ex-husband. 'Can we talk outside, please? Alone.'

'Is this a surprise to you?' Hana asks. 'Or to Marissa? Any of this?'

A stark white bulb burns above the staff entrance to Central Police Station. Hana and Jaye are alone in the empty doorway. Fifty metres away, waiting for Hana in the car, Stan can see the excruciating body language between the two.

'Because,' she continues, 'it's no surprise to me.'

Jaye knows exactly what Hana is saying. Addison is in first year at university, studying music and politics, her competing passions. At seventeen, she is young to be in tertiary education, but in Addison's heart and in her mind she'd long since moved on from high school, well before she walked out the front gates the final time. She had always moved fluidly between the houses of her two parents, but when she started university, she shifted into Marissa and Jaye's place full-time. It made sense; their house is in one of the leafy, well-heeled suburbs, much closer to the university campus. Marissa has Vita and Sammie, two pre-teen daughters by her first marriage, but there was lots of room and Addison took over the granny flat out the back.

But her motivations to move in with Jaye weren't just geographic.

When she was a baby, when she woke in the night, an exhausted Hana would tell Jaye, 'Put her in her cot, let her cry a bit, she'll go to sleep.' Jaye would smile and nod, yes, absolutely. Then, as Hana slept, he'd walk around the flat for the next few hours with Addison in his arms, doting on his baby girl, pulling dopey faces to make her laugh, holding her up to the big windows in their lounge to gurgle at the flickering lights of the city. As a senior cop responsible for one of the largest and busiest investigative units in the New Zealand police, Jaye is uncompromising, someone with a reputation for being utterly fair and utterly intolerant of any bullshit.

But with his daughter, he is a hopeless pushover.

Addison got her first tattoo the last year of high school. A schoolmate did it, her take on a female Māori figure, a wahine toa, a warrior woman. The idea was kind of perfect, a symbol for Addison's fierce spirit, but the execution was decidedly imperfect. Addison made sure she showed Jaye the tattoo first, explaining what it meant to her, getting him onside before she plucked up the courage to show

27

Hana. Her mother exploded at the sight. 'You're sixteen, you're not even legally allowed to go to a professional tattooist.' Jaye said that in point of fact, the schoolmate wasn't actually a professional, but was planning to do a tattoo apprenticeship after school. Hana couldn't understand. 'Why would you get your body permanently engraved by someone who doesn't even know what they're doing?' For Addison it was simple. 'My body, my mind, my choices.' To Hana's frustration, Jaye pointed out that that was exactly what they'd brought their daughter up to believe. 'Isn't it?'

Not many ways for Hana to argue against that. Because it was true. She wanted her daughter to be a woman in control of her own destiny, her own life. She would just really like it if Addison's choices were a lot better than this slightly lopsided tattoo.

Jaye and Marissa would much rather Addison had a joint with her friends in the granny flat than outside some back-alley tinny house. If she was going to hook up, better she felt comfortable enough to do it in a safe place rather than unprotected sex in the back seat of some car. For Addison, being able to say her dad's place was walking distance to university made things simple. But just as she was long overdue for getting rid of the itchy rigidity of her high school uniform, she was also ready to fly in many many other ways.

Living in the granny flat at Jaye and Marissa's place gave her room to spread her wings.

Above Jaye's head, a moth flits around the white bulb at the door of the police station. He takes a deep breath. 'We have our way of doing things. Might not be your way—'

'Our daughter smokes weed. In the house of a detective inspector.'

'Hana, *Christ*.' Jaye squirms. Really not wanting to have this particular conversation in this particular place. 'When Marissa and I moved in together, we made decisions, how we want to be, as a family. Marissa's kids, Addison—'

'A seventeen-year-old, doing what she wants. Dragging home a different guy every other night. Or girl.'

Sideways glances as two uniformed cops pass. News has spread fast that the team policing vans picked up the daughter of two of the most senior detectives in the station. It's not a great look. When the cops have safely disappeared, Jaye battles on. 'We'd rather know what she's doing than have her do it on street corners.'

'Well that worked.' Hana doesn't even try to hide the disdain in her voice.

'It's a phase,' Jaye attempts. 'Her whacky friends ... she's finding herself, experimenting. She's so talented, her music, her performances, we should be really proud of her.'

'I'm not very proud tonight. You?'

A street-sweeping truck rumbles past where Stan is waiting in the car, trying hard not to be too obviously interested in what's unfolding under the cold doorway light.

Hana watches Jaye turn the nub of one thumb between the forefinger and thumb of the other hand, one way then the other, like someone trying to coax loose a rusty resistant doorknob. Cops learn to hide their tics, the subconscious physical habits that give away their stress in moments of heightened tension. But Hana knows the thumb thing, she

29

knows it well. For a moment, there's a vivid image in her mind. Sixteen years before, telling Jaye she didn't want them to be together any more. Neither of them crying, their baby girl between them in the bed, asleep but starting to snuffle, the noises she made just before she woke. Jaye staring at a crack in the ceiling of their rented flat. Turning the nub of his thumb with his other hand.

Hana hasn't thought of that moment for a very long time.

A deeply uncomfortable silence. Finally Jaye sighs. 'What a fucking day.'

After the confrontation with Patrick Thompson in the parking building, Hana went straight to Jaye, told him what had happened, how the entitled prick got in her face, taunting her, talking trash about the victim he'd raped – all but saying he'd do the same to their daughter – wanting Hana to go for him. Jaye didn't spare Hana's feelings; he wouldn't be doing her any favours. 'He smashed his own face against a pillar?' he said, 'You know how that sounds, right?'

'Like a bad excuse for police brutality. But that's what happened.'

'Did you touch him? Lay a finger on him? I need to know.'

The question hung in the air between them. In the car on the way back to the station, Stan told Hana he'd support her story, make a statement that he saw everything. Hana gave him a dressing-down; she wasn't going to have a sworn officer lie for her, and she didn't want to hear him suggest anything like it again. She'd deal with it, whichever way it went.

'I shoved him backwards against the pillar. That's all. I realized what I was doing, I stopped myself. What happened to his face, he did that himself.'

'When his QC hauls you in front of the Independent Police Complaints Authority, you cross your heart and point to God and this whole thing disappears?'

'He threatened our daughter.'

Suggesting you were going to direct-message someone on Instagram wasn't actually a threat, Hana knew, not in any kind of way that could lead to actual charges. And Patrick Thompson was a lot of things but he wasn't a fool. He wasn't stupid enough to harass the daughter of the cop who'd successfully prosecuted him for sexual assault.

She wrote up a full statement about the incident. Stan did too, without perjuring himself. For the time being, there was nothing else Hana or Jaye could do.

Hana looks out to where Stan is waiting in the car on the street outside the station. Dark clouds hang over Auckland, the promise of rain before the night is through.

'Yeah,' she says. 'What a fucking day.'

'What do you want to do?' Jaye asks. 'About Addison?'

'She's like someone I used to know,' Hana says finally – not angry, not blaming Jaye or Marissa, just wishing it wasn't so. 'She's heading somewhere I don't understand. I hate it.'

Jaye has stopped the thing with his thumb now. Hana knows what that means. Whatever happens next, it's over to her.

'I want her to move in with me. I want her in my home. I want to know my daughter again.'

4

THE LAST FLAT ON THE SECOND FLOOR

'Know this place?' Hana asks, holding up the video on her phone so Stan can see.

The email had been niggling at the back of her mind ever since she'd received it that morning in the court-house, but after dealing with the incident in the car park, working through the possible fallout with Jaye and then discovering her daughter had been arrested, she hadn't had the time to look properly at the enigmatic video. As Stan drives through the night-time streets, heading away from Central Police Station, she plays it again.

'The Palace,' Stan says. He recognizes the condemned building; he went there more than once when he was in uniform, to serve arrest warrants, one time to deal with the messy week-old aftermath of a fatal overdose.

'Is Addison okay, D Senior?' Stan asks. Hana grunts a non-committal reply. She really doesn't want to revisit the excruciating last hour. She'd rather have something else to focus on. The video of the Palace.

'Take a left,' she says.

'Your house is straight on.'

'The Palace is left.'

'Boss. It's the middle of the night . . .'

Outside, the rain that has been threatening starts to fall. Stan hits the indicator. At the next corner, he takes a left.

The Palace looms in the darkness, a crumbling three-storey edifice. The electricity has been cut off for years, the owners waiting to see which happens first: a property developer with an impressively bulging wallet turning up to make the right offer, or one of the itinerants who drift in and out of the place falling asleep with a half-finished joint and burning the decaying structure down.

Across the road in a park, a swing moves gently in the rain. In Stan's car, Hana plays the video again, the image zooming in on one particular rusting iron balcony. The last flat on the second floor.

Stan retrieves flashlights from the trunk and they head for the entrance.

Hana hauls aside the CONDEMNED notice tacked across the front door, shines her torch into the darkness beyond, picking out the shapes of a couple of homeless covered in cardboard. Slurs of protest greet the dazzling

33

police flashlights. 'Just passing through, fellas, don't mind us,' Hana soothes as the two cops pick their way past.

She leads the way up a graffitied stairwell, most of the handrails broken. 'Jesus. Smell this place,' says Stan, as they head towards the farthest door on the second level, muffled noises coming from around the building.

Hana knocks on the last door in the hallway. 'Hello. Hello. Police.' No response.

Stan pushes the door. It swings open. Unlocked.

The beams of the two torches pick their way around the flat. It's one room, consisting of a bedroom slash kitchen area. The place has long since been gutted of anything that could be sold or slept on or burned for warmth.

There's a door to the outside balcony with its rusty railings, Hana forces it open. There's nothing to be seen on the rain-soaked platform. Looking through what remains of the cupboards and wardrobe, Stan says, 'Nothing here. Take you home, D Senior.'

It's raining harder now. Back in the car, Stan hits the wipers, starts the engine, and as he pulls away, Hana looks back at the Palace for a final time. Each of the poky apartments is laid out identically, she can see from this angle: the balcony, the windows.

The windows.

'*Stop*,' she says, urgent. Stan pulls over, perplexed.

'They all have a window to the side of the balcony. Every flat.'

Stan looks out through the rain. He can see that Hana's right: in each apartment there is an external window located away from the door to the balcony. But he has no idea why she's suddenly interested in boarding house design.

'If there's a window,' she tells him, 'there must be a room.'

'There *was* a room,' he points out. 'There was nothing in it.' His mind is on the last two episodes of the Netflix series he wants to watch tonight, if he ever actually gets home. He's suddenly aware of the look on Hana's face. A look he's familiar with. Hana in mentor mode, forever prodding the more junior detective towards pushing himself harder, thinking through every angle, looking at a problem from every side, always giving himself the best chance of reaching the right answer.

'Boss?'

'That's a second window,' she says. 'Means there's a second room.'

It takes a moment for Stan to twig. *Shit*.

'There was no second room . . .'

Stan, a few inches taller than Hana, climbs up onto the railing of the balcony outside the flat. Hana grasps him by the belt in case he slips. The rain is really coming down, and as he stretches, a cold stream of water plummeting from a rusted gutter somehow manages to aim its way straight down his collar. He gets his hand on the sill of the window, but it's just too far for him to see inside.

Hana helps him clamber down.

Inside the apartment, *tap tap tap*. Hana uses the rubber

end of her flashlight, tapping her way along the wall behind which the missing room should logically be. At a certain point, the sound changes, *tap tap thud*. Where the wall is thinner, where it's hollow behind. She taps around the space, finding the perimeter of the hollow area.

'About the size of a door,' Stan suggests. A door that's been sealed over.

Hana sounds out the hollow space, finding the middle point. She draws the flashlight back half a metre and . . .

She slams the end of the flashlight into the wall. It goes straight through. She scrapes away plaster, points the beam through the fist-sized hole, searching the dark room beyond.

The beam falls on something inside. But the hole in the wall is too small to see clearly what it is.

Hana steps back. She kicks at the wall, hard. The newly plastered-over section caves in, leaving an opening the size of a fireplace. Stan grimaces. 'Oh God.' His hand goes to his nose at a rush of rank air.

Lit by the beams of the two torches is a body. A rope is noosed around its neck. The body is suspended from a rafter.

It sways gently. It's a man. Late twenties. Naked. He's dead. The beam of Hana's flashlight picks out his arms. His hands are bound in front of his torso, the feet tied at the ankle.

She studies the strange scene in the hidden room.

Outside, the rain keeps falling.

5

THE MESSAGE

The night before, the looming edifice of the Palace was laden with omen and portent. By day, it's just sad. Old, shitty, broken-down and sad. Police crime-scene tape surrounds the building now. Uniformed cops keep journalists at a distance, officers interview the homeless from the building, locals gather, passers-by with takeaway coffees pause on the way to work, trying to find out what's going on.

Stan's car pulls up alongside a row of uniform police cars, wagons holding the forensics equipment used by scene-of-crime officers, unmarked detective cars. Behind the wheel, he yawns. After finding the walled-in room, he didn't get to see those last two episodes of his Netflix series.

The flat at the far end of the second floor has been transformed. Plastic covers every inch of floor, square plastic stepping stones make a sterile access path, work lights have been erected. SOCO officers in white paper overalls and masks work in quiet, focused activity, testing every inch for fingerprints, DNA, blood traces.

The body is still where it was found, and as a forensic photographer takes photos of the crime scene, Hana crouches in a corner of the room with a sketch pad in her hand, a sharpened artist's pencil, carefully sketching the strange ritualistic pose the victim was left in. Like the sketches on the walls of her home, her drawing is intricate. Precise.

The photographer takes a final series of photos, and Hana moves to a different angle, starts a new sketch. From this angle she can see a wound on the victim's forehead, a horizontal impact mark, a single lethal strike from some kind of weapon.

Out in the corridor, the photographer packs up her camera. 'What's the deal with D Senior?' she asks quietly as Stan approaches. 'There's these things called crime-scene photos. My livelihood is based on them. How come the pad and pencil?'

Stan pulls on sterile gloves and a mask from the piles waiting at the door. 'The boss trusts her eyes more than photos,' he tells her. 'Nothing personal.'

Stan picks his way over the stepping stones and into the crime scene. He crouches by Hana, speaking quietly as he updates her. 'Digital forensics are going to town on the email. But they're not expecting a miracle. Looks like the video was sent via an untraceable proxy site.'

Which is pretty much what Hana was expecting.

Stan has better news from fingerprints lifted from the victim. He hands over a printout of an arrest sheet from nearly ten years earlier. Hana puts it side by side with one of her sketches.

In the arrest sheet photo, the young man glares out at the world bristling, taunting, ready to fight. In Hana's sketch, the angry eyes are concealed beneath dead eyelids, and there's the wound on the forehead, which she has shaded and detailed to pick out the split skin, the ridges beneath made by cranial bone splintered from the impact of the blunt-force trauma. But the two faces are the same.

She reads the name in the summary of charges against the young man, formerly offender, now victim. Terrence Sean McElvoy.

A west Auckland suburb. High fences, cars in front yards jacked up on concrete blocks, the sound of barking dogs from up and down the street. Stan's unmarked car pulls up outside a house. It's long overdue for a coat of paint and the corrugated iron roof is rusting and patched. There's a sign nailed above the front deck.

JUSTINE'S HAIR AND NAILS

A woman waits under the sign, nursing a lit ciggie, watching Hana and Stan as they approach. She gets straight to the question she's wanted to ask since Stan called to tell her they were coming because of an incident involving her ex-partner. 'Is he dead?' she asks. Aware of the curious looks from neighbouring houses, Stan says,

'It'd be better if we talk inside.' Which pretty much gives her the answer to her question.

Her ciggie is only a third finished, but she stubs it out on the handrail. Brushes the ash away into the garden. Brushing it into nothingness.

'Thank fuck,' she says.

What was once a living room has been repurposed as a hair and nail salon. 'Hair makes more money than nails,' Justine tells Hana and Stan. 'But touching people's hair gives me the jeebies. It's, I dunno. Intimate. What lovers do. Maybe I'm in the wrong job,' she says, pacing, nervous. 'Nails are different. I like it. It's aesthetic. I can do yours,' she offers. 'While we talk . . .'

Hana can see how tense she is. Something familiar, something comfortable might just help. She holds out her hands. 'Warning,' she smiles, 'I'm a gardener.'

Justine looks at Hana's nails, surprised at the cop's warmth. 'Uh-huh, what a mess.' She gets her nail kit. 'You must have Terry's records. His court file. What do you want from me?' she asks.

'Whatever you can tell us.'

Justine uses her file. Hana's nails are short and practical; it's going to be an effort to give the corners a pleasing curve. She and the dead man were together only a couple of years, she tells Hana. They were eighteen years old, being eighteen-year-olds. Booze. Drugs. Sex. A twenty-four-hour party.

'Then something happened. *She* happened,' Justine says, looking up at a framed photo hanging on the wall above the hairdressing mirror. It's a photo of a baby, a few months old, wrapped in white. Fast asleep.

When she found out Darleen was coming, Justine said she knew she couldn't be eighteen any more, she knew she had to grow up. 'Be a mum. But Terry, he wasn't ready to grow up. The baby didn't fit his world view. He never understood why the hell he had to change his life to make space for something he never asked for in the first place.'

Justine finishes filing Hana's nails. She offers her a range of polishes, and nods knowingly at Hana's choice, a neutral shade. She can tell Hana's not a local; clients from out west tend to go for something louder.

As Justine applies the polish, Hana feels the grip tighten on her hands. Justine is getting to the tough part. The part she'd rather not revisit. 'I was studying,' she says. 'Hair and nails. I'd leave the baby with him, days when Mum couldn't look after her.' She trails away. Carefully, carefully running the polish to the edge of one nail. 'It was the first day we did hair spirals. I came home. He's out back with his mates. Four in the afternoon, already on crate number two. My little girl was in her cot. She looked real peaceful. Then I realized . . .'

Justine finishes Hana's left hand. Is Hana sure this is the right colour, she can try something else? Hana tells her, 'The colour is good. It's perfect.'

Justine pours all her concentration into Hana's right hand.

'I picked her up. My girl. My baby. She was cold. I just started screaming.'

Determination in her face. She's not going to cry. She's not going to fucking cry.

She tells Hana that Terry denied everything. 'Finally one of his mates got a fucking conscience, said what happened. Baby was crying, wouldn't stop. Terry shook her, which just made things worse. Problem was, he was already half cut. My baby slipped out of his hands. Hit the floor. Baby stopped crying. So he got to get back to drinking, undisturbed. The doctors said later that she fell on her head. She would've died within an hour.'

The tears that were threatening are gone. Replaced by anger. Hana can see this has maybe been a familiar rhythm for Justine for some time now. 'Three years,' Justine says. 'For manslaughter. Why is it called manslaughter? It wasn't a man he killed. Not someone big, someone who could defend himself. She was a baby. She was *my* baby.'

Justine has finished the final nail. But she doesn't let go of Hana's hand.

'When did you see him last?' Stan asks, gently.

'The day he was sentenced.'

'Nothing since? Haven't heard from him?'

Justine shakes her head, no.

'After I knew she was passed,' she says, almost an afterthought, 'I realized she hadn't even been round long enough for me to take a photo. Not one. Mum took that, before they took my baby away . . . '

Hana realizes, the baby in the framed photo, she isn't sleeping.

Justine lets go of Hana's hand. 'There you go. I've been known to work miracles.'

Hana realizes there are tears in Justine's eyes, with this human contact, holding Hana's hands, then having to let them go again. She can't hold them back any more.

'I heard he was living on the streets,' she says, composing herself. 'Fucked up on crack. Same old, same old. That how he died?'

'He was murdered.' Hana sees the reaction, an involuntary flinch. However much anger and ill-will Justine has for her ex, the news is a jolt. It takes some processing.

'The universe,' she finally says, quietly. 'Goes round, comes round. Might take a month. Or years. No bad deed goes unpunished.'

As Stan heads out to wait in the car, Hana tells Justine, 'Thanks for your time. And I'm sorry.'

'I'm not.'

Hana says, 'I don't mean about him.'

The start of a homicide inquiry is sugar meeting yeast. The reaction is instantaneous. In the few hours since the hidden room was discovered, more than a dozen detectives have been drafted into Hana's section on the eighth floor of Central Police Station, and a good number of uniformed cops. New desks and chairs have been requisitioned, computer stations, whiteboards erected; blown-up images from the crime scene are displayed across large pinboards. On a big television screen, the anonymous video of the Palace plays on a loop.

It's the first morning briefing for the full investigation team, what will be a daily event for as long as the inquiry runs. 'The cause of death was a single blow to the temple,' Hana tells the gathering. 'The striking edge was ten to eleven centimetres, the weapon hasn't been located.' Stan distributes a series of hard-copy files with everything they have on the victim so far, printouts of the crime-scene photos. 'Convicted of the manslaughter of his kid,' he summarizes. 'Long-term homeless after he was paroled, and long-term junkie, with all the shit that comes with that territory.'

Hana reports back on the interview with Justine. 'We'll bring her in for further questioning,' she says, 'Due diligence. She's not going to shed any tears for him. No doubts there. But . . . '

'But?' Jaye asks, at Hana's side. As detective inspector of the criminal investigation branch, he oversees all active inquiries.

'A mother's baby is killed by the father. When she lashes out, it's going to be angry. Ugly. Messy. It won't be a carefully arranged shopfront window display, like we found last night.' Hana's instinct is firmly that it's not the ex-girlfriend.

'There's something else,' she tells the team. 'The initial results from the autopsy examination. The pathologist believes the abrasions and markings from the ropes on the wrists and neck are post mortem.'

Murmurs among the other detectives. The case is already strange as hell, and this detail is even stranger. One of them asks, 'The victim was deceased before he was tied up and hanged? Why hang him by the neck if he's already dead?'

'Whoever did this,' Hana says, 'they wanted their handiwork found. They laid a trail of breadcrumbs. Sent the video to take us to what they'd prepared in that room. Planned. Considered. A posed tableau.'

She looks at a blown-up photo of the crime scene. The body hanging, the wrists bound in front, the feet tied at the ankles.

'This is a message,' she tells her team. 'We have to find out what that message means.'

'Thompson's QC called this morning.' Jaye closes the door of his office. 'It wasn't a social chat.'

Hana's lips tighten. It's not that she wasn't expecting this. Both she and Jaye knew it was coming. But the timing, today of all possible days, the start of a murder inquiry, an investigation where Hana is officer in charge, the lead detective.

'The kid's nose is broken,' Jaye tells her.

'He's not a kid. Thompson is an eighteen-year-old man who drugged and raped a woman.'

'His nose is still broken.' The QC spent twenty minutes throwing threats at him, so Jaye's not going to sugar-coat it.

He shifts course for a moment, to something that's been niggling at him about their case. Someone gets away with murder, literally, then sends a calling card to reveal what they've done. 'The video,' he asks Hana, 'why was it sent to you?'

Hana doesn't have an answer. Her email isn't a secret; it's on every card she hands out. But she's been asking herself the same question.

She puts her hands in the pockets of her jacket. The gloves she used at the crime scene are still there. The feeling of cold latex and talcum powder is unpleasant. Like touching old burst balloons.

'Thompson,' she says, eager to finish the conversation and get back to work. 'What's going to happen?'

'I don't know. But it's not going away.'

The video. Hana watches the footage as it loops through again and again on her phone. She's standing outside the Palace. It's getting dark now; the crime-scene tape still surrounds the building, but the energized activity of the first few hours of a new investigation is slowing, the deceased has been removed, the SOCO officers are packing up their forensics equipment.

Why her? The question Jaye asked, the question Hana can't answer, still running through her mind. Of all the cops in this city, why was this thing sent to her?

The amateurish footage is almost mesmerizing as it plays on repeat. As she watches, she tries putting herself in the killer's place. She imagines them plastering the wall. Closing the door of the empty dark flat. Walking across the road to the children's park. Standing there in the middle of the night, shooting crappy phone footage. Why? What was going through their head?

She keeps moving, changing angle, comparing her position with the video. Finally she finds a point where her perspective matches the perspective on the phone screen. She looks around. The nearby play area, the swings and slides and climbing nets, is deserted, parents deciding that the scene of a murder inquiry isn't the best place to take the kids today.

In front of her, a park bench. Something catches her eye. On one of the concrete legs there's a faint marking, close to where the leg is set into the ground. The marking is hard to see in the growing dark; could be just a discoloration in the concrete. She turns on the torch on her phone. In the stark beam, the marking looks like a faint red splodge.

She frowns. Could be nothing. But then again . . .

Outside the Palace, flood lamps are being loaded into police vehicles, testing kits are packed away. Hana approaches a SOCO officer who is comparing theories with Stan.

'Borrow you for a tick?' she asks the SOCO guy. 'Bring your kit.'

Back at the park bench, it's getting darker still. Stan has set up one of the battery-powered flood lamps. On hands and knees, the SOCO officer paints the leg of the bench with luminol.

'Out of interest, D Senior,' he says, 'why luminol? Why do you think there might be blood out here?' Hana doesn't have an answer.

The SOCO officer finishes painting the luminol. He steps

away, readying a camera, giving the chemical process long enough to react. 'Okay,' he says.

Stan flicks the switch, turning off the floodlight. The lamp dies to darkness, and instantly the surface of the concrete leg glows. The dark red splodge becomes luminescent purple. It's small, smaller than a child's palm. The iridescent glow in the darkness is at once strangely beautiful and disturbing. A positive indication of the presence of blood.

The SOCO guy starts taking photos; he has maybe thirty seconds before the glow from the chemical reaction fades.

Hana gets closer to the glowing shape. She can see that the luminescent purple is no random splodge. Not at all. It's a very carefully crafted pattern. An inward-turning spiral. Precisely, deliberately drawn. She takes her sketchbook from her bag. She sketches fast, replicating the shape on her page.

Then the glow fades. Darkness falls again. Hana switches on the flood lamp, and in the pool of artificial light in the middle of the dark park, a hundred metres from where she found the hanging body the night before, she studies the drawing.

The shape on her page is like something from nature, the perfect spiral on a hermit crab shell. The inward-circling meteorological map of a cyclone approaching landfall. The fragile pattern of water as it flows down a sink. A shape that's organic, harmonious, pleasing to the eye.

Until you remember it was drawn in blood.

6

A DOWNWIND POSITION

His movements are careful, precise, with the sureness and speed of a practised artisan.

This blade he has used, he has used it so many times before. It's the knife she gave him, the one she showed him how to keep sharp like the beak of a bird, so sharp that the thrust of the blade into the deer's heart will not be cruel, so the animal's life will end quickly and with mercifully little suffering.

The sharp point of the knife tip is being used for another purpose. It digs clean into the concrete wall. Tiny, exact perforations. One dot, then the next, dot after tiny dot, each puncture made by the knife tip adding to an overall shape, like the microscopic fronds of a snowflake that cumulatively form the greater pattern, making a perfect balanced whole.

He remembers hunting with his mother. His father died

young, so young he barely knew his son, and after that she was mother and father both to him. 'Find a downwind position,' she'd whisper, her mouth close to his ear, when the telltale signs of fresh tracks or droppings would lead them to their first glimpse of the distant deer. 'A deer's sense of smell is much greater than his hearing, a thousand times greater than our sense of smell. Find a downwind position so your scent doesn't carry his way. If he smells you, he is gone.'

As he uses the knife his mother gave him, dot after dot, each dot making the greater whole, he listens. Outside the door, above the distant hum of traffic far below, he hears the man now. He knows what the man will be doing. He knows he doesn't need to hurry, he has been in this place before, he has watched the man more than once, he knows his habits well.

With the sharp point of his knife he carefully, precisely etches the last few marks in the wall. He brushes away the concrete dust. He studies the patterns, the markings.

He slips the knife back into his kitbag. A rolled-up woven flax mat, a whāriki, is strapped to the kitbag. He takes the whāriki, places it on the concrete floor, unrolls it. With care and reverence, he takes the long, carved weapon from the mat. A taiaha, crafted in a traditional style. But this spear is unusual. It has two striking heads. Hardened wood. Inlays of polished pounamu* make the cutting edges more deadly. An awesome weapon. He weighs it in his hand. Running through his head what will happen

---

* Pounamu – greenstone, New Zealand river jade

next, a few moments from now. Visualizing what he must do, the way his mother had him rehearse: how she would place a sack of potatoes at the base of the washing line pole, guiding his hand as he practised the killing of the deer, so that the plunge of the knife would become second nature and the deer would be finished in its death throes cleanly and fast, so he would not falter in the adrenaline of the moment.

He bows his head.

He speaks low and quiet under his breath, sending his words up to the heavens.

'Ka tūāumutia e au te mata o taku rākau – kāore e ora i a au. Ahakoa he pūhuki te mata o te rākau – kia pā ki te tinana o te tangata – mate tonu atu.'*

The whispered words trail away. His eyes open. In his face, great pain. An inner torment. He is doing the thing he knows he must. But doing it tears him in two. His hands tremble. Tears form. Panic builds. He falls to his knees. He retches, soiling the concrete floor.

On his knees, he is distraught. In complete doubt. Ready to walk away from the thing he is doing, from the thing that is destroying him.

With an effort of will, he steadies himself.

The difference between man and the animals is the ability to understand suffering, to feel the pain of other living things. As his mother taught him with the deer, there will be no unnecessary suffering today. He will do that which

---

* 'I consecrate the edge of my weapon, and no enemy can withstand me. Although the edge of my weapon be blunt, let it but strike the body of man, and he perishes.'

must be done quickly and with precision. He is ready, and it will be fast and merciful.

Afterwards, after it is done, he will return his weapon to its place, he will roll it in the woven mat he took from his mother's bed after she died, he will strap the mat back onto his kitbag. Soon after that, he will disappear into the crowded streets, making his way in the opposite direction to the sirens that will by then be coming.

He looks once more towards the patterns he has carved on the concrete wall. Then he quietly eases open the door. The light from the distant setting sun hits his face.

The man is there, his back turned, silhouetted by the pinkening sky.

With a man, it is different to a deer. The sense of smell in a man is imprecise and clumsy and blunt. The man will not smell his scent on the wind. He will have no warning.

He tightens his grasp on the long shaft of the two-headed weapon. Then he walks out of the door, towards his prey.

7

NOTHINGNESS

Hot water runs down Hana's back, the mixer turned nearly to full, the way she likes it, just under the point where it might actually risk burning human flesh.

It was a cold, drizzling rain this morning as she ran through the dark inner-city Auckland streets, circling around the glowing needle of the Sky Tower, a soaring symphony playing in her earphones. Every morning, 10.13 kilometres, the same route step for step. A creature of routine, that's what Hana is, but it's more than that. Other people try meditation, mantras, Eastern metaphysics, visiting Peru to ingest cocktails of beta-carboline alkaloids in shamanic ayahuasca ceremonies, all in pursuit of the same thing: to attain a state of mental nothingness, to unclutter the forebrain and settle the self into the ancient areas in the back of the cerebrum. To reboot, to give clarity. That's what 10.13 kilometres in the pre-dawn dark does for Hana. Sometimes it works. Not today.

She was in bed finally at three in the morning after going over the forensics transcripts again, studying the pathologist's report, looking at the autopsy photographs and her own sketches of the deadly mark left by the unidentified weapon with a ten-to-eleven-centimetre striking blade. She was on the wet pre-dawn streets at five a.m. as always, and before that she hadn't slept a solid twenty minutes in the couple of hours she forced herself to lie between the sheets of her bed. This morning's run didn't bring clarity; there was no reboot, no chance of nothingness. Just a constant shuffling of the strange jigsaw pieces – why did the body end up bound hand and foot hanging in a sealed room, why was the video sent to her, what is the spiral marked out in blood?

Her bathroom is full of steam. She wipes the glass wall of the shower, studying the foggy image of her face.

If you want to achieve mental clarity, if you seek nothingness, become a Buddhist monk. For fuck sake don't decide to be a career cop.

Hana juggles a black coffee as she gathers her files and notebook, half watching an item on morning television about the body found in a condemned inner-city building. She pauses to look again at her sketchbook. She runs her finger around the inward curving lines of the drawing she made of the symbol on the park bench. From her collection of pencils, she finds the right dull red. As she shades the spiral shape, the buzzing of a phone alert interrupts her. Probably Stan saying he's running late to pick her up, Auckland traffic. But it's an email. The sent-by address is an anonymous series of numbers, like the email that held the video of the Palace.

No message in the body of this new email, and once again, a video attached.

She swallows the last mouthful of coffee, tense and not because of the caffeine. But before she can open the video, there's a knock at the door. 'Come in, Stan,' she calls.

'Hey, Mum.'

It's not Stan.

Addison hauls in a backpack bulging with her worldly possessions – a collection of op-shop clothes and a turntable. 'I took an Uber. Couldn't bear half an hour trapped in a car with Marissa and her classic rock radio station,' she tells her mother.

'Love,' Hana says, 'you're here.' Trying to hide the fact that with the events of the last thirty-six hours, she had completely forgotten Addison was about to arrive, and the timing is now about as bad as it can possibly be. Addison knows her well enough to be stung by the equivocal tone in her voice.

'Yeah, I'm here. Like you wanted. That still okay?'

Hana smiles at her daughter. She pockets her phone. The video will have to wait. 'It's more than okay.' She hugs her. 'It's wonderful.' And she means it.

She tells Addison she'll have to dig a trail through the

piles of canvases and sketchbooks to get to her bed. 'I meant to make things tidy for you,' she apologizes.

'Dad said something big is happening,' Addison says, looking at the news item about the murder at the Palace on the television. 'Is it that, Mum?'

Hana shoulders her bag, making no response, but Addison wasn't expecting an answer. She knows well enough that her parents can't talk about their work lives.

Stan arrives at the door, surprised to see Addison. 'Hey, Detective Stan.' Addison beams at him. At twenty-three years old, he is much closer in age to her daughter than to Hana, and in the year he has been working alongside her, he and Addison have developed a bit of a big brother/ little sister relationship, where Addison's favourite sport is embarrassing the hell out of the slightly awkward young detective. Now she compliments him on his shoes. 'Takes true style to make a twenty-buck pair of Warehouse slip-ons look kind of good.'

Stan reddens. Hana tries not to smile.

'I'm playing Sailor Bar Thursday week,' Addison tells him. 'Come along. I'll introduce you to my friends. You'll fit right in with us little freaks.' She is taking the piss, knowing full well the clean-cut young white cop would be painfully out of place with her crowd.

'Ready when you are, Senior,' Stan says as he heads back out the door. Addison pulls a gun finger. *Boom.* Stan pulls a gun finger back. Both barrels. *Boom boom.* He blows off smoke. Addison bursts into laughter.

'Too try-hard?' Stan asks.

'How'd you guess?'

Following Stan out the door, Hana pauses. 'You all right? After the other night?' she asks her daughter.

'Yeah,' says Addison, and now the false bravado from the interview room is gone. She adds quietly, 'If ... if I maybe went too far, Mum ...'

'Not maybe,' says Hana. 'Not if. You went too far.'

Lots of unspoken and unresolved stuff swirling from what happened at the back-yard party, and the aftermath in Central Station. Hana is determined, with Addison moving back in, that she's going to start this off the right way. She's not going to leave stuff unsaid.

'I feel so lame,' Addison says. 'Falling apart. Crying. In front of Marissa, too. For fuck sake.'

'Don't be so hard on her. Marissa cares about you. She loves you.'

There's no old-partner/new-partner animosity between Hana and Marissa. Hana knows how much Jaye feels for Marissa, and she knows why, and she couldn't be happier, for both of them. Jaye and Marissa got together a few years earlier. Marissa's husband – a member of an armed offenders squad, the specialist armed units who respond to high-risk incidents – was killed in the line of duty. He was one of Jaye's closest friends. The relationship between Marissa and Jaye began as a process of shared mourning, both working through their grief about someone they loved deeply, until slowly the comfort they found in each other's pain shifted into something else. It wasn't a fiery, passionate romance; it wasn't fireworks and starry nights. It was two wounded, damaged people seeking solace. Solace that became love.

Marissa is a vet because of an aching empathy for all living things. When she loses an animal in surgery, it still cuts deep, though she's been doing the job for years. Hana knows that Marissa is exactly the kind of partner a cop should have – someone whose world is the magnetic opposite to theirs.

'Yeah, she loves me,' Addison says. 'Marissa loves everyone, so much it gets hard to breathe. Maybe that's okay if you're eight years old or a Labrador with an infected paw, but honestly, Mum . . .'

Hana kisses her, heads for the door. 'I'll bring home takeaway.'

'I know you want me to pull my head in, Mum.'

'I want you to be you.'

'And pull my head in.'

'And pull your head in.'

'I'll try.'

Hana smiles. 'That's a start.'

As their unmarked police car heads towards Central Police Station, Hana opens the new video. It plays for twenty seconds or so, shorter than the footage of the Palace. It's a very wide shot of Auckland's skyline, the city at sunset. She rewinds, watches again. It's hand-held, someone shooting on their phone, like the other video.

Stan hangs up from a call. 'Forensics report on the blood from the park bench. It matches the victim.' Hana expected this, but Stan is gobsmacked. 'What kind of balls does that take? Kill a guy, string him up in a deserted flat, take some blood, wander across to the kids' park and calmly sketch a symbol.'

Stan glances at the phone screen as Hana plays the video again. 'What do you think, Senior, is it from the same person?' Hana has sent the new video to digital forensics, but if it is from the same source, she knows the sender will have been just as careful to keep themselves anonymous.

Where the first video was a trail of crumbs leading straight to the last flat on the second floor of the Palace, this one is different. It's not specific. A broad expanse of the central city, office blocks and apartment buildings and commercial towers. There's no clue in the video of exactly what they are meant to be looking at.

A few hundred metres from Central Station, the car passes a mass of police vehicles pulled up outside a tall mirror-glass office tower. Hana looks out at the emergency tape surrounding almost the whole block.

'Suicide,' Stan tells her. 'Last evening. Summers' case, he says the guy jumped from the top floor.'

Hana leans into the windscreen, looking up to the top of the building. She can just see the radio mast hundreds of feet above, the strong red light of the aircraft warning beacon flashing. Her eyes drop, tracking in her mind the trajectory of the falling man, down to a grey emergency services tent, erected on the footpath, covering the body of the deceased.

'Twenty storeys,' Stan says. 'Poor bastard.'

The media briefing room is on the ground floor, a large space in Central Police Station purpose-built for press conferences. Hana heads down the corridor scanning the notes she's made. Through the glass doors there's a good-sized contingent of reporters. A murder in Auckland is still a big deal.

She steps through the doors. She stops dead.

'The victim's name is Terrence Sean McElvoy.' It's Jaye, he's at the lectern, already briefing the cameras and rows of microphones. 'Last address unknown, occupation unknown.' He passes on the number of the police hotline about the case, inviting any information that might be of assistance, guaranteeing anonymity if that's required.

Hana stands still, her notes in her hand, furious. Jaye has taken on the briefing she should be giving. He's elbowed her sideways.

'If you're going to pull rank,' Hana says as they climb the stairwell afterwards, 'warn me before I walk in there and humiliate myself.' The staircase is dark, her mood is darker.

'The decision wasn't mine,' Jaye tells her. 'The district commander doesn't want you on every television screen, reminding Patrick Thompson's QC how much he wants to bring lawsuits against you and the Tāmaki Makaurau police force.'

'You're sidelining me.'

'I'm trying to protect you.'

At the exit from the stairwell, Jaye pauses. 'Something else. I've requested a programme of counselling sessions with the police psych unit. To deal with any potential anger-management issues. I expect you to attend. Every one of them.'

'This is *bullshit*! You know it is. *Issues?* The guy broke his own nose! *Fuck*.'

The green exit light above the door flickers, making the two of them look unwell. And that's exactly how they're both feeling.

Hana and Jaye have both tried very hard never to arrive at this kind of place in their professional relationship. They'd made a commitment when they split up, promising two things. They'd work together to both stay part of their daughter's life. And as born cops, neither would sacrifice the career they loved. Being in the same city for Addison, they'd inevitably be working together, and as tricky as that might be, they'd deal with it. Over the years, they have been meticulous in keeping to the word and the spirit of the undertaking they made. They're professionals first and ex-partners a distant second. It might get hard, but they make it work.

Standing under the sickly green exit light, Hana knows it just got hard.

'I'm running interference for you,' Jaye tells her. 'So I can tell the district commander we're addressing the situation. So you can do your job. So you can *keep* your job.'

The words are out of his mouth before he even realizes what he's saying, but it's too late to soften the edges; it's already been said. Hana raises her eyebrows. Okay then. Now she knows how far Jaye's conversation with the district commander went.

'Go to the counselling programme,' says Jaye, quietly now, feeling for her. 'Please.'

The new video is distributed internally throughout the inquiry team. With no identifying markers to give geography, it's impossible to figure out where it was shot from. Meanwhile, the spiral from the park bench opens up a new slew of speculation. Is it a graffiti artist's symbol, maybe the tag of some kind of drug gang? Perhaps a cult thing, wannabe Satanists. One of the team discovers that a florist shop in Wellington has a very similar logo, based on the spiral frond of the mamaku,* but the elderly owner is approaching seventy. Not high on the list of potential murder suspects.

The existence of the videos and the spiral symbol painted in blood is deliberately kept from the media; it's 'special knowledge', a detail known only to the cops. And whoever committed the crime.

'This thing isn't going to be straightforward,' Hana tells her team at the end-of-day meeting. 'It's not one plus one equals two. Any long shot, any half-hunch. Come to me. Follow up. Trust your instincts. Dig holes in unexpected places. This is going to be all about the unexpected.'

---

* Mamaku – a tall tree fern

As Stan drops her home, she looks again at the new video. A postcard of the whole city of Auckland. If the same person who strung a dead man up in a sealed-off room sent her this, what the hell do they want her to see this time?

And why are the videos being sent to *her*?

Even at rest, PLUS 1 is a live wire. Eyes always moving, leg bouncing, hands constantly adjusting the sprawl of dreads that tumble down across their discoloured cheekbone and eye socket, the aftermath of their overzealous confrontation with the cops in the cul-de-sac.

Hana brought home Korean, Addison's favourite. The three sit around the kitchen table passing vegetarian bibimbap and a rich seaweed soup.

PLUS 1 tells Hana, 'My dad got me a lawyer. She's fucking expensive. Dad says fucking expensive means fucking good.'

'It can just mean expensive,' says Hana.

'Dad told me to ask if you could put in a good word for me. With, you know, the hierarchy. Get the charges dropped?'

Addison rolls her eyes, knowing just how this is going to land.

'No,' says Hana, spearing a piece of chilli-coated tofu with her wooden chopsticks. 'Of course I can't. Don't be a dick, PLUS 1. And don't ask again.'

'One of our mates filmed what the cops did,' PLUS 1 continues, utterly undeterred. 'Attacking a bunch of peaceful partygoers, it's all there in living colour! I can show you if you like?'

'Eat your soup,' Hana says. 'The chilli is really good.'

PLUS 1 knows perfectly well that Hana can't compromise herself by having any official part in the charges against Addison or her friends. Hana knows PLUS 1 knows. Knows this is all playful. Hana likes PLUS 1, a lot.

'Before I go to sleep, I've got four days' work to do in four hours,' she says as she finishes her food. 'There's vines strangling my kawakawa, I just want to deal with them first. You two clean up.'

As Hana heads for the door to the garden, Addison pulls something from her pocket. A joint. She lights it. Takes a drag. Very aware that her mother has paused in the doorway.

'This is pulling your head in?' Hana asks.

PLUS 1's feet make rapid circles, one way, then the other, intrigued by where is this going.

'You asked me to live here,' Addison says. 'I'm good with that. I'm really happy. But I'm still me.'

As her daughter passes the joint to PLUS 1, Hana considers her words carefully. She knows that how this plays out will define how their relationship works from here on. 'Yes, you're you,' she says. 'And you're extraordinary. Your friends are extraordinary too.' She takes the joint out of PLUS 1's hand. 'You want to talk about how it's going to be here? We'll talk. But don't give me ultimatums, and I won't either. Deal?' She stubs the joint in the sink. Washes it down the plug. 'Better be a deal. 'Cos that's what's going to happen.'

With that, she heads out to the garden.

'Your mum,' says PLUS 1. 'Far out.'

Addison hasn't been talked to like that for a while. She's quietly impressed. 'Yeah. She's staunch.'

'And fucking hot,' PLUS 1 says. 'Those eyes.'

Addison punches PLUS 1 in the arm. Hard.

The shadows in the garden are getting longer. It's a clear night, and Hana is starting to sweat as she takes to a mass of vines with a sharpened stainless-steel machete. The vines have wrapped themselves around the stand of kawakawa and have started on the other trees nearby. They're the sticky kind with masses of clinging tendrils, and she has to use the flat side of the machete to scrape them off the branches.

She has her clip-in earphones in. Orchestral music playing. As she works, she turns the volume up, loud. Her hands in the soil, music in her ears. Five minutes of nothingness before she has to go in and open the bulging briefcase again, at least that's something.

She pauses. A feeling in her spine. She looks up. Trying to see what's unsettling her. She can't see anything. She goes back to scraping a branch with the machete. But . . . the feeling again. Someone walking across her grave. She stands up and moves, shifting angles, looking out past the branches of the trees, across the picket fence, to the street beyond.

She sees something. Two hundred metres away, on the street. A figure. Standing. The sun is setting over the western ranges behind the figure, shining straight into Hana's eyes. It's impossible to tell if the figure is looking at her, or if they just happen to be paused in the street.

A moment and . . .

Hana slips off her earphones. She crosses the garden, heads towards the fence. Opens the gate. Careful, calm. But walking steadily towards the figure.

Then . . .

The figure silently walks off.

'Hey,' Hana calls. The figure disappears down a side street. She follows.

She jogs down a parallel side street, trying to get ahead of whoever it is. Coming to the next cross street, she glimpses the figure moving at pace, crossing the side street and disappearing again. Hana turns down this street, picking up her pace, running now; she turns the next corner, emerging out onto a main arterial route and . . .

The street is empty. Nothing.

The figure has gone. No sign of anybody.

Hana looks around in the growing darkness. Heart racing. A kid on a bike passes, staring at her. She realizes she's still clutching her machete, probably wild-eyed, looking like a crazy woman.

She knows she's under huge stress. With the investigation, the potential fallout from the confrontation with Patrick Thompson, her daughter moving in. Is that taking its toll? Is she imagining things? Freaking out about some poor person who was just pausing to look at the setting sun?

She tucks the machete away discreetly under her jacket. No point alarming the public.

She turns back towards home.

8

THE TIPPING POINT

There was a bridge Hana used to jump off, in the green speck of a farming town where she grew up. Her and a bunch of cousins the same age, boys and girls, would go swimming in their football shorts and hand-me-down rugby jerseys, all of them country kids shy of displaying their fast-changing bodies, huddling on the riverbank sharing ciggie butts marked with their mums' or aunties' lipstick sneakily retrieved from the metal tin ashtrays out back of the local marae.* Hana still remembers the slightly queasy, slightly ecstatic sensation located some-where between her abdomen and her pelvis as she picked her way out to the edge of the long suspension strut that jutted out from the side of the bridge, the one that pro-jected outwards above the big rock in the river ten metres

---

* Marae – the communal buildings and meeting place of a tribe

below. Her favourite thing was standing at the very end of that strut, arms spread, leaning slowly forward. Inch by inch. Slowly slowly. There's this point you reach where you still have options, where you can stop, turn around, climb back in from the end of the strut, clamber back over the rusty wire railing, to be met by the mocking voices, the jeers of your older cousin, Ngahuia, 'Yellow belly, wimpy chicken shit!' But you don't turn around and go back, hell no! You're not going to endure the taunts and laughter, so you keep leaning, the delicious/awful feeling in your gut building and building, you got this, leaning forward more and more and more, and then you find yourself at the tipping point. A moment later, you're gone.

Hana loved that feeling.

The tipping point, after which nothing is in your control any more, it's in the hands of the gods, AKA the forces of gravity, your whole being surrendered to something much bigger and more unknowable than your skinny brown teenage body. No handbrake to pull like she could on her bike, no foot brake to push like when Dad would teach her to drive around the rugby field of the local school.

You go past the tipping point. You are gone.

And it's beautiful.

At a certain point, Hana lost her love of the sensation. If she could articulate it to herself in a clear-headed and unguarded way, she'd be able to put a time and a place and an event to where things changed for her. To when everything changed, when the current of her river altered course for ever. The before, the tipping point and the after. Before, she was Hana, the smart, athletic local girl from the small town who'd gone to the big city and done well, coming top of her class in police college, meeting the good-looking Pākehā boy with the big smile. Then, after the tipping point, she became the other person. The person who would be talked about behind her back when she came home to the marae in her town for tangi* or family weddings. She heard cousin Ngahuia one time, talking in the kitchen of the wharekai† when she didn't know Hana had come to the doorway. Ngahuia had a couple of kids by then, one balanced on her hip as she dried dishes from the hākari.‡ Motherhood had made her softer around the edges physically, but she was just as sharp-edged as the taunting teenage girl on the bridge chanting insults at anyone who didn't have the courage to jump.

'You saw her on TV, right?' Hana heard Ngahuia say to a handful of the other cousins. 'On that mountain, in her blue uniform, turning on Māori. Turning on her own. Fucking traitor. She made her choice. Dunno why she even bothers coming back here.'

Soon after that, Hana stopped returning.

She hasn't been back to her home town for years now. She has no intention of going back. With her parents now gone, with the talking behind her back, the success story suddenly turned into a story of shame, it is too hard, too ugly, too painful. She threw herself into her career, into making good on the promise shown in police college; she steadily climbed the ranks, a tenacious, unflinching

---

* Tangi – funeral rituals
† Wharekai – dining hall
‡ Hākari – feast shared after a major event such as a funeral

investigator, the town becoming just a place she used to live, her home now the big city.

Like jumping off a bridge. There was the before, there was the tipping point, then there was the after. And it feels to Hana as if now, she's once again leaning into some kind of tipping point.

This strange, enigmatic killing, the weight she's carrying, not only as lead detective of the investigation, but as the person the killer sent the video to. Her daughter, so amazing and driven and alive, but someone Hana feels she has to learn to know all over again, before it's too late. The finality of actually divorcing Jaye, the thing that for some unknown reason they'd never actually quite got around to despite all those years apart, but an act of completion Jaye now wants, with him and Marissa making a life together. The approaching tornado of the law student and his QC, the unearned and unjust disaster she knows is slowly and relentlessly bearing down on her.

She feels like she's out on the end of the longest strut of the bridge again, wavering on the very edge of the tipping point. But now, it's not the joy of leaning forward, it's the fear of being shoved from behind, the weight of momentum pushing her to tumble downwards, not a willing rider of the glorious pull of gravity but a victim of its unfightable forces, falling involuntarily and out of control into the cold water below.

'What are you thinking about, Detective Senior Sergeant?' Dr Silao asks gently.

Hana hasn't said a word for several minutes now; she is well aware of it, and actually she's in absolutely no hurry to speak. Her obligations to this farce of a process end when she walks in the police psych counsellor's office. After that, it's just a matter of running down the clock, counting the minutes till she can walk back out the door.

She runs her finger along a join in the pale green upholstery of the couch she's sitting on. The furniture, the cheap and uninspiring abstract prints on the wall, even the lampshades – everything in this office is designed to be calming and relaxing. The result for Hana is neither calm nor relaxed, just a vague indignation at the lack of aesthetic boldness or taste.

She just wants to get back to the eighth floor, back to her investigation.

'No cop who walks in this door wants to walk in this door,' Dr Silao says. 'Cops are doers. You solve. You apprehend. You don't sit around talking about internal stuff. More's the pity.'

It's not admonishing or accusing. Dr Silao is amiable. She is maddeningly amiable. 'I've got to write a report on each of our six sessions,' she says. 'It's up to you if that report says "DSS Westerman is very interested in identifying and addressing potential issues." Or if it says "She is very interested in the clock on the wall."'

Hana thinks vaguely for a moment: what would happen if she talked to this soft-spoken counsellor about the tipping point? About the footage on television that Ngahuia saw, how what happened that day on the mountain eighteen years ago changed everything? About the feeling dwelling deep in her gut like she's balanced precariously at a fragile fulcrum, a place so tenuous it's sometimes

71

hard to breathe, just waiting for the hard, vicious shove from behind?

The before. The tipping point. And the after.

Before she's even finished the thought, she knows she's not going to share a thing with this woman. Fuck her.

'I didn't touch the guy,' she says. 'I'm here because my boss says I have to be here, not because I want to, and certainly not because I've got any underlying issues to deal with.'

She leaves the muted tones of the office. The amiable woman will write whatever she wants to write in her report. That's her job.

Hana's got her own job to do.

With the Palace, the video is specific. Starts wide. Zooms in on the flat on the second floor, telling them exactly what to look for. With an hour of the day already wasted, Hana is head down, renewed urgency, sitting with Stan at her desk in the open-plan area, comparing the videos side by side on Stan's laptop.

She flips to the second video, the footage of inner-city Auckland. 'It's the whole city,' she says. 'Thousands of buildings and homes and offices, hundreds of thousands of people. What are we meant to be looking at? What are we supposed to see?'

The video loops once more. Hana watches a final time. Already in her head she's moving on to the list of several dozen things she needs to get updates on from the several dozen officers in her team, the afternoon briefing with the new leads she wants pursued. Time to keep moving forward.

Then something catches her eye on the laptop screen.

The *flash-flash-flash* of a regularly repeating blinking red light.

'Zoom in on that,' she says to Stan, indicating the flashing. Stan toggles his mouse. It doesn't even need repositioning; the repeating red light is dead centre of the frame. On the laptop screen, the buildings of Auckland enlarge, getting more pixelated as the image zooms in further, finally centring on one particular mirror-glass building.

It's the tall office tower Hana and Stan pass every day on the way to Central Police Station. The flashing light is the radio mast atop the building, the red aircraft warning beacon.

The place where a man so recently fell twenty storeys to his death.

Footsteps echo in dark, cold corridors beneath the main city hospital. Hana and Stan are with a pathologist and another cop, DSS Summers, an older guy with greying hair, the detective in charge of the suicide investigation. They descend concrete stairs, further down into the gloom.

In the mortuary four floors beneath ground level, harsh white lights spark to life.

Lining one side of the windowless room, a row of dull metal hatches like a series of refrigerator doors. Which is what they are. The pathologist opens one door; the cold steel examination tray slides out on its rollers. Stan shivers, and it's only partly because of the icy temperature the mortuary is kept at. The body is fully covered by a blanket.

'We're all professionals,' the pathologist says. 'Still. It was a long way down. Just be ready,' she cautions as she removes the blanket.

Hana doesn't flinch. Although there's good reason to do so. It's not that she's unempathetic, not at all. But twenty years into the job, you learn to check emotion at the mortuary door. When you approach these sliding steel trays, your job is to look with the eyes of an investigator in search of evidence. Especially try not to look too deeply into the face, try not to imagine the contours when the deceased was talking, the wrinkling of the lines around the eyes when they smiled.

Try not to give your dreaming self any material to work with in the precious sleeping hours.

'Daniel Waterford. Just turned sixty. He was CEO of a property development company,' says Summers, standing at the foot of the examination tray that holds the deceased's remains. After Hana took the exams to become a detective, she worked with Summers for a year or so, the kind of mentoring relationship she now has with Stan. They're close. But today Summers is impatient. Unhappy about being dragged in to rehash an investigation that is all but done and dusted, especially when he's only a few months away from retirement.

'The property development company have offices on the eighteenth and nineteenth floors,' he tells them.

'Was there a suicide note, Gary?' Hana asks. 'A final call? Any hint?'

'Nothing. Shock to everyone, apparently. But then again . . . maybe it wasn't.'

Waterford had recently found out that he had advanced prostate cancer, his wife had told Summers. It hit him hard. He did triathlons, ocean swimming. An athlete. At sixty years old, he'd get changed into running gear at the end of work each day, go to the rooftop, watch the sun go down as he stretched. Then he'd run nine kilo-metres home.

Hana takes out her sketchbook, chooses a pencil. She moves around the stainless-steel tray, carefully drawing what she is seeing.

'A long, slow decline,' Summers tells them. 'That would be hell on earth for a guy like Waterford. A quick, fast descent might have been the more attractive option. His wife said as much.'

As Hana keeps sketching, Summers meets Stan's eye. The thing with the sketchbooks was something Hana started doing later, after she'd been plain clothes for a few years, a way to record in graphite and lead what she was actually seeing through the eye, which she found again and again could be very different to what was seen through the flattening lens of a camera. Stan can tell the sketchbook and pencil is a habit that an old-school cop like Summers has no time for.

'I already put everything in my 258.' Summers hands

a copy of his file notes to Stan. 'It's ready to go to the coronial inquest. That is, once we're done here,' he adds, pointedly. Hana recognizes the tone in her friend's voice. She has worked with Summers closely enough to know he doesn't mince words. He can be tetchy and terse if he feels he's being mucked around. But she isn't done yet. 'Do you have spare gloves?' she asks the pathologist.

Summers leans against one of the metal doors, unimpressed. Clearly this isn't finishing any time soon.

Hana pulls on a pair of surgical gloves. 'Can we tilt the head?' she asks the pathologist. 'Is that all right?'

The pathologist joins her and they work together. It's delicate work; the head of the deceased has suffered awful damage. The body is about to be given back to the family, and before the funeral an undertaker will do whatever reconstruction is possible, but with the best will in the world and the most able of reconstructive skills, Daniel Waterford won't be having an open-casket funeral.

With the head moved to a slightly different position, Hana studies the deceased's forehead. The flesh has been ruptured by the fall. On the two areas that have been split apart, she can see two separate marks. Both straight lines. Very, very carefully, she eases the pieces of ruptured flesh back together, aligning them as they were before the man fell. The two separate marks line up perfectly to form one straight line.

'Can you measure this wound, please?' she asks.

The pathologist retrieves her tape measure. 'Eleven centimetres.'

'The victim from the Palace, the fatal blow was from a

straight-edged weapon, ten to eleven centimetres. Almost identical,' Hana says, taking off her gloves. She starts sketching the forehead wound.

'Can we have a quiet word?' Summers asks her. 'Outside?' He's annoyed. Not even trying to hide it now.

'We can talk here, Gary.'

Summers nods, fine. 'You fall twenty storeys, you're gonna get all kinds of damage. Straight line, jagged line, every kind of damn line. Look at the guy.'

'I'm exploring possibilities. It's my job.'

'You're making some crazy connection between a murder and a suicide.'

'I'm not saying there's a link,' Hana says. 'I'm following a possibility.'

'You're kicking up dust in my case. It's disrespectful. I don't appreciate it.'

'I'm sorry you feel like that. I'll get out of your way as soon as I'm done.' She keeps sketching.

Summers has had enough. 'I heard what you've been saying to your team,' he snaps. 'This won't be one plus one equals two. Dig holes in unexpected places. Your bloody scribbling in your picture books. I've been doing this a few moons. I know when I see someone on the scent of something. And I know when I see a dog barking at passing cars.'

Hana's back straightens. That stings. 'Gary. We've always treated each other with respect. Don't patronize me.' With the ruined body lying between them, they stare at each other. Eyes locked in a silent battle of wills.

Finally Summers turns and walks away, waiting outside the door of the mortuary for Hana to finish her sketching.

The sun goes down over the inner city as Stan follows Hana up through the stairwell and out onto the open rooftop of the office block. In the distance, the sky is turning red over the Waitākere ranges, which divide greater Auckland from the wild beaches of the west coast.

It's just after six p.m. The streets twenty storeys below are jammed with cars and buses as the city sheds its work-force at the end of the working day. The same time of day that Daniel Waterford fell, Hana observes.

Stan has the file of case notes that Summers gave him. He moves around the rooftop, referencing the file, working through the police reconstruction of the fatal fall. They go to the western edge, the part of the roof Waterford fell from. There's a waist-high barrier. Stan and Hana look at the drop. It's a very long way down.

Hana turns. It makes sense that Waterford would come to the west-facing side of the building, the last glow of sunset warming his face as he stretched. She'd do the same.

She looks around the rooftop. There are banks of air-conditioning units. The big radio mast, the flashing red light on top. Cell phone masts surround the perimeter.

'If you knew his habits, if you knew he came here every day at the same time, after work, and you were up here waiting for him . . . where would you wait?'

On the other side of the rooftop, there's a utilities shed. The size of a large home garden shed. Hana tries the door. It's padlocked. Stan retrieves his Swiss Army knife. It takes some fiddling before the padlock springs free. Hana goes into the small dark structure, turning to look out through the open door. There's a clear line of view across to the western side of the building. 'Can you go back to where he fell,' she asks Stan.

Stan stands where Daniel Waterford would likely have stood, at the guardrail at the western edge. Hana closes the door of the shed most of the way. She looks through the sliver of a gap. She can see Stan perfectly. She eases the door open and walks fast across the rooftop, talking as she goes. 'It's fifteen, twenty paces at most. I cover the distance in five, maybe six seconds. I get close. He hears me, turns . . .'

She raises an imaginary weapon in her hand. Stan turns. Hana brings the weapon down. 'One strike,' she says, 'across the forehead. If it's not already over, the fall does the rest.'

Stan clears his throat. An uncomfortable, embar-rassed sound.

Hana can see he is as awkward now as he is whenever he's around her daughter. But with Addison, it's discomfort in an enjoyable way. There's something else in Stan's eyes now. Something that looks like pity.

'Say it,' she tells him. 'Say what you're thinking.'

'I'm not saying you're wrong, Senior . . .' Stan trails away.

'Yes you are.'

'I'm sorry, boss. But *why*? Why kill a homeless junkie one day and a wealthy property developer the next? What possible connection could there be?'

'I have no idea,' says Hana bluntly. She doesn't. There's absolutely nothing to link the two victims.

Stan feels like a Year 6 student telling the maths teacher

79

they might have the fifth decimal place of pi wrong. 'A guy who's all about physical strength,' he says. 'Pushing himself to the limit every day, living for the adrenaline and the aching muscles. Then he finds out his body's betraying him. The suicide scenario. One plus one, D Senior. Sometimes it just equals two.'

Hana knows she's been doing what she asked her team to do, following instinct and intuition, looking for the unexpected. But what if following your instincts is just a pretty way of saying you have no fucking idea, you're taking a random lurching stab in the dark?

'A dog barking at passing cars,' she says.

'Summers was being a dick. No call for that.'

Far below, the street lights are starting to flicker to life around the maze of streets. Hana sighs. 'The thing with Patrick Thompson,' she says quietly to Stan. 'If he takes it further, Jaye's going to have to stand me down. He's trying to dodge it – the bloody anger counselling – but if the QC lays a formal complaint, he won't have a choice. At least I'll have some time with Addison.'

It's not self-pity. Just a cold, unflinching look at reality. But it's painful for Stan to watch.

As Hana heads towards the entry to the stairwell, Stan goes back to lock the utilities shed. He's about to close the door when he sees something inside, the last rays of the pink sunset hitting something on the rear wall of the shed.

'*Shit*. Boss.'

Hana hears the tone in his voice. She hurries to join him. 'Look,' says Stan.

When she was in the shed, Hana was focused on the view

from inside, looking out towards the edge of the building where Daniel Waterford fell. Now she is looking the other way, into the shed, and for the first time she sees carved into the concrete, meticulously engraved, a shape. It has been made with a series of dots, by some very sharp object, a fine chisel or meticulously sharpened knife.

She has seen the shape before. So has Stan. The first time they saw it, it was shining luminol purple in the darkness.

An inward-turning spiral. Like something from nature, like the perfect spiral on a hermit crab shell, the circling of a cyclone approaching land.

The same symbol that was on the leg of the park bench outside the Palace. But this time, it's not just one spiral.

'Jesus,' says Stan, his voice shaky. 'Two. There's two of them.'

As day becomes night in Auckland city, Hana stares at two identical spirals etched side by side into the concrete wall.

Her hunch was right. The Palace was number one. The CEO is number two.

She's not in charge of a one-off homicide inquiry.

She is hunting someone who has murdered twice.

Someone who may well kill again.

9

HERE SHOWS MUCH AMISS

'Come, for the third, Laertes. You do but dally! I pray you, pass with your best violence. I am afeard you make a wanton of me.'

The actor playing Hamlet is not a big man, not someone who commands the stage by physical size. He is lean and wiry, but he has the swagger and the dangerous edge of a cornered street fighter. There is an adrenaline-fuelled desperation in his eyes; his honed and tattooed biceps bulge as he leaps effortlessly around the stage, sword flailing as he madly pursues hapless Laertes. The staging is a clever imagining of Elsinore as a modern-day Auckland city street, Hamlet and Laertes facing off atop a rusting rubbish dumpster, eye to eye, steel flashing as their swords strike.

'Have at you now!' explodes Laertes. He leaps forward, his sword's poisoned tip piercing Hamlet's chest. Both men tumble from the dumpster to the ground; in the process, both lose their weapons. Hamlet is the faster to his feet,

and by chance he grabs Laertes' poisoned sword. Laertes picks up Hamlet's blade to desperately defend himself. But Hamlet has the advantage now. He backs Laertes up against a street light and beneath a *No Parking* sign; the blades flash in the disconcerting flickering light of a faulty sodium bulb.

Hamlet lunges, thrusting the sword into his opponent's shoulder, unknowingly condemning Laertes with the same powerful poison that will soon kill Hamlet himself.

But even as he taunts Laertes – '*Nay, come, again!*' – his mother, Gertrude, falls to the litter-strewn concrete footpath. White froth forms at the edges of her mouth. The poison from the chalice she mistakenly drank from is already taking hold.

Mother and son will soon die together, surrounded by numerous other dead.

'*Take up the bodies!*' Prince Fortinbras implores his men with the last words of the play. '*Such a sight as this becomes the field, but here shows much amiss. Go, bid the soldiers shoot.*'

The soldiers bear the dead bodies solemnly from the stage. The stage lights fade. Only the sporadic flickerings of the sodium bulb remain. Gunshots sound, ten in all, one for every death in this bloody tragedy. The final shot echoes away to silence.

The orange street light flickers one final time, and dies. Then, darkness.

The lights brighten again on the cast gathered hand in hand at the front of the stage. The audience rises in acclaim for a spectacular and singular performance.

In the middle of the line of their fellow cast members, Hamlet and Gertrude stand side by side. They beam at the rapturous applause.

The water falls blood red onto the floor of the shower.

The actor who played Hamlet hums under the shower head as flowing water washes away the stage blood. The song Simon Masterton hums has neither words nor tune. A melody-free hybrid between a Buddhist chant and a half-remembered nursery rhyme. The mantra is something Masterton has learned to use, a way to transition from the energy and fury and adrenaline and despair of a role like Hamlet, back into the blandness of real life. He'd bought a nice eggplant that afternoon. Deep purple, nearly black, the just-right midpoint between taut and pliant. He's already planning the meal he'll make when he gets home. Cut the eggplant into inch-thick circles, dip in egg and panko, slow-fry in heaps of olive oil.

After the curtain fell, Laertes invited everyone back to his local for a vodka or three. The younger cast members are better equipped for that kind of carry-on, the night after night of going out after the show, swapping stories and sinking drink after drink, maybe ending up in each other's beds and spending the rest of the season cleaning up the awkward fallout. All that, it's a younger actor's game. Masterton would rather keep the drama where it belongs, on the stage.

He dries himself and pulls on trousers and a shirt, sits at

the make-up mirror, removes his contact lenses, carefully puts them in their plastic case.

Behind him, the door to the changing room quietly opens. The actor looks towards the shape in the doorway. Without his glasses on, the figure is just a vague blur. How the hell did the short-sighted ever perform intricate sword fights before contact lenses were invented? he wonders vaguely to himself.

'Peter, I won't make it tonight,' he says, assuming the actor playing Laertes is there to follow up on the invitation to vodka. 'I'm going to grab a bite to eat, take the dog for a walk. Have a Stoli for me.'

No response. The door shuts, but the vague shape is still there. Masterton hears a click, the sound of his dressing room door being locked.

'Peter?' he tries again, peeved at the silent treatment he is apparently being given. What grave offence did I commit now? he wonders. Maybe the plastic retractable blade of the rapier didn't retract. Maybe he spoke across one of Laertes' lines, and the fragile ego of his stage partner will never allow the slight to be forgotten.

He reaches for his glasses. Tortoiseshell and Italian, a splash-out present he bought himself at the start of the season; playing Hamlet is something to celebrate. As he puts them on, he catches a glimpse of a movement reflected in the mirror, something falling towards his head, moving very fast, a movement not unlike the flash of the swords on stage just a few minutes earlier.

The taste of blood fills the back of his throat. It's not stage blood.

In his last moments of consciousness, the actor realizes he has somehow fallen heavily to the floor of his dressing room. His glasses are still on his face, but one of the lenses is smashed. The world is a strange blur, the cracked lines of the broken glass and a red tint where his own blood has hit the other lens.

He tries to reach out, to raise himself up from the floor, but for some reason his arm isn't working. He makes to speak, to protest at whatever the hell just happened, but the hard, precise blow to his temple has fractured his skull and caused instant and irreversible damage to the area of the frontal cortex in which words are formed. If he were to live, from this moment on Masterton would only be capable of vocalizations remarkably similar to the mantra-like sounds he was using to unwind in the shower. He would never again be able to work at the job he has done his entire adult life. He wouldn't be able to drive a car. He would struggle to ever learn again to sign his name. If he was very lucky, after several years of intensive physical therapy, he might one day haltingly walk.

But Simon Masterton is not going to live.

Once more the flash of the weapon, moving fast through the air. A sickening dull thud. Then darkness.

Afterwards, after he has prayed for the long dead and the newly dead, after he has wiped the blood from the striking edge of his weapon, after he has rolled the weapon once more in the woven mat, he looks at his hands. They are shaking.

A feeling of dull nausea aches deep within him. The haunting and involuntary reaction of his body, the lower functions of his consciousness battling against the decisions his higher reasoning has committed him to, the course of action he has determined and is following.

With an effort of will, a sheer act of resolute concentration, the way his mother showed him when they were hunting deer and his hands were trembling as he lined up the animal in his sights, he controls his breathing.

He closes his eyes.

He remembers holding his mother's hand as she was dying.

He remembers how she was eaten alive from inside; not like Hamlet's mother, with poison administered in a chalice, but devoured by another poison, the cancer that overtook her. And also devoured by the poison of despair. The loss of all hope that the wrongs committed against her people in the generations before her would ever be fixed, that things would be put right for the generations that would follow her. Poisoned by a mourning that never died, that couldn't die, until she died. The poison of despair that consumed his mother, now eating him from within as well, as surely as the poison Gertrude swallowed.

He breathes. He puts aside the memory of his mother.

His heart rate returns to something like normal.

He opens his eyes. His hands are steady now.

He returns the weapon to his kitbag.

He has so much to do before morning.

10

CARVED INTO SKIN

Hana hasn't slept.

When Stan dropped her home, it was already long past midnight and there was no point in going through the charade of lying down in bed. She'd pulled on her running shoes instead. Running 10.13 kilometres at two in the morning isn't exactly a recommended replacement for eight hours of REM sleep, but for Hana it's better than the alternative. Lying under the sheets looking at her ceiling, trying to fit together the baffling pieces of this puzzle.

Addison and PLUS 1 had been in Addison's room, cutting the music video for her new song on PLUS 1's laptop. 'You need to sleep,' Hana told them.

'You can talk, Mum,' said Addison.

Hana runs the dark night-time streets, the events of the last few hours rolling through her head. The evening meeting where she told the Operation Palace team they were now investigating two separate but connected murders. Two photos side by side on a whiteboard now – Daniel Waterford, the CEO of a property development company, a guy who owns a ten-million-dollar house in one of the best parts of town. And Terrence Sean McElvoy, a crack junkie without a cent to his name, a former inmate convicted of the manslaughter of his own child.

'Something connects these two men,' Hana told her team. 'We don't know what the connection is. But we're going to find it.'

She said the words with utter conviction, with the authority and belief a leader has to instil in those who follow. But it's bewildering. What could possibly tie these two vastly different individuals? Some kind of drug supply connection, the CEO at the top of the pyramid, the junkie at the bottom? Sexual perversion, the mainstay of so many violent crimes, a degenerate human sex-trafficking ring? A dozen scenarios were brainstormed, the responsibilities of following up on each possibility divided among the ever-expanding team of detectives.

With her discovery of the two carved symbols on the rooftop, any questions about Hana's leadership disappeared. A breathtaking collision of instinct and deduction had led her to the utilities shed on the rooftop of the high-rise building. Every officer on the eighth floor of Central Station had renewed respect for the woman at the front of the room.

At the meeting, Jaye was beside Hana. This is uncharted territory for everyone on the eighth floor. These cops have suddenly found themselves involved in the biggest homicide case of their careers; of course as officer in charge of the criminal investigation branch Jaye will be hands-on. But Hana is also aware of an unspoken undercurrent, the long shadow that hangs over her. The incident with the law student. With legal action threatening, if criminal charges are brought, she will find herself suspended in the middle of the investigation. Jaye was there at her side to ensure that if the worst happens, there is continuity. If Hana is not standing in front of that room in a week's time, he can step seamlessly into the breach.

Hana pauses in the light of an all-night takeaway bar. The smell of old canola wafts, oil that has fried way too many scoops of chips. She reaches for her phone, checks her emails, something she has been doing every fifteen minutes, every ten minutes. The killer is expertly managing the flow of information, and it's driving her crazy. On the one hand, there's the two videos, the carefully laid trail of breadcrumbs leading to the two bodies. On the other, each of the murder scenes was left pristine, not even a partial fingerprint or the faintest hint of DNA. Hana finds herself willing another anonymous video to arrive. A fresh set of breadcrumbs to follow.

The sound of quiet sobbing. A middle-aged woman leaning against the wall of the takeaway bar, considerably worse for wear, tears leaking, her mascara painting unintended abstract designs on her cheeks. Hana has spent enough time on the beat to know there's no point inviting a half-hour of melancholic drunk-speak about heartbreak and broken dreams.

'Are you able to tell me your address?' she asks the

woman, straight to the point. The woman says a street name and house number, slurred but recognizable.

Hana takes her arm, guides her firmly to a nearby taxi, gives the driver a twenty-dollar note and tells him the address. As the taxi disappears into the darkness, she checks her phone again.

There are no new emails in her inbox.

The light is off in Addison's room when Hana gets home. But Addison puts her head into Hana's room as she's getting ready to shower. 'Are you okay, Mum?'

'Yes. Yeah, I'm good. You?'

Addison is fizzing, the new song they're working on, she thinks it's going to explode. 'The gig at Sailor Bar,' she says. 'Any chance you can make it?'

Hana smiles. 'I'll try.'

Addison can read the look in Hana's face. There's no way her mum is going to be able to get there. She comes and sits on the bed beside her. 'It's big, isn't it? This new case. Like, seriously big?'

Hana puts her arm around her daughter. She holds her for a long moment.

When she was Addison's age, Hana was sporty, athletic. Like Addison, she was always the smart kid, curious about the world. And bold as hell, a born leader. When she first got her driving licence, she drove her mates to the movie theatre in the town twenty kilometres away. On the way home, they passed an accident, a car that had run off the side of the road. Hana pulled over. The girlfriends she was with sat in the car, terrified, but Hana didn't think twice; she scrambled down the bank and dragged the guy out. He was drunk and bleeding like hell where his forehead had gone through the windscreen. By the time the others pulled themselves together and came down to help, Hana had the drunk guy in recovery position; she'd cleared his mouth of vomit and staunched his bleeding.

Growing up, she sometimes visited her great-uncle at his house. He was a legend for her family. He'd been in the 28th Māori Battalion in World War II, the unit of young Māori soldiers who went to Europe and Africa to fight for the country that had colonized Māori, that had stolen their land. It was an entirely voluntary battalion; Māori weren't actually eligible for conscription. But you couldn't stop young men like her great-uncle from enlisting, they signed up in droves.

The British commanders routinely sent the 28th in first to every confrontation. Cannon fodder. You can take the colony away from the colonizer, but don't even try to take away his mindset.

Unsurprisingly, the Māori battalion casualty rate was devastatingly high, but they were legendary in their fear-lessness, and their bravery turned the course of battle after battle. In truth, though, it wasn't so much that these young soldiers were fighting for king and country. That wasn't why men like Hana's great-uncle enlisted. They signed up for the adventure of their lives. To go to the other side of the world, to do something exciting and extraordinary. They were fighting for their mates and their whānau; they were fighting for the people the Nazis were exterminating. They were fighting against the bad bastards.

When Hana started seriously thinking about what she wanted to do, the cops was the obvious choice. A career that asks for physicality, nerve, brainpower. She applied for the police as soon as she turned eighteen, a few months older than Addison is now. The job was perfect for someone like her, someone who'd scramble down a bank in the dark to save some stupid drunk bugger from drowning in his own vomit.

Someone who understood the idea of stopping the bad bastards doing what they do.

Hana kisses Addison's head. Her finger traces the grooves and lines of her daughter's skull, where the bone structure shows beneath the clean-shaven skin. 'Your beautiful hair. Are you ever going to grow it back?'

Very quietly, she answers Addison's question, about the investigation.

'Yeah, love. The case is big. Really big.'

Hana stands under the shower. The mixer nearly on full heat, the extractor fan doing its best but the bathroom steadily filling with steam. Her sketchbooks now have several pages of detailed drawings of the inward-turning spiral shape, the symbol painted in blood at one murder site, carved with a sharpened point into the wall on the twentieth floor. She reaches out with her index finger. In the steam on the glass wall of the shower she carefully, meticulously crafts the symbol. She doesn't need to look at her sketchbook; the tip of her finger delicately inscribes the inward spiral, the line becoming finer and finer until the taper ends.

Then her eyes shift focus.

In the mirror outside the shower, her own reflection. The spiral she has made in the steam seems to sit on her cheek as she looks at her image in the mirror. A strange effect, like the unintentional abstract mascara designs on the drunk woman's face. Almost like a tattoo.

She pauses. She looks again at herself in the mirror. Exactly like a tattoo.

A facial tattoo.

In the black and white photograph, the fine edge of a carefully sharpened stone chisel cuts deep into the face of a man. Blood seeps from his cheek. The tā moko, the traditional tattoo, given to the wearer in a sacred ritual. Each as distinctive and unique as a fingerprint. The facial moko carries as much information about the one who bears it as the helix spirals of their DNA, telling stories of their heritage, the tribe and sub-tribe they belong to, their ancestors, the things they have achieved in their lives, the status and honour with which they are regarded.

A moko is much more than a tattoo. A moko is a living book. Not printed on paper. Carved into skin.

Hana and Stan have been in the restricted reading room of the museum for several hours. There's a growing pile of reference material around them. They started with books and manuscripts devoted to the art of tā moko. The librarian, excited to assist the officers and their impressive police identification cards, has steadily returned with more and more old books, anything that might have some photographic or painted representation of traditional tattooing, helpfully marking relevant pages with slips of acid-free paper. She has issued them with white gloves and insisted they remain on at all times.

When Hana or Stan finds a tā moko symbol that resembles the inward-curving spiral, Stan photographs the image and feeds it into his laptop, overlaying it on top of images of the symbols taken from the Palace and the twentieth floor. While the spiral or koru shape is universal among Māori carving and tattoos, each koru is different and distinct. There are many designs that have similarities to the symbols left at the locations of the two murders. But scanned onto the laptop, none of the koru matches exactly.

Hana finishes with the collection of black and white photos and moves on to another book. Reproductions of beautiful nineteenth-century oil paintings of kaumātua and kuia, the respected older men and women of a tribe. It is not just men who bear the moko. The finely chiselled female moko kauae are a form of tattoo reserved for only the chin, not the full face. Moko kauae were common once among Māori women, the blue-green etchings signalling prestige and standing, as well as being an adornment of great delicacy and beauty.

Hana turns the pages, not letting herself give in to the

temptation to stop and stare at the haunting images of the long-dead elders.

Stan reaches for another book. He opens it to the page the librarian has marked, but the image doesn't seem relevant. He's about to close it and add it to the pile to be returned to the shelves. 'Hang on,' says Hana. Something has caught her eye. She goes to stand behind him. The book is open to a full-size image, a group photo from the nineteenth century.

A troop of English colonial soldiers are gathered under a large tree. But when you look more closely, the image suddenly becomes macabre. Suspended from the tree behind the six soldiers, a naked body. A Māori man. Older, perhaps in his fifties. He is dead, strung up by the neck. His body and face are covered in tā moko.

'His hands and feet,' Hana says quietly. Stan realizes what has caught her attention. The executed prisoner's feet and hands are bound in the exact same position as the man they found at the Palace.

The librarian approaches, curious at their interest in this particular book. 'It's a collection of daguerreotypes,' she explains. 'Images from the very dawn of the age of photography. The work of a nineteenth-century English artist, sent to New Zealand by the British Army. A kind of proto war photographer.'

Stan works fast, photographing the daguerreotype, focusing in on the body of the dead Māori prisoner. He downloads the image onto his laptop, magnifying the tā moko on the man's body and face.

'The daguerreotype was taken in the early 1860s,' the librarian says.

'Where?' asks Hana.

'Auckland. The other side of the harbour. Mount Suffolk.'

Hearing the name of the volcanic peak, Hana is uneasy. She knows Mount Suffolk well. She has history there.

'Look,' Stan says, excitement in his voice. He magnifies one particular area of tā moko, a prominent part of the design from the deceased man's face. It's an inward-curving spiral shape.

A koru.

He lines up the koru from the dead man's moko over the image of the carved spirals taken from the murder sites. He works carefully, adjusting the relative sizes of the images, changing the tilt and orientation. It's fiddly and exacting, the images delicately aligned and realigned, then adjusted yet again.

As Stan works, Hana studies the strange tableau captured on the page of the book. The chilling moment frozen in time. The dead chief, stripped, humiliated, hanging by his neck from a tree. Below, the men who took his life, standing straight and proud, the brass buttons of their army uniforms polished, as if they are on parade for visiting nobility.

Stan makes a last adjustment. The images are precisely lined up. He looks at Hana.

'It's the same, D Senior,' he says. 'An exact match.'

Hana slides off her white gloves. She rubs her jawbone, the part of her body where she carries tension. Of all the places on earth this could lead her back to. The last place she ever wanted to go to again.

Mount Suffolk.

11

LINES OF DESCENT

Mount Suffolk lies on a headland directly across the harbour from the mirror-glass high-rise buildings of downtown Auckland's central business district. The mountain is five kilometres as the gull flies from Central Police Station, but unless you take a commuter ferry or own one of the thousands of yachts in the many marinas around the harbour, getting there involves a convoluted twenty-kilometre drive from the city, across the harbour bridge and through the suburbs of the lower north shore.

As Stan drives across the bridge, Hana sees the distinctive shape of the volcanic outcrop in the distance. She tries to remember the details of the last time she went to this place. It was with a contingent of nearly a hundred officers. How exactly did they get there? Did they take police vans? The junior cops like Hana, were they moved in buses? Was it a convoy, a trail of vehicles with their red and blue flashing lights lighting up the harbour bridge in the pre-dawn darkness, like something from the movies?

She can't remember. So much of that day has been packed away in a box and deliberately pushed to a dark corner of her consciousness. Strangely, she remembers breakfast. Maybe it was because she'd become so sensitive to food smells. Of all the things that could stay in her head about that day, nearly two decades later . . . the scrambled eggs Jaye cooked that morning.

She was just over three months. She'd stopped drinking coffee because the smell she used to love so much now made her feel sick. She'd given up fish, she couldn't have the smoked salmon Jaye had with his eggs.

Hana hadn't told anyone at the station that she was pregnant, not yet. It was still early on; they decided there was no hurry, they wanted to make sure everything was fine.

Her shift were given an especially early call that day. The bosses kept the nature of what was planned confidential. None of the shift had any idea what was happening. Jaye was in a different unit and it was his rostered day off, but he got up early and made her scrambled eggs, toast. Juice instead of the coffee she couldn't drink any more.

She remembers finishing her eggs, Jaye dropping her at the station. It was still dark as he kissed her goodbye. 'Have a nice day,' he told her.

Neither of them realized this day would change everything. For Hana. For both of them.

Hana remembers waiting in the car park near the top of Mount Suffolk. The cops could see the protesters' camp on the summit, a hundred yards away. The shanty town of tents and temporary buildings. The fluttering red, white and black tino rangatiratanga* flags. Big hand-painted signs, decorated in cheerful bright colours, with daisies and sunflowers added by the children, but carrying serious and insistent messages.

HONOUR THE TREATY

MAUNGA WHAKAIROIRO IS MĀORI LAND

RETURN WHAT WAS STOLEN FROM TE TINI-O-TAI

As Stan drives through the well-heeled suburbs towards Mount Suffolk, he can feel Hana's growing tension.

'What happened up there, Senior, on the mountain. The big protest,' he says, tentative. 'It was way before my time. I would've been five years old, at most. But I read about it. I heard you were up there.'

'Yeah,' says Hana. 'I was there.'

Stan's car passes the marae at the base of the mountain, the home of the local tribe, Te Tini-o-Tai. The beautiful carvings of the meeting house. The wooden tekoteko† atop the apex, the carved representation of the ancestor of the tribe, the captain who led his people on a twin-hulled canoe across vast expanses of uncharted ocean, a journey equal parts awe-inspiring courage and incomprehensible recklessness, a storm-tossed voyage of thousands of kilometres to reach these islands at the bottom of the Pacific.

'The tribe wanted the land returned from the Defence Department, right?' asks Stan as the car heads up the narrow access road towards the summit. 'They built a shanty town. Refused to go anywhere until their land was

---

* Tino rangatiratanga – Māori autonomy, self-rule, sovereignty
† Tekoteko – carved figure on the gable of a meeting house, usually representing an ancestor of the tribe

returned. It got embarrassing for the government, a law-and-order issue. Cops went in to evict them.' He glances at Hana in the passenger seat. 'I heard they put the Māori cops on the front line?'

Hana makes no reply.

The car pulls into the car park near the peak of the hill. It is empty today, but eighteen years ago, there were dozens of junior cops like Hana here. Another twenty or so experienced senior staff co-ordinating the operation. Hana remembers looking around at the other younger cops as the riot gear was handed out. Long batons, shields. So many faces like hers, young and brown. The Māori cops looking at each other, at the protesters camped above, only realizing at the last minute what the police hierarchy had done, the decision that had been made without consultation with those most affected.

Māori cops sent to break up a Māori land protest.

Māori cops ordered to haul away peaceful Māori protesters.

'The bosses went round us.' Hana finally replies to Stan's question. 'They told us it was down to us. We were the best equipped. The right people for the job . . .'

She unbuckles her seat belt.

'That's just wrong,' Stan says, and he means it. 'That's bullshit, boss.'

In the daguerreotype, the pūriri tree on the crest of Mount Suffolk already stands a good ten metres tall, a strong young adult tree jutting forth from the surrounding stand of ancient bush. In the intervening years, the other trees have long since been cleared. The pūriri is easily twice the height now, but he has become an old man. The once dense leafage is patchy, like a lush head of hair slowly being stripped back year after year to a bald pate. The eccentric patterns of the gnarled and twisted branches seem to sag, as if the old man's arms are no longer much interested in reaching upwards to the sun, as if now he is looking downwards, searching for a suitable resting place on the ground. A century and a half of storms and lightning strikes and possums and insect blight haven't helped.

The old pūriri tree is still standing. But he isn't long for this world.

Stan pats the peeling bark of the tree's huge trunk. 'Seen better days,' he comments.

Hana keeps her distance. Something about seeing the awful image of the dead body hanging from these same branches leaves her wary.

She circles the summit. Auckland harbour is spread out below. Ferries shuttle between the various docks. A twelve-storey behemoth of a cruise ship is piloted into the downtown terminal. Turning her back away from the central city, she looks past the islands of the gulf, out towards the open water beyond.

When the Te Tini-o-Tai tribe first made the peak their home nearly a thousand years earlier, they named the volcanic headland Maunga Whakairoiro, remembering Kākahi Whakairoiro, the great mottled orca who in the tribe's tradition guided their canoe across the ocean to this place, then threw herself ashore, her mighty body transforming into the sacred mountain. When newly arrived English settlers petitioned the fledgling New Zealand parliament to support their acquisition of the prime piece of real estate, the land was confiscated, with the support of the colonial forces. Māori objections to the forced land grab were quelled. The mountain of the guardian orca became the far less lyrical Mount Suffolk.

The view from the headland was the reason the Defence Department took control of the area over the course of the two world wars, to build lookouts and defence posts and even cannon bunkers to guard against the deeply unlikely event that German U-boats would bother to make the fifteen-thousand-nautical-mile journey to invade sleepy Auckland.

It was a most improbable scenario. But New Zealanders are a cautious bunch.

Down the northern slope of the mountain, Hana sees an area of dense foliage. In the middle of the bushes and scrub, a glimpse of a concrete structure.

Making her way down the hill, she tells Stan how a maze of old tunnels were dug under the hill over the century the Defence Department had possession of the land. They were used for storage for ammunition, weapons, engineering supplies. When the protesters tried to take back the mountain peak, the tunnels had long stood empty, the entrances sealed.

She pushes through the bushes, approaching the concrete shape. It's an entrance to the tunnels. She emerges through a final gap in the undergrowth.

The wall is covered in graffiti, the metal door is red-brown with rust. Hana immediately sees that the weld sealing the door has been gas-axed through. She runs her finger along the exposed metal around the four edges. It is fresh, burned free of rust. Both detectives can see that whoever broke into these tunnels, they did it recently.

The door is heavy, the joints creaky. With Stan and Hana working together, they manage to pull it open.

Beyond, the dark tunnels of the cave system.

'I'll get the flashlights from the car,' Stan says. But Hana doesn't want to wait.

She takes a few steps from the sunlight into gloom. Stan joins her. It's cold, a surprising and abrupt drop in temperature. Hana zips up her windbreaker. As their eyes adjust, they see the tunnels are narrow, with a high ceiling. Moss covers the walls; there is a constant dripping of water.

Hana turns on the torch app on her phone. Stan does the same. The lights reflect off puddles on the roughly excavated rock floor. They start into the darkness.

They move carefully, illuminating gaps and recesses with their phones. Rusting army equipment lies abandoned in dark corners. There are bends in the tunnel. Any number of shadowy places where someone could hide.

They make their way deeper. Stan knows Hana well enough by now not to ask what they're looking for. Some cops treat a crime like algebra, work out the equation, figure out the divisor of x and y, make their way step by logical step to the solution. For Hana, it's not maths, it's instinct.

The phone torches are less powerful than their police-issue flashlights; they only penetrate a few yards into the blanket blackness of the tunnel. Stan pauses by a rusted metal pipe long forgotten in a crevasse in the rock. Maybe street kids have taken over this place to sniff glue and party. Could be a convenient place for drug deals. He picks up the metal pipe. Just in case.

As Hana leads the way towards a fork where two branches split from the main tunnel, Stan checks the reception on his phone. 'There's no bars, Senior. We're too far under.'

'You want to order a pizza?' Hana asks, turning her light in his direction.

'My phone's running low,' he tells her. 'Torchlight chews up phone power. Don't wanna run out of battery halfway under this bloody mountain.'

They stand in silence, realizing for the first time just how quiet it is in this place. All around, the steady *drip-drip-drip* of water falling from the ceiling.

'A local uniform can come and check the place out properly,' Hana says. 'Make sure no homeless have moved in. Then they'll seal the door up again.'

As Stan heads back the way they came, Hana pauses a moment longer. The light from her torch moves across one of the forks in the tunnel. A last careful look. Nothing.

Drip-drip-drip.

Something occurs to her as she stands there alone in the darkness. Something she's thought of often since the day she was sent to this mountain. If she'd made the decision to tell her senior officers she was pregnant, she would have been on desk duties that day. She certainly wouldn't have been rostered on the front line.

That was then. This is now.

She turns to the other fork, taking one last look before she leaves. The light from her phone sweeps over a puddle on the floor, twenty metres away. There's a shape in the water. Something dropped there. She approaches the puddle, lifts the object from the water, turns it in her hands.

'Boss?' Stan comes hurrying back. Hana shows him what she's found.

A pair of tortoiseshell glasses. Expensive. Italian-made. One of the lenses is smashed.

But Stan's eyes have already gone to something else, something Hana didn't see before. His phone lights up the wall of the tunnel directly behind her.

On the wall, a photocopied photo. Technically, it's not actually a photo. It's a daguerreotype. Hana and Stan have seen the image before. Six men in the uniform of the nineteenth-century British colonial army. Standing in a posed semicircle under the pūriri tree. The dead body of the chief they just killed hanging by the neck above them.

Hana moves her phone, looking closer at the wall. Below the copy of the daguerreotype, three other images are taped to the rock. From the first soldier in the photo, a piece of cord runs down to a clipping from a recent newspaper report.

The article is about the unsolved murder in the Palace. The photo is of the victim Hana and Stan found in the sealed-up room.

From the second soldier, another length of cord connects to a second image on the wall. A photo neatly cut from the prospectus of a property development company with its headquarters based in downtown Auckland. The photo is of the CEO who fell to his death from the twentieth floor of his office block.

Hana looks at the resulting effect. The men from a

hundred and sixty years ago linked to images of the two murder victims today.

'What does it remind you of?' Her voice echoes off the rock walls.

'A family tree,' says Stan.

Hana's face is grim. 'It's whakapapa. Lines of descent.'

A third length of cord runs from the third soldier down to a flyer taped to the wall, an advertisement for a production of *Hamlet*. On the poster, the lead actor brandishes his sword, leaping after Laertes, a look of mad vengeance on his face.

'*Hamlet*,' says Hana quietly. 'Isn't that on stage now?'

With a low beep, Stan's battery dies. The tunnel is lit only by Hana's phone now. The darkness seems to close in. Stan's grip tightens on the length of rusty iron pipe.

Hana sees something below the *Hamlet* flyer. The moss growing on the stone wall has been carved into, carefully, painstakingly. It's a series of finely rendered symbols. Inward turning spirals, like a curling fern frond. The same koru symbol.

'Three of them,' Stan says.

With her torch still on, Hana takes photos of the tableau. As she moves her phone closer to the theatre flyer, she realizes something. She cautiously touches the flyer, draws her finger away.

The end of her finger is red.

As she photographs the blood on the flyer, another red drop falls from above. *Plop!* It splatters across her screen.

She gasps. Her phone slips from her hand, falls to the hard floor, the screen dies.

Complete darkness.

As she fumbles in the blackness, searching for her phone, Stan's eyes scan the vague shapes of the openings and forks of the tunnels. Both cops stay completely silent, listening for any movement. There are a hundred places someone could be concealed in the enveloping blackness of this maze.

And the only things they have to defend themselves are two phones and a length of rusty pipe.

Hana's fingers grope along the cold, wet stone floor. Finally she finds the plastic casing of her phone. She presses the on button. Nothing happens. Fuck, is it broken? She presses the button again, and again, and at last . . .

The screen lights up. She opens the torch app once more. She glances at Stan. Both of them know that the drop of blood fell from somewhere above them.

Hana turns the light of her phone upwards.

'Jesus, D Senior. Fuck.'

Two metres above them, a rocky shelf. Suspended from the outcrop, tied and bound, the actor who played Hamlet. Hana can just make out a deep wound on the side of his head, his temple, the source of the falling drops of blood. She can't see the wound clearly in the dim light of her phone. But she doesn't need to wait for a pathologist's report to have a good hunch as to how Simon Masterton was killed.

Blunt-force trauma, caused by a blow from an unknown weapon. A striking weapon with a blade ten to eleven centimetres long.

12

WE WILL MEET AGAIN

'Utu' is a word with no precise equivalent in the English language. Because there's no idea in English culture or law that is exactly similar. The words 'balance' or 'reciprocation' are perhaps close, but utu does not carry the sense of simple vengeance, an eye for an eye. It is about giving and receiving, maintaining a sense of equity and balance – for both positive and negative actions.

If a gift is given, it is necessary for your mana,[*] for your pride and standing, that a gift of equal or greater value is given in return. You have a dinner party, someone brings a nice bottle of Prosecco; when you're invited to their place, you take a good Prosecco or maybe upgrade to an affordable champagne. If a great honour is made by one group to another, a gesture of equal or greater magnitude

---

*   Mana – status, authority, spiritual power

should be returned. If the honour is not repaid, it becomes a source of lingering shame, even dishonour.

On the flipside, if someone is wronged or harmed or insulted or even killed, a debt is created. An imbalance exists. Just as with gifts and honours, so too should a wrong be repaid, in order to return to a state of harmony and balance.

Importantly, utu doesn't fit the punitive retribution of the Anglo-Saxon version. In the European legal model, if someone is hit with a stick, the one who swung that stick must be dragged in chains to face their punishment. With utu, just as honour and standing is shared collectively, a debt is held collectively – by a group, a tribe, a family. It is not just the one who wielded the stick who holds the debt. It is owed by all members of the group. Recompense can be extracted from those whose hand never touched the stick, those who are entirely innocent of the original transgression.

Better the blood of the innocent than no blood at all. And a debt doesn't diminish with the passing of time.

A debt disappears only when balance is finally restored.

Thwock thwock thwock. The helicopter circles low over the pūriri tree, the down-blast of the rotors sending leaves flying across the summit. 'You're kidding me,' Jaye yells into his police radio, maddened. 'This whole damn area is an exclusion zone. What are they doing?'

It's a TV network chopper and the camerawoman

kneeling at the open door is beside herself. Her camera sweeps across the summit, which is now crawling with cops carrying out grid searches. The white boiler suits of SOCO officers carrying their forensics testing gear come and go from the concrete opening to the tunnels; uniformed police stand guard over all the access points to the mountainside. The camerawoman knows that everything she's shooting is going straight on the early-evening bulletin.

Jaye has to shout into his handset to be heard above the helicopter rotors. 'Tell them to get the fuck out of here, now!' The TV chopper finally gets the message, rising away to a position above the harbour, just far enough to be outside the exclusion zone but still get an awesome panoramic shot of the entire mountainside for the six o'clock news.

'Fucking parasites,' Jaye mutters. He fights the urge to give the chopper the finger. Wouldn't be a great look on screen, and the last thing he needs is the media getting a sniff of the kind of pressure the cops are under, reeling from the onslaught of a developing case on a scale unlike anything anyone involved has experienced before.

Base camp is a series of E-Z Ups in the car park near the summit, surrounded by large white police situation response trucks. Jaye joins Hana in one of the trucks. The photos she took inside the tunnels have been downloaded from her phone onto a laptop. Jaye has looked at the images dozens of times now, he's been down in the tunnels, he's seen for himself the third victim hanging from the rock shelf, the daguerreotype with the lines of descent mapped out on the wall. The macabre scene is no less shocking no matter how many times he looks at it.

Even harder to come to terms with is the why. For any investigation, understanding motive is the holy grail, the key that nine times out of ten unlocks everything. They have a motive now, they've found the thing that forges a link between the murders of three complete strangers. But it's the strangest, most unsettling motive imaginable.

'Three murders,' Jaye says, still struggling to comprehend what is unfolding. 'One descendant executed for each of the six soldiers. Three more killings to go.'

It's just over five hours since Hana and Stan first entered the tunnels, following Hana's hunch, and already the investigation has branched into entirely new directions. Still more detectives have been drafted into the inquiry, and a specialist team of investigators has been established to work with genealogists and historians to identify the six soldiers, then to craft the complex webs of ancestry from the mid-nineteenth century to the descendants alive today, creating a pool of all the potential victims.

'Vengeance after one hundred and sixty years, after eight generations,' Jaye says. 'Why?'

Hana once more looks at the image of the daguerreotype on the tunnel wall, the lines of descent from the three soldiers, the three other lines waiting to be completed.

'Vengeance isn't the right word,' she says quietly. 'This is utu.'

The cops standing guard at the base of the mountain watch as the old woman approaches, followed by twenty or so others. The kuia* is dressed in the carefully pressed bleached whites of her bowling club uniform. It was ladies' day at the lawn bowls club; she'd just rolled the jack for her second end of the morning when her grandson turned up.

'Something's happening on the maunga,† Nan,' he told her.

She didn't even collect her jack; she left the cracked old leather carry bag that holds her bowling balls. She got in her grandson's car, went straight to the marae at the base of the mountain. A couple of dozen of the tribe were already there, bewildered, unable to get any information from the uniformed cops guarding the access road.

'They won't tell us a thing, whaea.'‡

The old woman buttoned up her white cardigan. 'This is our maunga,' she said, with the quiet gravitas and power of her status as a respected elder, a senior leader of her tribe. And she walked out the gate of the marae, towards the police cars.

At the cordon the young cops try their best to tell the old woman that this is a police operation, there's no public access to the summit. Holding her grandson's arm, back straight, head high, she says with restraint and dignity, 'It's *our* maunga.'

And she walks straight past the cop cars.

---

* Kuia – elderly woman, respected female elder of a tribe
† Maunga – mountain
‡ Whaea – mother; also used as a term of respect for an older woman

The uniformed cops urgently call ahead to base camp on the summit, 'There's a group coming up from the local marae, maybe twenty people. They refused to stop; do we arrest them?'

Hana says, 'Let them come.'

She is waiting with Jaye as the group approaches.

It takes a moment for the old woman to gather her breath. Time enough to look around the mountain. To see the sheer numbers of police and forensics people.

'What has happened here?' she asks.

'We're not able to give out that information,' Hana tells her. 'I'm sorry.'

'So many police,' the old woman says. 'If someone has died, there are things we need to do. The mountain must be isolated, the tapu* acknowledged. We won't stop you doing your work. But we have our own work to do. It may be different to yours. But that doesn't make it any less important. You have to tell us.'

'Yes. Someone is dead.'

The old woman's eyes fall to the name on Hana's swing badge. She looks again at her face. Hana can see a glint of recognition.

The old woman's fingers entwine with the fingers of her grandson. 'The mauri† of the mountain is harmed again,' she says, her voice trembling. 'Violence has returned to our maunga. Another life taken here.'

Among the locals, tears are falling. There are other

* Tapu – state of sacredness or spiritual restriction. A place, person or object that is considered tapu cannot be touched or, often, even approached.
† Mauri – life force, vital essence

older women in the group. Some are quietly keening, the low sounds of mourning for a departed spirit.

Hana has a copy of the daguerreotype, the photocopy from the library. She unfolds it, gives it to the old woman. 'The man in the photograph,' she says. 'Can you tell us about him?'

The grandson takes the photocopy, he holds it for his grandmother to study. 'This has something to do with our tupuna?'* the old woman asks.

'Whatever you can tell us,' Hana says, 'it will help us understand what happened here.'

The kuia looks up to the pūriri tree. Clasping her grandson's hand, she makes her way the hundred or so yards up from the car park, the others following. The ground is steep, but the old woman is determined. At the tree, her hand reaches out, touching the huge ancient trunk. Deeply lined skin gently touching deeply lined bark.

'Detective Westerman,' she says.

'Detective Senior Sergeant,' Hana says. She was right. The old woman had recognized her.

'You ask to know about our tupuna.' The kuia wipes away tears from her eyes. 'You will know. You will know everything.' She holds firmly to her grandson's arm. There is a grim resolve in her face. 'Te Tini-o-Tai have lived here continuously for centuries,' she begins. 'After the long voyage across the oceans, we made our pā† here on the mountain. Our children were born, grew old and

---

* Tupuna – ancestor
† Pā – village

115

died here. Generation after generation. Our land. Our soil. *Here*.'

The kuia looks out over the harbour. The sails of pleasure craft dot the waters. 'Then they came. They came in their boats with the tall white sails. The English, the Pākehā. No sooner did Pākehā set foot on our land than they wanted to take it. Our people would not sell. But the settlers who wanted to take our mountain, to cut down the trees and make it into their farms and their grand houses – they would not take no for an answer.'

The kuia trails away. For a moment she is silent. 'Our ancestor's name is Hahona Tuakana,' she says finally. Her voice is low, respectful, as she speaks the name. Her grandson gently pats her hand. But she doesn't want to be comforted. 'The white settlers drove their stakes into the ground,' she continues. 'Hahona Tuakana told our people they would not respond with violence. The Pākehā are reasonable men, they are civilized men, he said. We tell them this place is sacred, then the Pākehā will listen. We treat our visitors with dignity and respect, our visitors will do the same.'

The kuia smiles sadly at the innocence of the notion, a naïveté quickly corrected by the course of history. 'The Pākehā did not listen. Men with brass-buttoned uniforms and iron guns stood at the side of the settlers. But still my ancestor refused to take up arms. Tuakana refused to let his people fight. He found his own way to resist. By day the Pākehā drove in their stakes. By night, Tuakana pulled them out.'

The kuia looks around the summit. 'When they built stables all across this place,' she says, 'when their horses shitted all over our sacred headland, then Hahona Tuakana finally understood. These visitors would not treat his people with dignity or respect. They were not reasonable men, they were not civilized men. They coveted the land with a great hunger, and nothing would stand in the way of that want.' She pauses to gather breath.

'Could you come to the marae later, after my grandmother has rested?' the grandson asks.

'No,' the old woman insists. 'Detective Senior Sergeant Westerman has asked about our ancestor. I want her to know. My ancestor burned the buildings,' she continues. 'He took a dozen men, disappeared into the shadows of a distant forest. From there they waged war. But his was a war of disobedience, of resistance, not a war of violence. A war where one side refused to bear arms. When the settlers erected a building on this mountain, it was burned to the ground. The troops chased my ancestor for months. He made a hiding place deep in the darkness of the woods, and from there he returned, again and again. He and his men made the mighty British Army look like fools. But at last he was captured.'

The kuia turns her eyes towards the tree towering above her. They search for the place where her ancestor was hanged.

'October 1863,' she says, her voice low. 'My tupuna was strung up by his neck. Here, not ten feet from where we stand.' She draws a long breath. '*That* ... that is the story of your photograph. Nā te ahi ka tahuna he ahi anō.*

---

* Literally, 'Fire ignites more fires'

Violence begets violence. This place has a history of violence. Yesterday. And today. You should know that well, Detective Senior Sergeant Westerman.'

She turns from the great tree to Hana.

'You wore a uniform when you were last here,' she says. 'That time, you did not bother to ask about our tupuna. You did not think to ask about the history of this land. You came here with your helmets, with your batons. You did the things you did. This land has not forgotten what happened. We have not forgotten. We remember what was done by those who came here in their uniforms a hundred and sixty years ago. We remember what was done by those who came in different uniforms eighteen years ago.'

Her eyes stay fixed on Hana, 'We remember.'

Hana's eyes don't fall. It's an effort of will, in the face of the strength of emotion etched over the older woman's face.

Finally the kuia hands the photocopy to Jaye. She straightens the collar of her white cardigan. 'Whatever has happened,' she says, talking directly to Jaye now, 'our people will help. We will do all we can to assist the police. But Detective Senior Sergeant Westerman is not welcome here.'

The media briefing is standing room only. Journalists are shoulder to shoulder, vying for the best position. There's a relentless and rising hubbub of voices, theories being traded about the new investigation on Mount

Suffolk on top of everything else that's happened in the last few days.

Outside the door of the briefing room, Jaye pauses to take a moment alone with Hana. He is certain how the situation needs to be handled. 'We keep a lid on this,' he tells her. 'What you found down in the tunnels has to be kept away from the eyes of the public. Whoever did this, they want panic, they want fear. They want people to look at the lines of descent, to look at the gaps waiting to be filled. They want people to wonder, is my name next? They want an audience to terrorize. We're not going to give them one. We work fast, we find this person and stop them.'

Through the glass panel in the door, they can see that the journalists are getting restless.

Jaye turns to look at Hana. 'Are you okay?' he asks. 'With what happened up there? The old woman?'

'She can't tell us how to run our investigation,' Hana says.

'She's not going to. But we have a job. Find the person doing this. Stop them. Put them away for a very long time. If it means someone else deals with the tribe so that we can do what we have to do, that's what's going to happen. But that's not what I mean,' Jaye continues. 'I know it would have been hard. Going back there.'

Hana is surprised at the tone in his voice.

This isn't her boss talking. This is someone who knows her, who knows her history, what it meant for her going back to the mountain. Someone who knows how her life was changed by what happened when she was a junior cop.

Behind the lectern, facing the banks of cameras and

microphones, Jaye keeps doggedly to script. He confirms that there are three separate murder inquiries under way in the Tāmaki Makaurau policing district, it's a challenging time for the criminal investigation branch, but useful lines of inquiry are being followed in all three investigations. 'Public assistance is being sought from anyone who has information about any of the incidents – the event at the Palace, the death at the central city office block, or the discovery of a body in the tunnels under Mount Suffolk.'

As Jaye continues, Hana, watching from the back of the media room, becomes aware of a ripple moving through the mass of journalists. Phones vibrate with incoming messages. Texts and emails are being opened. Journalists look at each other, murmurs rise.

'Did you get this?'

'You too?'

'Fuck.'

Hana moves so she can see the screen of one journalist's phone. A video is playing. It's a scene she is very familiar with. The video popping up on every phone screen was taken in the tunnels. It shows the daguerreotype on the wall, the lines of descent to the three murder victims. The very thing Jaye is so determined to keep out of the media.

A journalist raises his hand. 'I'm sorry, Detective Inspector, when you say there are three separate inquiries, do you mean the investigations are unrelated?'

'We have three separate investigations,' Jaye repeats.

'The three killings are unconnected?' the journalist asks. 'You're saying those killings have nothing to do with a historic execution?'

Clang.

Before Jaye can even try to answer the curveball question, a TV news reporter asks, 'Has evidence been found that indicates these three murders are connected? Committed by the same person? The person who sent this video? Yes or no?' She steps forward, showing Jaye the screen of her tablet. 'This was just sent to all the major news outlets,' she says, the cameras still rolling.

Jaye looks at the footage. The thing he was desperately trying to keep a lid on, now in the hands of every news organization. And by this evening, on every TV screen in the country.

Around the room, a cacophony of competing voices rises.

'Do you know who sent the video?'

'Who are the people in the old photo?'

'What does the army troop have to do with the killings?'

'Why are the police denying a connection between the three murders, treating the press like idiots? And the public as well?'

'What should we tell the public, Detective Inspector? Are the lives of ordinary New Zealanders in danger?'

As Hana and Jaye return from the chaotic media conference, the video footage that was emailed to the various media outlets is on the screens on the eighth floor, already being broadcast on a breaking news bulletin on the main TV channel.

'We've lost control of the damn investigation,' Jaye says, furious. 'This fucker is calling the shots. He wants everyone admiring his handiwork.'

As the video plays down, replaced by footage taken from the helicopter at the mountain, Hana's phone starts to vibrate. It's a private number. She answers. 'DSS Hana Westerman.'

'I wanted to send the video of the tunnels to you first, Detective. Give you a heads-up, since you worked out my other two messages so quickly. But you got there ahead of me.' The voice on the other end of the phone is calm, considered. 'I'm impressed,' he says.

Hana hits the mute button, urgently hushing the others, *be quiet!* Silence falls around the office.

She unmutes, putting her phone on loudspeaker. Jaye moves closer. 'Do you have information about the killings?' she asks.

A long pause. 'Kōrero Māori mai,'* he says.

Hana says, 'We don't want anyone else hurt. I want to find out what it is you want, how we can work together to stop this. Can we meet—'

'If you want me to answer you,' the man interrupts, 'use our language.' Around the eighth floor, all eyes are on Hana.

'Who is this?' she asks in te reo. 'What do you know about the crimes?'

'So you remember your language. That's something. But you have long since forsaken everything else about you that is Māori.'

---

* 'Speak to me in Māori'

Hana's phone beeps, an incoming email message.

'I just sent you something,' the man on the phone says. 'Open it.'

She presses the email icon. It's an image, a screenshot from archival TV footage of the land protest from eighteen years before. Rows of blue-uniformed cops advancing on the protester camp on the summit of Mount Suffolk. She recognizes, in the front line of the uniformed police, her own face.

'Do you see yourself, Detective Senior Sergeant?' the man asks.

From the street far below, the sound of a siren can be heard, heading past the station.

'Look. Look long and hard at yourself. Does that not shame you, Detective?'

In the following moment of silence, a sound can be heard from the other end of the line. A siren. Everyone realizes at once, it's the same siren! Stan and the other detectives rush for the windows, looking down to where the police car is racing along the street, lights flashing.

The man on the other end of the phone speaks again. 'Ka tūtaki anō tāua.'

The call goes dead.

At the window, Stan spots something, 'There!' Eight floors below, a figure hurries across the street, pocketing a phone, heading for a back alley.

It's a headlong rush for the lifts. Some detectives stab elevator buttons, Hana and Jaye and Stan slam through the stairwell door, down the stairs, leaping the steps four at a time. On the ground floor, they sprint out past the reception area, onto the street, the younger and fitter Stan leading the way, rushing towards where the figure disappeared.

As other detectives and uniformed cops pour out of the building, Stan gets to the end of the side alley, to where the street opens up into a much bigger thoroughfare. The sidewalks are busy; it's early evening, workers are heading towards public transport to go home, others going out for a drink. As cars and buses pass, Hana, Jaye and Stan scan the crowded streets. But the man is gone.

'Again.'

'Boss?'

'The last words he said. "Ka tūtaki anō tāua",' Hana says. 'It means "We will meet again."'

She has her phone in her hand. The stilled image is on the screen, herself on Mount Suffolk all those years before. 'This man knows me. That's why he sent the videos to me,' she tells Jaye. 'He wanted me to be the one who found what he'd done.'

The pieces are tumbling together.

'He was there eighteen years ago. He was there when I was there. He was on the mountain.'

13

FIRE AND SMOKE

The video footage is off-speed, slow-motion. Dream-like in quality.

On the screen, the protesters are massed together near the pūriri tree. Around them the corrugated iron of their temporary shelters, the hand-painted signs of defiance. The police have been assigned into a series of lines; they move in unison up the slopes towards the summit, coming at the protesters from all sides, a co-ordinated pincer movement. They carry long batons, truncheons. Some protesters have loud hailers; they lead the rest, sometimes chanting, sometimes in song. The cops get closer to the protest lines. An order goes out for them to draw their batons. The protesters' chants rise, louder and louder. The singing rises, louder and louder. Orders are barked from senior police: 'You are trespassing on public lands, move now or be forcibly evicted!' The lines of cops keep advancing. 'Move, move, go, go!'

The viewing room is a grey concrete bunker in the bowels of the film and television archive. Like the whole of the archive's storage area, it's cold down here, the facility maintained at the best temperature to preserve ageing video and film materials.

It's a deeply painful watch for Hana. But she doesn't give in to the temptation of the fast-forward button. She watches the hours of footage in real time, making herself remember the day she has tried so hard for so long to forget. Now she has no choice. Four words have changed everything.

'Ka tūtaki anō tāua.' We will meet again.

One sentence, spoken in a calm, measured voice. And with that one sentence, the police action in the breaking-up of the protest on Mount Suffolk and Hana's role that day have suddenly become inseparably entwined with the murder inquiries now consuming the criminal investigation branch.

Watching the screen, Hana searches her long-buried memories as closely as she searches the footage. Looking for faces, trying to remember people, what happened, how it happened. She remembers thinking that day, as the cops moved into the group of protesters, how still they all were. Men, women, children, old people. It wasn't silent, far from it. There was the singing, the chanting, occasionally there were insults, especially at the Māori cops, calling them Uncle Toms. Collaborators. But what is remarkable is how still the protesters were. It would have been easier if they were confrontational, aggressive, violent. But they weren't. Some had chained themselves to fences; their chains had to be cut off. Others just sat there, their arms linked.

Hana remembers something she hasn't thought of for years: seeing two young kids on the south side of the summit holding out daisies to the cops. She remembers the feeling in her gut as she saw that.

Feeling more thrown and overwhelmed by it than by any insult.

For the Māori cops it was a nightmare. You learn your whole life to treat your elders with respect, to give others the dignity they deserve, to come to resolution through words, the way of the marae. Then you wake up one morning, you pull on your uniform. The man you love makes you scrambled eggs on toast, no salmon because you're three months pregnant and you've given up fish. You get dropped off at work. And that morning you realize, your history, your background, the things you got taught on marae, none of that matters. You're a person with a uniform. And a truncheon. That's all you are.

Hana remembers some of the Māori cops who had been out of police college a bit longer trying to talk to their seniors, asking them, 'Please, don't make us do this.' The senior staff didn't want to know. 'This is what you were trained to do,' they said. 'These people are breaking the law, they've defied every court order that's been put in front of them. It's a law-and-order issue, it's a sanitation issue, those shitty falling-down shacks, it's a health and safety issue. Just do your job.'

Just do your job.

On the screen, a section of footage Hana knows well. The excerpt that was broadcast again and again on television, in the days and weeks and months after the protest was forcibly disbanded. In the footage, a fire has broken out. The temporary structures are being pulled down with hooks and chains; a kerosene lantern must have overturned and ignited, the flames quickly racing through the blankets and duvets and plywood walls. In the background of the shot, fire and smoke, a trail of black haze rising into the branches of the pūriri tree.

Closer to camera, Hana is handcuffing a middle-aged woman in a rainbow-striped knitted cardigan. The woman is at least thirty years older than Hana, her hair tied in a bun, streaks of silver.

The camera holds on the pair. The woman is crying, but it's more than crying, it's guttural wailing, it's like she is at a tangi, like she is sitting beside a deceased loved one as the lid closes on the coffin, her heart breaking, her torment falling in tears and visceral cries. Hana tries again and again to haul her to her feet, to persuade her to walk of her own volition to the convoy of police vans waiting in the car park, but the woman is limp and unco-operative, refusing to move, unable to move. Behind, fire and smoke against the blue skies as the jerry-built structures closest to the burning building also catch fire. The camera moves even closer on Hana and the woman, and finally Hana knows she has no choice, she has to do her job. She takes her baton and slides it around the woman's chest from behind. As the woman struggles, Hana forcibly drags her past the burning buildings, down to the vans beyond.

This was the footage Hana's cousin Ngahuia saw. This was what Ngahuia gossiped about in the kitchen of the marae, unaware that Hana was in earshot. Betraying other Māori, she said to the other young cousins the same age as Hana. 'Turning on her own. Fucking traitor. Dunno why she even bothers coming back.'

The TV news camera didn't follow Hana and the woman in the rainbow-coloured cardigan to the car park. The camera moved on to the drama of the flames rapidly engulfing more buildings, then to more brown cops dragging away brown protesters. If the camera had been there with Hana, it would've witnessed something else; cousin Ngahuia would have seen something different. After Hana put the wailing woman in the police van, after the cage door was closed and none of the arrested protesters inside could see her, she paused for a moment. Tears in her own eyes.

But just for a moment.

Then she wiped the tears away with the sleeve of her blue police uniform and got back to work. Back up the hill to arrest and drag away another protester. And another. And another.

Fire and smoke. The same footage plays on a laptop screen, but in a very different space. It's a room with floors and walls of rough hand-hewn wood. Shadows, semi-dark. There is another door to the back of this windowless room. A heavy bar on it. As if this room had been created to hold something captive. Or someone.

The room is full of tools and equipment. An electric cable from a solar panel powers the laptop and the low-wattage bulbs that light the space. On one end of the bench, a kitbag that holds a rolled-up woven mat, and inside the mat, the long carved weapon, a spear with two striking heads. The blades of the striking heads, if one was to put a tape measure against them, would be perhaps four inches in the old measurements.

Ten or eleven centimetres in metric measure.

On the wall above the workbench there's an old daguerreotype photo. Six members of a colonial army troop, staring solemnly at the camera, no smiles on their faces, because after all, was Christ smiling in da Vinci's *Last Supper*? Above the six, a naked body, bound hand and foot, strung up from a high branch, hanging by his neck.

On the laptop screen, smoke and fire rise into the sky. It's a chaotic scene on Mount Suffolk, protesters wailing, men and women in blue uniforms forcibly dragging them away. The camera closes on two people. A young Māori female cop, and a late-middle-aged woman in a rainbow-coloured cardigan. The cop places a long baton around the woman's chest, lifting her from behind, dragging her away.

In the room with the rough-hewn walls, a hand hits the pause button. The image is stilled.

The man watches the laptop, silhouetted against the brightness of the screen.

Fire and smoke. Buildings burning. Protest signs decorated with colourful flowers torn to the ground. A young Māori cop, and the protester she is arresting.

It's silent in the room. The only sounds come from somewhere outside the locked wooden door.

The sound of a distant river. A bird screeches as it takes flight.

'I shouldn't have confronted DSS Westerman in the car park. I know it was wrong. I can't tell you what I was thinking. I guess — well, I was upset. After everything that was said about me. I wanted to tell her the things I hadn't been able to say in court. How all this derailed my family. I got name suppression, sure. But all Mum and Dad's friends know. Of course they do! My grandmother can't look me in the eye.'

The meeting room in the district commander's offices is two storeys above the criminal investigation branch floor. The view is spectacular, the whole of Auckland spreading out below. The district commander is at the head of the table, in his formal uniform, as befits the gravity of the meeting. A senior police legal adviser sits beside him. Patrick Thompson is on the opposite side from Hana and Jaye. His father and his QC sit either side of the young man. Hana notices that father and son wear the same brand of linen shirt. Tailored. Impeccable. And she doesn't miss the fact that Thompson's mother isn't present.

'I shouldn't have gone down to the car park. It was dopey. Impulsive. I guess I just wanted to say to you, I've been punished, lady. I've been punished more than you could ever know. But I shouldn't have done it. I'm sorry I did it. I apologize. I apologize to you.'

Thompson folds his hands in front of him. He's said his piece.

Hana can feel the eyes of the district commander and the legal adviser turning towards her. Waiting for her response. Willing her to follow in kind, offer some form of acknowledgement and reconciliation.

She says nothing.

The QC distributes copies of a document around the room.

'This is a notice of claim,' he says, standing, ever the courtroom performer. When Patrick Thompson spoke, his voice was shaky, fighting his emotions as he gave his apology to Hana. But his silver-haired lawyer's voice is monotone, all business. 'My client has outlined in full his sworn recollection of the events,' he says. 'As you heard, he takes full responsibility for his poor decision in confronting DSS Westerman. But he is quite clear he made no physical threat to the officer and that was never his intention. In response to seeing my client on the lower level of the car park, Detective Senior Sergeant Westerman immediately took him into a headlock. She smashed his head against a concrete pillar. Her actions caused bruising, lacerations, impairment of his vision, possibly permanent.'

The QC pauses, reaching for his handkerchief. Perhaps

a slight allergic response. But the timing creates a dramatic pause of great effect.

'My client asserts that the officer's actions were unprovoked, unwarranted,' he continues. 'In his view, DSS Westerman was frustrated with the outcome, and believing the sentence was insufficiently punitive, she took justice into her own hands.'

He directs the others to the final page of the statement of claim.

'My client demands compensation to an amount to be mutually negotiated. A public apology from both the detective senior sergeant and the Commissioner of Police. And a personal and unequivocal apology from DSS Westerman.'

The QC takes his seat. All eyes turn to Hana.

Jaye sees the look on her face. It's a look he recognizes. He turns to the police legal adviser. 'Can we speak privately, he says, 'so DSS Westerman can receive appropriate legal advice before she makes any response.'

'Thank you, DI Hamilton. That's not necessary,' says Hana. 'I'll apologize.'

A ripple of relief around the police staff in the room. But it's fleeting.

'I'll apologize to the girl whose life you destroyed,' Hana says. 'I'll apologize to her family. I promised them that if she spoke out about what you did, they'd get justice. I'll apologize to them.'

Sitting beside Hana, Jaye's eyes are fixed on the polished wood surface of the long oval table. He knows there's nothing he can do to prevent what is coming. He knows this woman so very well; he knows the train is rolling and there's nothing he or anyone else can do to stop it.

Hana isn't emotional. This isn't impulsive or reactive; she has thought this through. She continues, 'I'll apologize to the other girls who will be hurt because entitled sociopaths like you get away with whatever they want. But I'm not apologizing to you. You and I both know that I never touched you. Go fuck yourself.'

The meeting disbands. No polite shaking of hands. The QC leaves copies of the statement of claim. As the door closes behind Thompson and his father and the lawyer, the district commander takes his hat. He adjusts it as he looks out across the city. There are no sails on the harbour today. A big squall is moving in from the north.

'I don't give a shit that you're O/C of these murder investigations,' he tells Hana. 'I don't care that you're leading the biggest inquiry in the history of this region. You're an extraordinary investigator, yes, but no cop is bigger than the police force they serve. No one's indispensable. If you can't control yourself, you're a liability.' He heads for the door.

'Sir,' Jaye says, knowing the answer before he even asks the question. 'What does that mean?'

'What the hell do you think,' the district commander snaps. 'You're stood down, Detective Senior Sergeant Westerman. On leave without pay, pending further action. You're off the case and out of the building. Effective immediately.'

14

CAR WASH

An inner-city service station. Late at night. Taxi drivers fill their vehicles. At the till, there's a man, late forties. He's tall, wiry. Observant eyes. Māori. A carefully trimmed goatee.

A TV screen behind the till shows the late-night news on mute. The man watches as helicopter footage plays of the police operation on Mount Suffolk. At the bottom of the screen, there's a chyron scroll: *THE WHAKAPAPA* KILLINGS*. The phrase that has quickly become the go-to descriptor in the press for the three murders. The man reaches the front of the queue. 'Pump six,' he says. 'And a car wash, thanks. And a pie. I'm bloody starving.'

'You're him, eh?' the attendant asks.

'Depends who *him* is,' the man replies.

---

*   Whakapapa – genealogy, line of descent

That day's newspaper is open on the counter in front of the attendant. There's an opinion piece with an image of the journalist who wrote it, Grant Wirapa. In the photo, the same observant eyes as the man buying his gas, the same goatee.

'I like your column. Always read it,' says the attendant. 'You say it like it is. Stuff that needs saying.'

Wirapa swipes his cash card, not in the least interested in engaging in conversation. The attendant gestures towards the TV screen. The story has moved on to the uploaded video footage from the tunnels under Mount Suffolk, the daguerreotype and the lines of descent.

'What do you think of all this?' the attendant asks. 'The whakapapa killings?'

Wirapa pockets his receipt. 'It's a fancy name for straight-out cold-blooded, gutless murder. Why polish it up? Some lunatic is chasing headlines. Taking a sick fucked-up shot at a day in the limelight. We're giving the prick exactly what he wants.'

'You're right,' agrees the attendant. 'Just giving the prick what he wants.'

But the journalist is already walking back out towards his vehicle.

The SUV manoeuvres into the car wash. The stop/go lights turn red. The washer rollers descend. The stereo is up loud as Grant Wirapa thumbs through a news app on his phone. Humming to the music, he unwraps his pie.

The cylindrical plastic brushes of the rollers spin; from the top of the car wash a spray head rolls slowly down a track dispersing red liquid detergent the length of the SUV. Torrents of water shoot from high-pressure jets, hitting the vehicle from all directions at once, a low thunder rising as the heavy spray meets the metalwork. Wirapa has never actually been in the eye of a tropical typhoon, but maybe it feels a bit like this. He vaguely wonders what would happen if he opened the door and got out. The roller things must be pressure-sensitive, he thinks; if they hit something unexpected, like a human or a dog, they would surely pull away. Then again, it's a car wash. How high-tech can it be? Would it just keep spraying and spinning? Would it wash him to death?

As he takes a bite of his pie, he contemplates what the subbies would do with that headline. *Prize-winning journalist killed by car wash.*

He is about to take another bite when he becomes aware of a smell. A waft of something. A slightly sweet chemical odour. The car-wash detergent? Surely it wouldn't have that kind of chemical tang, he thinks; that couldn't be good for the paintwork.

A movement from the back seat catches his eye.

Before he can react, a hand reaches forward, holding a piece of cloth. The cloth goes over his nose and mouth, pulling his head back hard against the headrest. Out in the forecourt, whatever is happening inside the car is obscured by the spinning rollers, the cascading jets of water.

The prize-winning journalist struggles. But the hand holding the chloroform-soaked fabric to his face is strong.

The car wash hasn't quite reached the rinse cycle when Grant Wirapa's body becomes very still.

The rollers stop. The roller arms ascend. The stop/go light turns green. The SUV emerges, shiny, clean, waxed. As the vehicle waits to join the traffic, for a moment the headlights of a passing car hit the face of the driver.

It's a man. He doesn't have a goatee.

The SUV pulls out from the service station and drives off into the night.

15

THE SCREAMING BOY

Running, for Hana, is all about control.

You lace up your Allbirds running shoes, you start the watch, you hit the streets. The same 10.13 kilometres every day, the first three hundred metres a steady rise, take a quick cut across the pedestrian overbridge, then on through a maze of inner-city streets towards the illuminated beacon of the Sky Tower. The route so familiar you could run it eyes closed, pushing yourself on the uphill sections, keeping your heart rate read-out on the watch plumb in the middle of the orange band, the fat-burning and cardio-building zone, rarely dipping down into yellow, never green. Control of your heart rate, the cadence of your footfalls, your breathing, in through your nose, out through your mouth.

Control.

Hana keeps running. Hard. Her breath coming in jagged, urgent gasps. Heart and mind racing.

There's no control this morning.

'What the fuck is this, Mum?'

A few hours earlier, after the meeting with the QC and Patrick Thompson, where Hana spoke her mind and the district commander immediately suspended her, Stan dropped her home. As he pulled up outside her house, an awkward moment. 'Boss, I know we don't have this kind of relationship. And you probably don't want to talk right now, but if you do . . .'

'You're right, I don't want to talk,' Hana snapped. She got out of the car, but before she'd taken two steps towards her house, she regretted her reaction, her tone. She turned around, went back to Stan's window. Apologized.

'Nothing to say sorry for, boss. This whole thing is fucked.'

He tentatively squeezed her hand, where it was resting on his open window. Embarrassed as soon as he'd made the gesture. But Hana appreciated it. It was probably the first time they'd touched since she shook his hand the day they met a year earlier, when Stan, having freshly passed his detectives' exams with flying colours, was assigned to work alongside her. She put her other hand on top of his. Returning the gesture. Despite the huge gap between them in miles on the road, in seniority, in life experience, they are friends of a sort.

As Stan drove away, before Hana even opened her front

door, she heard the sound coming from inside the house.

Her laptop playing.

The sound of protesters chanting, singing. And other voices. Voices amplified through loudhailers. Urgent, threatening voices. 'You are trespassing on public lands, move now or be forcibly evicted!'

She opened the door. Addison looked up from the laptop screen, her face ashen.

'What the fuck is this, Mum? What did you do?'

Addison had come home from uni, found her tablet wasn't working, gone to use her mother's laptop. Hana had been watching a copy of the Mount Suffolk video from the archives every spare moment she had, believing that whoever was behind the killings was on that footage somewhere. When Addison opened the laptop, turned on the screen, the news video from eighteen years earlier was there, paused. She found herself looking at the image of Hana, only a few years older than she herself is now. Despite the years between, her mum's face was unmistakable. Her mother in blue police uniform. Dragging away Māori protesters.

'Why didn't you ...?' Addison didn't finish the sentence. 'Stupid question. I know why you never told me. You're ashamed.'

In the doorway, Hana hesitated. Trying to pull together an explanation that would make sense to her daughter, to this young woman whose music and politics stood for everything that was against what she was watching her mother do on the old grainy footage.

'At least I hope you're ashamed. You *should* be fucking ashamed, Mum.'

'You don't understand ...'

'Yeah, I do. It's there on the screen.'

'I was a junior cop, the bottom of the pole. We were given orders, we had no choice.'

Addison stared at her mother, a bemused smile on her face. 'No choice? Do you actually believe what you're saying?' After Addison recognized her mother in the footage, she'd googled the land protests and the police actions. 'They were innocent protesters, on their iwi* land, land their people had lived on for centuries before it was stolen from them at gunpoint.'

'They were breaking the law.'

'*Whose law?*' Addison's barely suppressed explosion startled both of them. It took Hana a moment to gather herself.

'Jesus, Addison, don't lecture me, not today.'

'A brown woman with a badge. Doing that to your own people.' Addison slammed down the screen of the laptop. 'You're a fucking kūpapa.'†

The word hung in the air between them, a slap, brutal. For Addison, it was the worst insult she could fling at her mother. Kūpapa, the word for those Māori who during the land wars of the nineteenth century collaborated with the colonizers, took up arms alongside the British, against other Māori fighting desperately in their last-ditch attempts to hold their sacred lands in the face of the mightiest force on the planet, the British Army.

---

* Iwi – tribe
† Kūpapa – collaborator, traitor

Addison headed to the open door. Pausing beside her mother.

'I'm staying the night at PLUS 1's flat.'

She wiped her eyes with her sleeve.

And she walked out the door.

Hana sprints across the overbridge, risking twisting an ankle as she races down the steps three at a time, a horn blaring as she runs across the road without even looking for traffic. There's a street light out on one of the back roads, and after the brightness of the main streets it's like running into a black hole, but she doesn't slow at all, running blind. Sweat pouring despite the cold.

She runs across a four-lane highway. Pushing herself even harder now, jaw set. It's punishing, but she welcomes the ache of the jarring joints, the painful spikes of lactic acid in her calves. She springs up onto the traffic island in the middle of the road, a ten-inch ridge she's navigated without incident every morning for literally years, but this time she's travelling faster; she misjudges, stumbles, falls sprawling across the island, rolling face-first, grazing her knees and palms on the rough concrete as she manages to stop herself barely a metre before she would have tumbled into oncoming traffic.

She picks herself up. Checks her heart rate. It's at the very top of the red zone.

She sees herself reflected in the window of a shop on the other side of the road. Lit by a street light, she sees the blood on her knee. Chest heaving, heart racing. Ready to throw up, she's pushed herself so hard.

For Hana, running is all about control. But there's no control this morning.

A buzzing. It's a call from Jaye. She doesn't answer.

Back home, as the sun comes up, Hana collects handfuls of kawakawa leaves from her tree. She makes tea, scoring each leaf to release the peppery bite into the boiling water. Sitting in her kitchen, she forces herself to go back to the laptop, to look again at the footage from eighteen years before.

A way of not thinking about Addison wiping away her tears with her sleeve. A way of not thinking about being taken off the case.

But it's more than that.

The killer was on that mountain. He is on this video, somewhere. She is off the investigation, she is bruised and reeling, personally, professionally. Doesn't mean she's not still involved. Doesn't mean she doesn't want to do everything she can to help find the bastard who is doing these things.

She scrolls at half-speed through the archival footage of the police operation. There were over a hundred people on the mountain, dozens of arrests. She studies the faces of the protesters being dragged away past the news cameras. Some cursing, struggling, resisting. But most silent, dignified. Many weeping.

'We will meet again.' He was there. But who?

The protesters who were fifty years old or more back then would be at least seventy now. They wouldn't be physically capable of doing the things this guy has done, Hana figures. He's meticulous. He's strong. He knows exactly what he's doing. He's skilled with breaking and entering, skilled at the hunt.

He's *very* skilled with his weapon.

As she watches the footage, Hana thinks back to the phone call.

The voice on the other end of the phone was articulate. Educated. His voice was like some of her uncles, proud men who spoke English better than the English. Men who lived in both worlds, Māori and Pākehā, effortlessly, comfortable.

She pauses the footage. The blood from the cut on her leg where she'd fallen earlier is dripping. Her body reacting to the tumult she is feeling inside.

'Does that not shame you, Detective?'

'You *should* be fucking ashamed, Mum.'

Almost the same words. From a killer. And from her daughter.

Shame.

Yeah, Hana felt shame after Mount Suffolk.

More than that. What happened on the mountain that day changed her. She was dragged through the mud, her face on every television screen, her cousins talking about her behind her back. It broke a part of her. And if she was really honest, it broke her relationship with Jaye.

Jaye had held her. He was there for her, of course he was. As in, he was in the same physical proximity, the house they shared, the bed they slept in together, the two of them and their baby girl. He did the things he was capable of doing. The problem was, what Jaye was capable of doing wasn't what Hana needed.

'We just have to move on,' he told her. 'We have jobs to do. We have to put our heads down. Carry on. Keep moving forward.'

As if there was ever a 'we' in it.

Jaye's face wasn't on the television screen, in newspapers, the public image of the heavy-handed police tactics brought to bear on peaceful protesters. Jaye wasn't there, and even if he had been, there would have been a profound difference. Skin tone. He wasn't the colour of the people at the protest.

Hana was.

It wasn't that he was blind to the fact Hana was hurting. He tried his level best. What he didn't understand was how deep the damage cut. By following the orders she'd been given, by shackling those protesters, by confronting and arresting Māori standing up for Māori rights, by hauling them away with her police baton drawn and ready to use – by all these things, Hana crossed a line. Jaye didn't know, he didn't understand how completely she was broken. And because he didn't know, he didn't know how to fix her.

And neither did Hana.

She thought about quitting the cops. She thought about it long and hard. Just walking away. That would be the easy answer. But it was the wrong answer. For Hana, being a cop wasn't just a job. It was all she'd ever wanted to do. The fearless young woman scrambling down the bank to save the old drunk who'd crashed his car. But then the job you were born to do damages you. It damages you deep. But because it's destiny, because there's nothing else on earth you can imagine being, you find a way to live with the damage.

You find a way to live with being broken.

Like Jaye told her to, she moved on. She kept pushing forward. She stopped going back to the marae. Stopped going to tangi, stopped going to weddings back home. It was too hard, knowing the cousins were smiling politely to her face then talking about her behind her back in the kitchens. Hana put her head down, she did her job, she put every piece of her focus and her energy into looking forward, into climbing the ladder, doing the detectives' exams, carving a career, moving upwards.

And she made the decision to stop looking back.

After Mount Suffolk, Hana and Jaye lasted just under two years. They were two people sharing a child, Hana came to feel, sharing a bed, a home. They were intimate. But they were also strangers. Jaye couldn't ever truly understand the dark shadow that had taken residence somewhere in her core after that day on the mountain. How could he?

And if he couldn't ever know that, how could he truly ever know *her*?

Then came the morning, so bleakly inevitable, both of them lying in bed, baby Addison between them. Jaye looking at the crack in the ceiling as Hana told him it was over.

At her kitchen table, Hana takes a deep breath.

She forces herself back to focus on the video. She had

asked Stan to cross-reference the arrests from the mountain that day with the individuals or businesses who had requested footage of the police operation from the film and television archives. The man on the phone had a copy of this footage. If he accessed the material through the archives, there's going to be a trail.

She keeps scrolling. Concentrating on the younger protesters, men from their mid teens upwards. They'd be mid thirties now and older. So many faces.

Then her own face again, the footage that Addison watched with horror just a few hours earlier. Hana dragging away the older woman. Watching at half-speed, she sees something she hadn't seen before, or at least hadn't registered. She pauses, rewinds. Slows the footage down to ten per cent speed. As she drags the woman past the camera, the long baton wrapped around her chest, hard and unrelenting, there's a glimpse of something in the background. It's fleeting, only a couple of seconds on screen if you were playing the footage in real time, a passing blur.

But at tenth speed, the blur takes form. Human form. A face.

Unease tightens Hana's chest.

It's a boy. Not yet a teenager, younger. He is reaching out towards the woman Hana is dragging away.

He is screaming.

Her phone buzzes. Jaye again. This time, Hana answers before the second ring.

'Jaye, there's a boy, I never noticed him before. He's maybe eleven years old,' she says, doing the maths in her head as she's talking, 'which means he'd be late twenties now—'

Jaye cuts across her. 'His name is Poata Raki. Wish you'd answer your bloody phone. He was twelve at the time. Thirty years old now. The woman you arrested was his mother.' He can't hide the excitement in his voice. 'Raki requested a copy of the footage from the archives a year ago.'

Hana can barely breathe. Remembering what the killer said when he called her. 'Ka tūtaki anō tāua.' We will meet again.

'We'll be outside your house in five minutes. Be ready to go.' And Jaye hangs up.

Hana stares at the kawakawa tea. The steam swirls upwards, making elegant drifting shapes in a beam of morning light falling through the kitchen window, before a waft of breeze from the open door hits it and it disappears.

At last. A name.

Poata Raki.

The office of the Dean of Faculty is on the top floor of the law department. The office is grand. The view even grander, looking over the city, out to the harbour beyond. Hana stands at the window. Ten storeys below, the university quadrangle is pretty much empty. It's still early, only a few particularly diligent students heading towards the library.

'I should ask to see the warrant, being a professor of law and all that.' The dean has a wry smile. She is young, Hana guesses, at most late forties. Her handshake when Hana, Jaye and Stan entered her office was strong. Direct eye contact. Her pants and jacket tailored without being showy.

Stan hands her the search warrant. The dean glances over the document for discovery of any property, digital or physical records relating to Poata James Raki, former lecturer in the university law faculty. She looks up at Hana. 'If I were to ask why you're interested in Mr Raki, I'm guessing you wouldn't be able to tell me?' The question is rhetorical, asked with the same ironic smile, the dean knowing full well the detectives won't share this information. But Hana doesn't miss the fact that the question was directed at her. I could be friends with this woman, she thinks.

'Why was Mr Raki fired?' Jaye asks.

'Officially he's on administrative leave,' the dean replies. 'That was from September last year. There should have been a departmental hearing shortly afterwards. I believe that would have resulted in his censuring and dismissal. But the hearing never happened.'

'Why not?' asks Jaye.

'The faculty tried to contact him repeatedly. We haven't heard from him in six months.' The dean pauses. Hana can see there's a strong undercurrent of regret about whatever happened with Poata Raki. Maybe even sadness.

'I know this is difficult,' Hana says. 'But we need to know whatever you can tell us about Mr Raki.'

The dean fills a glass from a jug of water on her desk. She takes her time. Hana can see she is working through exactly how she wants to frame the narrative. 'Before he joined the faculty,' she finally says, 'Poata was a brilliant lawyer. Specialized in treaty claims. Land settlements for Māori. He was an extraordinary person. I don't use the word lightly. Fluent in te reo, a black-belt kendo competitor, he had several years' part-time training with the Army Territorials.'

Glances between the three cops. The man they're hunting is physically able. A fluent speaker of Māori. Tick. Tick.

'He graduated top of his class,' the dean continues. 'One of the youngest law graduates in the country. A firm specializing in lands rights claims head-hunted him. He was made lead legal adviser representing his iwi in their land claim. By all accounts, his work was second to none. His research, his grasp of oral history and whakapapa were impeccable. His arguments to the court were eloquent and passionate. After two years of arguing the case for his tribe as well as it could possibly be argued, Te Tini-o-Tai won. But the settlement . . . '

From the window, Hana can see Mount Suffolk on the far side of the harbour. Te Tini-o-Tai land. The threads of this case, she thinks, they all radiate out like a massive spider web, with the volcanic peak of Mount Suffolk in the middle of everything.

'The full and final settlement was the equivalent of two per cent of all land guaranteed under the Treaty of Waitangi.'* The dean lets the weight of that hang there.

---

* Treaty of Waitangi, or Te Tiriti o Waitangi – New Zealand's founding document, signed between the British Crown and over 500 Māori rangatira (chiefs) on 6 February 1840. The treaty has two versions, Māori and English, and the inconsistencies between the two remain contentious and problematic.

'The public don't realize,' she says, 'two per cent is stand-ard. It's the average figure across almost every settlement. A century and a half where the tribe was traumatized, killed, their lands stolen at gunpoint. And the result was just two per cent of what was rightfully theirs. When we did his final interview panel, I remember the way Poata phrased it. "The tribe was owed a fortune and an apol-ogy," he told us. "Instead, we were given breadcrumbs."'

The dean adjusts her glasses.

'Poata was upfront when he interviewed for a lecture-ship,' she continues. 'He told us he was deeply disillusioned by what he'd experienced. More than that. He used words like "heartbroken", "gutted". He'd worked within the system to get a result, for Māori, for his iwi. He'd won. But two per cent of what the tribe was rightfully owed. That was no win. It was an insult.'

'So he walked away from practice as a land rights lawyer?' Hana asks.

'His perspective was that the legal system was wrecked,' the dean explains. 'Change had to happen. He wanted to influence the next generation. To inspire the lawyers he taught to fight for systemic change.'

She gets out of her seat and walks to a wall of photos. Fifteen framed head shots. Hana's eyes search the images. Every one of them is a man. Every one of them a white man.

'The fifteen deans of the law faculty in the hundred and twenty years before me,' the dean tells them. 'One hun-dred and twenty years. I'm the first woman to sit in this office. I know what it means to swim against the tide. To fight to make a difference in an institution that's not even slightly interested in change.

'Some of the senior staff on the panel were worried about hiring Poata. For me, his perspective was utterly unique. His passion was exhilarating. There'd never been anyone like him in this faculty. There'd never been a voice like his talking to the lawyers of tomorrow. Yes, he was a risk. But he was a risk I thought we should take.'

The door of the office opens. It's a security guard. The dean hands the search warrant back to Stan. For a moment she is silent. Reflective. When she speaks again, her voice is uncharacteristically hesitant.

'After everything that happened. How things went. Maybe I was wrong.' She signals for the detectives to follow the security guard. 'Maybe the risk was too big,' she says, as they head for the elevator.

The elevator dings, the doors open at the basement level of the faculty. They follow the security guard as he unlocks the heavy door into the archives.

As he keys numbers into an alarm pad, Hana thinks about that morning. Stan's car had pulled up and by habit she'd gone straight to the front passenger seat. But it was already occupied. By Jaye. She took the back seat instead. In the car, she'd asked Jaye upfront, 'What am I doing here? I'm suspended.'

It took him a moment to answer.

'You're the epicentre of this. This is the biggest break

we've had, the only break we've got. I want your eyes on it. I don't want to miss something you would see in an instant. I need you there. What the district commander doesn't know won't hurt him.'

Stan glanced at Hana in the rear-view mirror. 'I told the DI you'd expect the front seat,' he grinned.

'Yeah?' said Hana, looking at Jaye. 'What'd you say?'

She could see the smile forming at the corners of her ex-husband's mouth. 'I said you're the epicentre,' said Jaye. 'But there are limits.'

The dean follows the security guard as he searches down the rows of archived materials. There's decades' worth of stuff, in plain boxes stacked on shelves the length of the room. 'I know I haven't answered your question, Detective Inspector,' she says. 'Why Poata was put on administrative leave.'

'No, you haven't,' says Jaye.

'The three years Poata was with us, he taught pre-colonial and colonial history, and its impact on the New Zealand legal system. His lectures were a thing of legend. He'd give the most reticent student a passion for the subject. But he trod a fine line. His work was often polemic. Doctrinal. Political.'

'What do you mean?' Hana asks.

'Whole tutorials were run where only Māori was allowed to be spoken. Poata would do classes on separatism. Self-determination. Tino rangatiratanga. Some students thrived on it. It was like the sixties. Fists in the air. Turning the old order upside down. But other students complained. I knew he was walking a knife edge,' the dean continues. 'But that's why I hired him. What Poata was teaching wasn't out of the textbooks. It was completely informed by his experiences. By the experiences of his ancestors. By the colour of his skin.'

The security guard has one of those big sliding ladder platforms that run on wheels. He moves it down the rows of shelving, searching through the boxes. The graunch of the ladder being slid across the concrete floor echoes.

'Then things started to change,' the dean says.

'Change how?' asks Jaye.

'About a year ago, the tone of his teaching shifted. I began to worry he was moving from critique to advocacy. He was encouraging students to join online groups, forums discussing political activism, protest groups related to land rights issues, some of them on the borderline between legitimate activism and illegal protests. There's challenging the status quo, and there's things that no faculty can be associated with.

'Then there was the field trip,' the dean says. 'He took a class to a mob HQ.'

'A gang pad?' Hana asks.

The dean nods, yes, clearly still incredulous at the memory. 'He didn't inform the faculty in advance, otherwise of course it would never have been approved. Afterwards, he was brought in front of a disciplinary hearing. An exercise in taking a privileged bunch of law students to see first-hand the long-term disenfranchising effects of colonialism was his reason in a nutshell. But it was a disaster.'

'What happened?' asks Jaye.

'One of the female students was groped by a junior gang member. Poata saw, and stepped in. The gang member took a swing, and Poata laid him flat on his back. It nearly ended in a class of our third-year law students being involved in an all-out brawl with one of the most feared gang chapters in the country.

'The disciplinary hearing put him on notice. But what none of us in the faculty knew was that at the time, his mother was in the last stages of liver failure. He was nursing her as she was dying. If we'd known that,' the dean says, 'it would have been different. We'd have put him on compassionate leave. Helped him with support and counselling if he needed it. We would have been more understanding. But we didn't know.'

For a moment, a flash in Hana's mind. The television footage. Smoke and fire in the background. The young Hana dragging the woman away. She looks up to see Jaye watching her. Knowing what she's thinking.

'The final straw,' the dean goes on. 'A Pākehā student presented a paper where he played devil's advocate. Giving hypothetical legal justifications for the historical appropriation of Māori land. Poata marked the paper inappropriately.'

'What kind of inappropriately?' Hana asks.

'He wiped his arse with it,' the dean says. 'The student got his paper back with an F, smeared in human faeces. That was six months ago. Poata was immediately suspended, pending a departmental hearing. We had no choice. We advised him to seek professional help. We persuaded the student not to lay charges. We found out later that this happened the week before his mother died. We haven't heard from him since.'

'Raki, Poata. This what you're after?' asks the security guard. He comes down the sliding ladder with an archive box labelled with Raki's name, and takes it to a table at the end of the room.

'It's what was cleared from his office,' the dean tells them. 'IT will give you full access to his emails and all the files associated with his university account.'

Jaye takes the lid off the box. It's full of staplers, pens, bulldog clips, nondescript office stuff. He takes out a pile of photos. Martin Luther King preaching to a huge crowd at the Lincoln Memorial in Washington DC. The lone protester staring down the tank in Tiananmen Square. The Buddhist monk who set fire to himself in Saigon in 1963, sitting calmly in the lotus position as his entire body is engulfed by flames.

At the bottom of the box, there's ripped-up paper. Jaye takes the pieces out, assembles them on the table. 'I understand that was found in his rubbish bin,' the dean explains. The shredded paper is Poata Raki's law degree, torn to pieces.

Jaye pulls out the final items in the box. A framed photo, the kind you sit on a desk. A woman. Hana instantly recognizes her. The woman she arrested on Mount Suffolk, Poata Raki's mother. Jaye retrieves Raki's university ID card.

Hana moves to his side. Together they look at the card. The man in the photo is thirty years old. Clean-shaven. A bright, open expression. Strong, intense eyes. It's impossible to miss the intelligence in his face. The face of the screaming boy from the mountaintop. That face, eighteen years older now.

'Hana,' says Jaye, quietly.

There's something at the very bottom of the box. A photocopy of an old daguerreotype. The image is of a troop of nineteenth-century English soldiers gathered under a large pūriri tree. Hanging above them, the naked, lifeless body of a Māori chief, strung up by the neck.

Grant Wirapa awakes on a floor made of rough hand-hewn timber. His head throbs, the worst hangover in the history of the universe. From somewhere far outside, the sound of a river flowing. And bird calls.

He tries to move, groans at a sharp pain around his wrists. He looks down to find his hands are bound in front with plastic fast-clip bands. He raises his eyes to the door, fighting panic. The door is heavy, wooden, reinforced. No handle or bolt.

There's no furniture in the room except a plastic bucket, a plastic water bottle.

Wirapa swallows. His throat is parched. The last thing he remembers is the car-wash rollers descending. Then the slightly sweet chemical smell. The same smell lingers as a taste in the back of his throat, making him want to puke.

After that smell, black nothingness. Until he woke up, in this place.

Trying to hold down the terror he is feeling, he struggles to his feet. He cautiously approaches the door. With his bound hands he tries to get purchase on the places where there's a corner join in the wood, or an indent in the boards. But the door doesn't budge.

He realizes that it is locked from the outside. He's in a prison cell.

Hands shaking, he takes the water bottle. He guzzles, thirstier than he has ever been. But it's too much too fast, and he pukes the water straight back up, a thin, ill-smelling mixture of bile and water.

From the other side of the door, a sound. A key turning in a lock. A heavy bolt sliding. Wirapa takes a stumbling step backwards. Getting as far from the door as he can. He wipes away the spittle, the vomit. His back straightening. Determined to give the impression, at least, of courage. Of someone who isn't frightened for his life.

Even if he is frightened for his life.

The door silently swings open. A figure comes into the room. A man with intense, intelligent eyes. Wirapa has no idea who the man is. He doesn't recognize the face.

It's the same face Hana saw on the ID card in the university archives.

Poata Raki.

16

NUMBER FOUR

Emergency lights flashing, sirens screaming, Stan's car races through heavy downtown traffic to where the police helicopter is housed on the waterfront. Jaye is on police comms, co-ordinating with the leader of the south Auckland policing region armed offenders squad. They have an address for Poata Raki. The house he shared with his mother, an isolated rural region to the south of the metro area.

On the police radio, the squad leader tells Jaye, 'There's a rugby field ten kilometres from the house. An armed unit will be waiting for you.'

'Nothing happens until we're there,' says Jaye. 'No one moves on his house until we arrive.'

Stan swings across two lanes of oncoming traffic. Ahead, the rotors of the police helicopter are already turning.

As the helicopter lifts into the air, Hana straps herself

in. In her hand, the ID card from the archival box. She studies Poata Raki's face. The face of a man she believes has killed, three times. Who she is certain intends to take three more lives.

Unless they stop him.

Grant Wirapa has a phone clutched in his bound hands. The other man said nothing as he gave the journalist the phone and set the video function to record. Not a word. No eye contact.

Wirapa's hands are bleeding, the plastic fast-clip bands biting deep into the soft flesh around his wrists. But he doesn't ask to have the bindings cut loose. He doesn't ask questions. He doesn't demand who are you, why are you doing this, what the fuck do you want? He doesn't say anything, anything that will make this terrible, confusing, shit situation worse than it already is.

He stands. Silent. Filming the other man with the phone.

Finally, the man's eyes rise. When he speaks, it is in te reo, formal. Like he is speaking on the paepae.[*]

'Mā āku mahi ka whakamaumaharatia, ka whakamanahia tōku tupuna a Hahona Tuakana. Ka whāia ōna tapuwae e au. Ngā tapuwae ā tō tātou Ariki.'[†]

He pauses. His eyes gaze into the camera. Intense,

---

[*] Paepae – the bench in front of a meeting house from which orators rise to speak on formal occasions
[†] 'With my actions, I remember my ancestor, Hahona Tuakana. I am walking in the footsteps of my ancestor, the great chief.'

but open. As if he wants to reach through the lens to those he is addressing, not to berate or chastise, but to share, to explain, to open himself to them and help them understand.

He continues, in English.

'Since my ancestor was brutally executed, what has changed? Māori must beg for our own lands. Only a fraction of our land is ever returned. This we accept, like lambs. Māori unemployment is twice that of Pākehā. When we work, our wage is little better than half. Like lambs, we accept. We have less access to health care, to education. We are imprisoned twenty times more than non-Māori. The most incarcerated indigenous race on the planet. We die ten years earlier. And we accept. Like lambs.'

His voice is powerful. Not strident. There's a lyricism to his tone, sometimes scaling, sometimes elongating syllables to emphasize a point. 'My ancestor was murdered, hanged from a sacred pūriri tree, surrounded by six men in British uniform. Māori may not be strung up by the neck now. But in the century and a half since my ancestor died, little else has changed.'

Hearing this, Wirapa's bound hands tremble. If he had any doubts before as to who has taken him captive, the crimes his kidnapper has committed, those doubts are now gone. The executed chief. The six soldiers. The old daguerreotype, an image he has seen on every newspaper and news show for the last few days. There's only one simple, clear goal now for Wirapa. He must do whatever he can, say whatever he must say, whatever it takes to stay alive.

He does not know the name of this man he is filming. But he knows the things this man has done.

Far below the spinning helicopter blades, it's gridlock on the motorway out of Auckland. The chopper flies high above the traffic, turning a ninety-minute high-speed drive to the meeting point at the rugby field into a fifteen-minute flight. Stan urges the pilot to make it ten. In the front seat of the chopper, Jaye is in radio contact with the armed offenders squad. Making sure there will be weapons for each of the criminal investigation branch detectives. There's no thought now of the consequences of Hana being involved in an armed operation while she is suspended. Only one thing matters. Getting to Poata Raki and taking him into custody before he can kill again.

The pilot banks away from the motorway, towards where Auckland's suburbs hit the farmland areas in the south of the city. The radio crackles again, the squad leader reporting back.

'We've got two snipers positioned on a ridge overlooking the house. High-powered binoculars. They're seeing movement in one room of the house,' he says.

'Our ancestors knew that the way of nature is balance. There is no balance for a people who have had all they cared for stolen. All that was precious and sacred, taken.'

The calmness of the voice surprises Wirapa. These words aren't the disorganized ramblings of a tortured, unstable mind. Even through his fear, the journalist can see the calm, the clarity in the speaker's eyes. The words are deeply considered. Thoughtful. Eloquent.

'A system has been forced on us that is not interested in balance. A legal system transplanted here from twenty thousand miles away, a set of laws that exists not to provide equality and recompense and honour and balance but to ensure that one side flourishes and the other is kept in the gutter. This we have accepted, like lambs.'

Poata Raki takes a step closer to the lens. His face filling the screen of the phone.

'The time of the lamb is over,' he says. 'By my actions, the spark is struck. It is time to return to the old ways. Of utu. To avenge that which has never been avenged. To take back that which has been stolen over the past two centuries.'

A drop of blood drips from the bindings cutting into Wirapa's wrists. His mouth is dry.

'Better the blood of the innocent than none at all.' Raki's head bows. Finished.

Wirapa lowers the phone. He breathes short, sharp breaths. He knows now that only by the grace of a miracle will he leave this room alive.

The police chopper swoops low over the main street of the rural town. Waiting in the local rugby field, two large black modified Nissan Patrols, heavy, grunty vehicles, reinforced windows, huge bull bars in front. The struts of the helicopter have barely made contact with the ground before Jaye, Hana and Stan are jumping down and into the open rear door of one of the vehicles.

In the back of the speeding 4WD, Hana, Stan and Jaye pull on full black bulletproof gear. Guns are handed to each of them. There are four AOS officers in this vehicle, eight in the following one.

The squad leader has a photo on his phone, the image of Poata Raki taken from the university ID. 'This is him?' he asks. 'We're sure he's the one?'

'Yes,' Hana confirms. 'He's the one.'

In the room, silence. The sound of bird calls from outside. Raki has finished. He takes his phone back from Wirapa. He turns off the video record.

For the first time, his eyes meet the other man's. It's all Wirapa can do not to gasp aloud.

'What's this?' Raki asks, pointing to his ear. 'Tell me the word, in Māori.' He indicates his hair. His nose. 'This? And this?'

Wirapa swallows. 'I know my ancestry. I have an uncle who is obsessed with the whole family tree thing.' His voice is shaking. 'I have European ancestors, like everyone; no one's one hundred per cent Māori any more. But I don't have a genealogical connection to those six soldiers, I swear it,' he pleads. '*I swear it.*'

'Six,' Raki says. 'What's "six" in our language?'

Wirapa doesn't reply. He can't. He doesn't know the answer. He doesn't know the word.

Raki retrieves something from his pocket. A swathe of cuttings, articles from newspapers, each with the image of the person who wrote them, the man in front of him. He hands Wirapa one of the articles. 'Read,' he says. 'Read the things you wrote.'

The journalist holds the article with his byline. His legs threaten to give way under him. Knowing he has no choice, he starts to read, his voice shaky. 'In ... in the end-less submissions from money-grabbing tribes to the land courts, no one asks the obvious. What gives us the right to claim every inch of this country because ... because our distant relatives happened to stumble on the place first?'

Raki takes another article. Hands it to Wirapa. 'This one. Read.'

'Before the English brought civilization, we were ... ' The journalist hesitates, his face drawn. Raki gestures: carry on. 'Before the English brought civilization, we were illiterate murderers intent on exterminating each other. Having no written language, that's something to be proud of? We are a few generations removed from cannibalism. What we Māori need is work ethic, self-discipline, not our dead language on every road sign.'

Raki takes the articles back. There are a dozen others in his hand. But his point is made. 'A Māori whose career is based on being the brown person more than willing to beat up on other Māori,' he says. 'Condemning te reo Māori as a useless language of dinosaurs. Blaming Māori for not lifting themselves up and breaking the cycle of poverty. All this damage, this vitriol and destruction, against your own people. And you don't even know the word for your nose?'

Wirapa slumps against the wall. His legs finally giving out, he slides down to the floor, his chest rising and falling fast, his breath coming in gasps. A stain spreads on his pants. He has pissed himself. Raki looks down at him. Slumped, humiliated, pathetic. Despite everything, he takes no joy in the spectacle. There's no pleasure in this.

It takes a moment for Wirapa to control his breathing enough to speak. 'Are you going to kill me?'

His voice is barely loud enough to register, the birds in the tall swaying trees outside drowning out his words. Raki's intense gaze doesn't leave his captive's eyes.

'Do you deserve to die?' he asks quietly.

The black AOS vehicles crest a hill, passing a police cordon. Turning off their emergency lights, they descend a ridge, turning to enter a long driveway. Along the driveway, tall pine trees move in the breeze.

The vehicles pull up a distance from the sprawling farmhouse. The doors slide open. Silent, efficient, the black-clad AOS officers spill out. Working with hand gestures, the squad leader signals the others. The officers fan out, moving in silent co-ordination towards the front door. Hana, Jaye and Stan follow them.

Hana adjusts the weight of her handgun. Prepared for whatever is about to happen.

The squad leader silently signals with raised fingers, three, two, one, and *WHAM!* An officer swings a hand-held battering ram, the door explodes. The officer with the ram steps aside, the next pair of officers kick out the debris of the shattered door.

The men move in waves through the house, weapons drawn, screaming, 'Police officers, we're armed!' Each door they come to is kicked open. Following side by side with Jaye, Hana sees that each room is empty. The leading pair of AOS officers reach the end of the corridor, the final room in the house. One officer kicks in the heavy wooden door, the squad leader steps forward, his automatic rifle raised. 'Keep your hands in the open! Don't move, do not move!'

Other officers take positions in the doorway. Their weapons trained into the room, ready to fire. 'Is there anyone else here?' the AOS squad leader shouts at whoever is in the room. 'Is there anyone else in the house?'

From further back in the corridor, Hana sees the body language of the officers in the doorway. The tension easing in their shoulders. The barrels of their guns dropping. One by one they fall back, returning to each room in turn, making sure they haven't missed anything.

Coming from the final room, the sound of terrified weeping. The squad leader gestures to Hana and Jaye, and they approach. It's a bedroom. On the bed, two kids, maybe fifteen, huddled together, half naked, their clothes scattered around them. They're shaking, confused.

'We didn't mean to do anything wrong,' the boy says, crying. 'We ... we only come here to ... to be alone ...'

The girl is trying to cover herself. Her face crimson. Tears falling.

Hana turns to the squad leader. 'I'll deal with this.'

The others back away. She picks up the scattered clothes and helps the young girl dress.

'Please don't kill us,' the girl says.

'No one's going to hurt you,' Hana tells her. 'It's okay, honey, you're going to be okay.'

Leaving the teenagers to gather themselves, Hana returns to Jaye and Stan in the corridor. The house is full of dust. Discarded alcohol cans and bottles, cigarette packets, from where other teenagers have used the place as a party venue since the previous occupant walked away.

Wherever Poata Raki is, he hasn't been in this house for months.

The journalist's SUV drives through the darkness of the south Auckland streets. In the back of the vehicle, Grant Wirapa lies flat on his back, tied and gagged and blindfolded. Unable to move or speak or see. But he is alive.

The SUV pulls over. Raki opens the rear door. He takes out the cigarette lighter and holds a nail against the glowing red coil. Carefully, quickly, he uses the hot nail to melt a shape into the vinyl of the car door. It's a shape that he has now made a number of times. A koru. He heats the nail again and again. Finally there are four perfectly etched koru symbols inscribed in the vinyl. He takes the blindfold off Wirapa. The journalist sees the four symbols. He knows exactly what they mean.

Raki has his phone in his hands. He has uploaded the video that was recorded in the locked room as a file to an email, addressed to all the major news organizations and websites in the country.

The SUV is parked outside an electrical appliance store. Through the security grilles over the front windows, the screens of several widescreen televisions on display can be seen. Something catches Raki's eye. The late evening news. A photo comes up, his photo, taken from his university ID. He raises his eyebrows. Not spooked, no panic.

'That was fast, Detective Westerman,' he says quietly, impressed.

He looks at Wirapa in the back of the SUV. 'You're nothing but a shitty delivery boy. All you've ever been. Delivering your poisonous messages of hatred and lies. Now, for once, you're delivering something truthful.'

Raki presses send on the email. Beep, it's instantly distributed to the dozens of recipients. At last he answers the question the journalist asked hours before.

'I'm not going to kill you.'

He places something on the floor of the SUV. It's a copy of the old daguerreotype, with a new line of descent, from the fourth soldier to a photo of a young man with long straggly blonde hair. Then Raki closes the door and walks away into the night.

Wirapa manages to haul himself up. He looks through

the rear window. The street is deserted, apart from the shadowy shape of Raki, briefly illuminated by a street light he is walking under. Then he is gone. With a jolt, the journalist realizes there's something else in the back of the SUV, on the deck next to him. Grunting with the effort, he manages to roll himself around to face whatever it is.

He starts screaming.

The screaming is muffled by the gag in his mouth. He desperately tries to struggle free of his bindings, tries to roll away from the thing next to him, but it's useless, there's nothing he can do.

Lying beside him is the shape of another person, completely bound in cloth, like a shroud. At the top of the shrouded figure's head there is a gap in the bindings. Straggly blonde hair flows out, matted red with blood. There's a dark stain on the cloth, in the place where the back of the head is. A stain from a wound where a weapon struck him.

The bloodied wound is eleven centimetres long.

17

WILD THINGS

Addison has lost track of time.

She has no idea how long she's been standing there, PLUS 1's arms wrapped around her, the two friends staring at themselves in the cracked bathroom mirror. Maybe five minutes. Maybe twenty-five. Maybe five hours. She doesn't know and she doesn't care. She could stand there for ever with her beautiful, beautiful mate. Not saying anything. Just being.

The door opens, the wall of sound from the dance floor hits Addison like a warm, joyous wave. Someone comes in, pauses for a moment, smiling at her. 'You were amazing up there. Like, just incredible. Superwoman. The Queen of Sailor Bar.'

Addison smiles at the girl. 'Oh babe. Thanks. That means the world to me.'

As the girl heads into a cubicle, Addison beams. It's true,

she knows it's true: the set tonight was something else. There's a point, she thinks to herself, when you stop going through the motions, when you aren't aware of how you are on stage any more, when you don't have to plan your next move, your next reach-out to the audience. There's a point that comes when you're not thinking, you're not consciously even performing any more. That's what it's like for Addison now when she's up there, when the stage lights are in her eyes, when she's not really seeing the audience so much as feeling the warmth, the joy and communion, like standing in the water at your favourite beach in the middle of a really hot summer with the strong, powerful, all-embracing tide wrapping itself around every single inch of you. That's what it was like tonight. You're not a performer. You're not a rapper, not a singer.

You're just being. You're just fucking being.

'You're just fucking being . . . what?' murmurs PLUS 1. Addison looks at them. 'Oh shit. I said that aloud?'

PLUS 1 smiles. 'You lost an earring.'

Addison's retinal focus sluggishly shifts to her ear, and she realizes PLUS 1 is right: one of her piercings is empty, occupational hazard of losing yourself so completely on stage; you might start losing the things attached to yourself. PLUS 1 reaches up under their dreadlocks, carefully takes out one of their own earrings, a dangly feather concoction. They reposition Addison's head, easing the earring into the vacant piercing. The two of them look at each other in the mirror. Matching earrings. Matching smiles. Matching.

Addison says, 'If either of us was the kind of person who fell in love, it'd be dangerous.'

PLUS 1 turns her to look at them. 'You said that aloud too.'

Addison nods, uh-huh. PLUS 1 kisses her on her nose. Gentle. 'Good thing neither of us is that kind of person, huh?'

Addison smiles. Yeah. Good thing. Though maybe right now, right here, together, feeling the way they both do, neither is entirely sure they aren't that kind of person.

Addison reaches into PLUS 1's camo jacket pocket. She pulls out a couple of pink tablets.

Up there on the Sailor Bar stage, for Addison it was transformation. Like it always is. Floating above. Singing about the stuff that matters so much to her, that means so much it hurts, the big ideas. Connecting with the music, with the audience, with the things she believes. But also, tonight, there was something else going on for her. It was not only connecting. It was a way to not think about what she'd seen on her mother's laptop. The old video footage.

Her mother, in a police uniform, dragging away Māori protesters.

Addison looks at the pink pills in her hand.

Now she's not on stage, now the music isn't pulsing through her, the images from the laptop are coming back to her. She really doesn't want those images in her head.

She slips one pink pill in PLUS 1's mouth. The other in her own.

'Two in one night. Not like you.'

She swallows her pill. 'I'm not me. I'm Queen of Sailor Bar.'

Out in the bar, the music changes. PLUS 1 heads for the door. Dancing time. 'See you out there.'

Alone in the bathroom, Addison's mouth is suddenly dry. She leans down to the tap, takes a long drink of water. When she stands up again ...

Urgh. A sudden dizzy feeling. A hazy mist descending in front of her eyes. She giggles, shit. But then the next moment, it's not so funny. She grabs the side of the sink, her legs threatening to give out beneath her. She goes into a stall. Locks the door. Puts down the toilet top, just need to sit for a moment, just need to sit.

Then ... *WHOMP*.

With a rush like the feeling when a plane takes off, all of a sudden there's no blood in her head. Before she even knows she's falling, she is on the floor. She tries to get up, but just lifting her head from the floor makes the haze suddenly more intense, like a dense fog settling in a valley, surrounding her. She realizes she can't stand; she tries to call out, but her vocal cords have stopped working.

'Two in one night. Not like you.' Shit.

She sees her phone, fallen from her pocket. She reaches out, and after a few tries she manages to grab it. With slow, painful movements she opens her phone book, finds PLUS 1's number. She hits call.

Out in front of the stage, PLUS 1 has their eyes closed, moving to the music, transfixed. In their pocket, their phone screen lights up with Addison's call. But the phone is on silent. PLUS 1 doesn't even notice.

On the floor of the toilets, Addison calls PLUS 1 again. It goes to voicemail again. She tries to pull herself to her feet once more, but already she's losing consciousness. She subsides to the floor, clinging to her phone.

She knows she's in trouble.

Stan's car pulls up outside Sailor Bar. He hurries for the front door; the bouncer looks him up and down, 'Not sure this is your kind of place, bro.' Stan pulls out his ID, pushes past, into the throbbing music.

He was just falling asleep when his phone buzzed, Addison's name on caller ID. He thought about not answering; as much as he enjoyed the teasing, hassling relationship the two of them had, this time of the night was a bit much.

Eventually he picked up. 'Addison? You know it's one o'clock, right? As in, one in the morning?' From the other end of the phone, no reply. Stan could hear the sound of music, bass thumping coming from somewhere nearby, but distant and distorted as if through a wall. 'Addison? What's up?' Still no reply. Assuming she was pocket-calling by mistake, he was about to hang up, but . . .

'Stan . . . ' Her voice was not much more than a gasp. Almost impossible to hear over the muffled music. But Stan could sense the fear.

'Addison. Where are you?'

The call disconnected. He immediately phoned her back. No answer. Suddenly worried, Stan remembered the mocking invite she had given him a few days earlier. 'I'm playing Sailor Bar Thursday week.'

Inside the bar, it's dimly lit, a hundred beautiful people

moving together, the lights and music all-encompassing if you're there to dance, chaotic if you're trying to find someone you think needs help. Stan shoves past people, ignoring the unimpressed glances, the smirks at what he's wearing, perfectly suitable for the eighth floor of Central Police Station, completely out of place here.

He looks around. No sign of Addison. He thinks about the way the music sounded on her distress call. Muffled. Like it was through a wall. He sees the sign to the women's toilets.

He pauses outside, really not wanting to do this. But he has no choice. He pushes in. Luckily there's no one else in the bathroom. He tries the cubicle doors; one of them is locked. 'Addison? You there?' He shoves against the door, hard, he forces it open, to see . . .

Addison there on the floor. Around her, a pool of vomit. Her eyes flicker and open, weakly. She looks up at him. Her hand rises weakly. She makes a finger gun at him. *Boom.*

Stan grabs a paper towel, cleans Addison's face. He picks her up in his arms. 'C'mon, you little freak.'

In the room with Hana's drawings all over the walls, Hana and Jaye sit either side of Addison's bed. Addison is feeling worse than she's felt in her whole life. Stan called Hana on the way to hospital. Hana met them there, Jaye soon after. For anyone who hasn't had their stomach pumped, think of the most disgusting thing you've ever felt and multiply by ten. The last few hours of Addison's life, she'd be really happy to forget.

It's quiet in the house. Addison looks at a drawing on the wall. One of the early drawings, three of them in the picture.

'Dad?'

'Yeah?'

'That book you used to read me? The one with Max?'

As Hana looks for the long-forgotten book, Jaye gets Addison to drink another glass of water. With everything that's journeyed up and down her oesophagus, her throat is raw and feels like hell, but she swallows it down. It takes a minute or two.

Hana finds the book tucked away under a pile of novels and criminology texts, unread for a decade, probably more. She passes it to Jaye. She didn't miss the fact that Addison asked Jaye about the book, not her. At the hospital, Addison clung to her hand while they inserted the gastric suction tube; she let Hana soothe her, stroke her hair as the awful-ness ensued. But the look Hana saw when Addison looked up from the footage on the laptop hasn't changed. The question unspoken now, but still there in her daughter's eyes.

'What the fuck is this, Mum? What did you do?'

Jaye opens the well-thumbed pages. Addison smiles as he uses the same silly voices for the different characters as he used to when she was the age she is in the drawing. He reads about mischievous Max in his home-made wolf suit playing with the scary-looking monsters, the wild things who are actually not scary at all but the sweetest creatures on the face of the planet, just terribly misunderstood.

Hana watches from the door until, on the bed, her daughter's eyes close.

Tequila was always their drink.

Hana and Jaye first got together over straight tequila at an epic wild party to mark the end of their cohort's first term at police college. Old habits die hard. Hana keeps a bottle in her freezer for the occasional night every month or so when work is just too hard to shrug off by sweating out 10.13 kilometres, but now the tequila is a decent brand, costs five times the kind that she and Jaye used to drink as junior cops.

'She wasn't there, Hana. She doesn't know. The things she talks about, the things she sings about, they're all in theory. They're not lived-in. She's seventeen.'

They're sitting out on Hana's steps, looking out into the dark leafiness of her back yard. A shot of tequila each. On the rocks, the way they always had it. Upstairs in her room, Addison is fast asleep, exhausted by the things her body has gone through. Hana told Jaye what had happened, how she walked in to find Addison at her laptop. The look in Addison's eyes. The violence of the word she used.

Kūpapa.

Traitor.

'What happened eighteen years ago. You had no choice,' Jaye says.

Hana downs her tequila. It burns. She wants to believe that what Jaye says is true, that she had no choice on the mountain; it's what she has clung to for years. She pours them both another. They drink, looking out into the night.

'When she was born,' Jaye says quietly, 'I'll never forget. She cried for like ten seconds. And that was it. It was almost perfunctory. Like she knew a baby has to cry, that's the deal. She got that out of the way and it was over. I held her while they cut the cord. She was staring up at me. I mean, I know all the stuff – they can't see anything, at that age their eyes are like baby dolphin eyes or something, it's just light and dark – but it felt like she was looking at me. Saying hello.'

Hana realizes Jaye is crying.

She can't remember seeing him cry before. It's silent crying, more a stray tear than something dramatic. But it's still hard as hell to see.

She holds him. They sit together on the top step, in the dark.

If you asked them later, neither would know how it happened. Did Hana take Jaye's tequila glass out of his hand, or was it Jaye? Did Jaye kiss Hana? Or the other way around? Neither could tell you, but before either could think or pause or consider, without a word spoken, they are in Hana's room.

Hana has had lovers over the years. Not a number that causes her embarrassment; not that any number would do that, there's no ignominy in being human. One guy, a landscape architect, the relationship lasted three years. They shared a dry sense of humour, the love of transforming dark soil into worlds of extraordinary green. But there were things they didn't share. He wanted simplicity. He wanted to move out of Auckland, find a place by the beach. Hana imagined the theory, the idea. A house with an amazing garden looking out over rolling waves and sand dunes. Maybe she would get a job at some local station, go back to uniform, sit at the edge of the fifty-kilometre-an-hour zone, pull over the local farmers and send them on their way with a warning, then do the same a week later. Every day, every week, the same thing over and over, in and out, like the endlessly repeating tides lapping the dunes below their garden.

Simplicity. His dream. Not hers.

In recent years, she downloaded a dating app. Hooking up in bars isn't her style, the idea leaves her cold, so those times when she feels restless or alone or just in need of fleeting release, she opens the app, finds someone who seems smart and kind, swipes right. For her, that is more than enough. She has long since come to realize she doesn't need another human to complete her.

What happens with Jaye tonight isn't romance, but at the same time neither is it whatever the opposite of romance might be. It's two people tied by unseen knots and binds, connections that can never be undone. Two people under unrelenting and escalating pressure in their professional world. Two people who, hours prior, accompanied a squad of armed officers into a house where they believed a dangerous serial killer was hiding and who knew, as every cop who ever draws a weapon knows, that the day might not end well for themselves, or for the people at their side. Two parents who that night looked at their fierce, remarkable daughter in a hospital bed and realized that any fear they ever had for themselves was as nothing compared to the fear they felt for her.

Two people who care for and love each other, and always will.

It's over fast. Not without passion, that's not really accurate. But it's without hope. Even as their bodies come together in a way that is, after so long, both deeply familiar and completely foreign, both of them know that this will never happen again, can never happen again, that it shouldn't be happening now.

But neither is able to stop.

Afterwards, Jaye gets dressed quickly. Hana rebuttons her clothes, tidies her hair. There's a moment when, in different circumstances, they might kiss goodbye. Both know that would be every bit as bad as what just happened.

No, it would be even worse.

'That morning, when Addison was a baby,' Hana says, very quietly. 'When I told you it was over. You didn't cry. You didn't fight for us.'

'If I'd fought,' Jaye asks, 'would it have made a difference?'

Hana doesn't answer.

She reaches under the bed, takes out the box she keeps there, retrieves the legal document from beneath the electricity bills and rates demands. 'Marissa is a good woman,' she says. She gives Jaye the divorce papers. She has already signed them. 'This never happened, Jaye.'

In the bathroom, Jaye washes his face. He climbs the stairs, kisses Addison, who is snoring like a truck driver.

Then he leaves.

18

THE WRONG QUESTION

'You know what? I admire him.'

Grant Wirapa sits on the edge of his bed. It's morning. He is in hospital for observation, to make sure there are no adverse effects from the fast-acting high-strength sedative he was given when he was abducted. There's a uniformed cop at the door to the ward. In case.

Jaye glances at Hana. Both surprised by the unexpected choice of words. They've been here for half an hour now. Wirapa has told them everything he can about the abduction, about the place where he was held. The room he was in was bare, a locked door, no windows. He was unconscious when he was dragged there; Raki used the same chemical to knock him out before he was taken away again. The one thing of use he could tell them was that in the distance he could hear the sound of flowing water.

It wasn't ebb and tide, it wasn't ocean. The sound was steady, relentless. A large river.

It's something. But it's not much. New Zealand is a country made of mountains and rivers.

'What do you mean,' asks Jaye, 'by "admire"?'

Wirapa looks through the steamed-up glass of the window. Outside, steady drips of rain from a leaking gutter. 'He hates everything about me. Everything I do. Everything I believe in. And why he hates me most . . .' He rolls up the sleeve of his hospital-issue gown and holds out his arm, the skin a deep brown in the pale morning light. 'Because I'm this colour. In his mind, the way his synapses spark, I should know better. He hates me for what I think, he hates me for everything I write about. He hates *me*.'

His voice trails away. His hand brushes the skin of his exposed forearm. Deep in thought.

'He hates me. But he didn't kill me. He could have. There was nothing I could have done to stop him. I was in the palm of his hand. He didn't kill me, because he has a moral code. He's playing by a set of rules, rules he won't break.'

Jaye and Hana both know this guy has been through one of the most traumatizing episodes a person could ever encounter. Kidnapped by a serial killer, anaesthetized, taken to the killer's hiding place. He had every reason to expect he was about to become the next victim. He could be forgiven for not quite thinking in straight lines. But all the same . . .

'He has murdered four people,' Jaye says quietly. 'He's planning to kill two more. I don't see anything to admire in that.'

After Jaye had left her house the night before, Hana was awake through the night with Addison. She'd woken her daughter periodically, making her drink water as the emergency room doctor had told her to. The doctor had told them that with the stomach lavage and the fact that Addison had already vomited copiously, any further toxic reaction was very unlikely. She'd feel like hell for a few days, and the best remedy in the next twenty-four hours would be sleep.

Then Hana got a call from Jaye, early. He told her about the abduction and return of the journalist, and the corpse that was left behind in the journalist's SUV, the shrouded body of the young man with the straggly blonde hair. Joseph Donald Camden, a descendant of the fourth soldier, a low-level dealer and user of cheap methamphetamine. Camden's disappearance a week before hadn't been much noticed, his associates assuming he was recovering from an overdose, or that maybe he'd disappeared to flee the consequences of a deal gone wrong.

For Hana and Jaye, the breakthrough in discovering Poata Raki's identity is overshadowed by the discovery of this fourth victim. And the kidnapping of the journalist, to humiliate him and to make him a messenger for the very public statement of what Raki is doing and why, shows them both that the killer is only growing bolder and more determined.

But Jaye's phone call was also to tell Hana that they had both been called in to the district commander's office. Immediately.

In the elevator heading up to the meeting, there was a strained silence between them. What had happened the night before wasn't going to be talked about again, both of them knew, not between them nor with anyone else, including Marissa. A car-crash collision of events that ended with them in Hana's bed. To talk about it would give oxygen to something that should not be allowed to change lives, that should not be allowed to hurt the many people it would hurt.

Both of them knew it would never happen again. Neither would allow it to happen again.

And both had to live with the knowledge of what they'd done.

Coming out of the lift, Hana had a pretty good idea what was about to happen. Jaye had unilaterally made the decision to ignore her suspension in order to have her there for the AOS raid. In the rigid hierarchical structure of the police, the district commander wasn't about to let this pass. But exactly what the consequences might look like, neither Hana nor Jaye knew.

When they were ushered into the district commander's office, to their surprise, others were already there. Patrick Thompson's mother, and Thompson's QC. Hana had seen the woman a number of times in the courtroom, but they had never had reason to speak. She remembered watching her in the moments after her son was sentenced, how she'd looked across the courtroom, meeting the victim's eyes for a moment. She vividly remembered how, even as her son and her husband were celebrating and hugging, the woman's eyes fell to the floor . . .

The QC cleared his throat. 'My client has instructed me that his mother is here to speak on his behalf.'

Mrs Thompson pushed her chair back. She got to her feet. Her voice was strong. Unequivocal. She looked directly at Hana. 'After my son was arrested, throughout the trial and the sentencing, you and I never talked. I never wanted to. I thought you were the enemy, Detective. I realize now that I was wrong.'

She told Hana that she'd been following the investigation into the killings; of course she had, like the whole of the country. She saw the work Hana was doing, the importance of that work. But there was more than that. 'I know you're a good detective. And an honest one.' She knew that Hana had uncovered the truth about her son, as uncomfortable and devastating as it was. 'If you are taken off this case because of my family, the shame I feel for the things my son did will be a hundred times worse.'

The QC stepped in. 'The Thompson family is withdrawing the complaint against you, Detective Senior Sergeant.' This wasn't a moment he was enjoying. The practice of law might take place in elegant courtrooms, played out in restrained and polite legal language, but it was a blood sport. Stepping away from a case against a high-profile senior detective that would inevitably be the stuff of headlines for months was painful.

But the mother wasn't finished. 'The accusations my son made against you—'

'Mrs Thompson . . . ' The QC tried to interject, to stop her saying what he knew she was about to say. She shot him a withering glare. And ignored him.

'I believe you, Detective. It hurts that I would take your word over that of my own son. But I know you didn't assault him.'

She had said everything she wanted to say. She walked around the table, pausing in front of Hana. She shook Hana's hand, then she and the QC left.

'This changes nothing.' The district commander had barely said a word while Mrs Thompson and the QC were in the room. With them gone, this was once more his domain. 'This is a disciplinary matter. You were suspended for appalling, unprofessional behaviour.' He turned to Jaye. 'Then five minutes later, you ignore my direct order and take a suspended officer to lead an AOS raid with you.'

Jaye was ready for this. 'I screwed up. It's indefensible.' He took something from his pocket. Placed it on the district commander's table. An envelope.

'What's this?' the district commander asked, already knowing the answer.

'You said it, sir, no one's bigger than this job. No one's indispensable. That's true of Detective Senior Sergeant Westerman, the person at the heart of this case, the cop who can actually solve it. And it's true of me. You have my resignation.'

Before Jaye even reached the elevator, the district commander was there.

'If this were any other situation. Any other fucking case.'

He shoved the envelope back in Jaye's hands. Turned his furious eyes on Hana.

'Find him. Stop him.'

In the hospital room, rain from a passing deluge hits the windows with force, making sounds like hard metal pellets striking the glass. Wirapa distractedly adjusts the sleeve of his gown, his hands shaking.

'I know this is hard,' Hana says. She is familiar enough with PTSD to understand that the aftermath of what happened to him will be with Wirapa for months to come, probably for years, maybe for ever. 'I'm sorry,' she says gently. 'We need to ask a few more questions. How did he seem to you?'

'You saw the video. That's how he was. That wasn't a performance. It wasn't a learned-by-rote diatribe. He was speaking from the heart.'

Hana has seen the video, of course, and she has to agree with this assessment. If Raki had been making a party political broadcast about global warming, the words you'd use to describe him would be 'credible', 'genuine', 'passionate'. But he isn't a politician. He's not talking about climate change. He's a murderer explaining his reasons for killing his fellow human beings.

'There are things we can't see on the video. I need to know what you saw, face to face with him.'

What Hana needs to know more than anything is Raki's mental state. Whether he's hanging by a thread. Or if the thread has already broken. 'Is he agitated? Anything unusual about his speech patterns? Moments of irrationality? Is he explosive? Unpredictable?'

The journalist considers her questions. 'He's whatever

the opposite of explosive is. So calm it's like the blood in his veins is moving at half-pace. He's how I imagine those guys who fly fighter jets to be.'

But Wirapa understands what it is Hana really wants to know. 'My sister . . .' he says. 'She suffered from paranoid schizophrenia her whole life. She jumped off Grafton Bridge on her twenty-first birthday. I know what you're asking. I didn't see any signs of psychosis. He was calm. Focused. He was more eloquent and measured and considered in his words and his actions than I could be in a dozen newspaper columns. He knew what he wanted to say. He knew what he was going to do. When I looked into his eyes, I didn't see a madman. I saw someone who was committed. Utterly, completely, irreversibly committed.'

Hana doesn't miss the word 'irreversibly'.

Wirapa finally turns away from the window. He looks at Hana and Jaye.

'If what you want to know is "Is he sane?" I think you're asking the wrong question,' he says.

'What's the right question?' Jaye asks.

Wirapa's eyes are steady. Strangely calm.

'Who's next?' he finally replies.

At the entrance to the hospital, Jaye and Hana stand in the doorway. The rain has eased from the earlier onslaught to a slow, steady fall. 'I hope he's right,' Jaye says. 'I hope Raki has a moral code. I hope he is sane. Whatever sane means, when he's killed four times.'

He tells Hana about a disturbing development digital forensics discovered when they hacked Poata Raki's Google searches for the last few months. He'd extensively researched the use of gelignite. Explosives. But it gets worse. 'Two weeks ago, a box of high-grade explosives and detonators was stolen from a construction site in Otorohanga over a long weekend. It hasn't been recovered.' His face is grim. 'It's enough to blow up an entire city block.'

And now Hana understands why Jaye is so desperate that Wirapa's assessment of Raki is accurate. A sane man with some kind of moral code is at least a known quantity. But an unstable man, a man deteriorating psychologically, someone who might unpredictably veer from six specific victims to many, someone who may have stolen a large quantity of gelignite and could be planning to use it – that shifts everything.

She buttons her coat, readying herself to head out into the weather.

'The envelope in your pocket,' she says quietly. 'Was it really your resignation? Or an old electricity bill?'

'It was my resignation.'

'Thank you.'

A few last drops ripple in a puddle on the ground in front of them, then the rain finally dies.

'Good to have you back', Jaye says.

19

ARE YOU OKAY?

PLUS 1 found Addison's missing earring.

As Stan was frantically searching for Addison in Sailor Bar, PLUS 1 was out on the dance floor, lost in their own world, a world of intense pulsing lights magically diffracted by the effects the beautiful pink pills were having on their optic nerves, a world of amplified bass notes that seemed to bypass the eardrums and surge straight into the spinal fluid, a world of movement and emotion and love for every life form. PLUS 1 was an energy machine, lean and naturally fit, and as Stan was driving through the dark city streets, the lights of his car flashing, rushing Addison to the emergency room, PLUS 1 was blissfully unaware, dancing like there was no greater purpose in life than to ride the perfect building waves of the beats coming from the speakers and the chemicals coursing through their veins, dancing like if this was how the world was going to end, really, that wouldn't be so bad, that could be all right, PLUS 1 would go with that.

Then it was three a.m. The house lights came on. The magical world of music and diffracted light transformed in a heartbeat into a dreary wood-panelled room, the DJ packed up his gear, the bouncer in his black shirt done up to the top button told PLUS 1 it was time to head off.

'I have to find my mate.'

'Addison? She went.' Everyone knew Addison.

'She went? Eh? When? How? With who?'

All the bouncer wanted was to get everyone the hell out of there so he could go home; he wasn't in the least interested in explaining about the guy who looked a lot like a pig who'd carried Addison out, barely conscious. PLUS 1 figured Addison must have found her own way home. As the bouncer hustled the last punters towards the door, PLUS 1 noticed something shining at the bottom of the stage.

A smile came to their face. It was Addison's lost earring.

'I found your earring, babe.'

PLUS 1 sits next to Addison on her bed, upstairs at Hana's place. When Addison felt well enough to call and tell them what had happened – Stan finding her and rushing her to the hospital, having her stomach pumped, the hideous day she'd just gone through – PLUS 1 hurried over to be with their friend. As they gently slide the earring into Addison's piercing, footage is playing on Addison's tablet. Raki's video. PLUS 1 has seen the video multiple times already; it's been broadcast and uploaded and had uncountable shares. But Addison, sleeping off the aftermath of Sailor Bar, knew nothing about it until PLUS 1 turned up with the lost earring and told her to open up YouTube.

'The time of the lamb is over,' Raki says. 'By my actions, the spark is struck. It is time to return to the old ways. Of utu. To avenge that which has never been avenged. To take back that which has been stolen over the past two centuries.'

Addison hasn't eaten, her raw tortured throat unable to deal with anything more than the water she craves so badly but that causes her hell when she swallows. Just speaking hurts. 'I can't believe it . . .' she rasps.

They both stare at the man on the screen. The dark, intense eyes. The two friends know this face.

Addison and PLUS 1 have met Poata Raki before.

Months earlier, there was a rally in the university quad, a protest gig in support of third-gender bathroom cubicles throughout the campus, a move the university hierarchy actively opposed because of budget shortfalls. Addison and PLUS 1 and their crew performed, and between songs Addison took to the microphone to attack the university's position.

'Staff cafeterias throughout the campus are being renovated to include barista stations. There are budget shortfalls when gender non-binary students ask for official status in this university, but plenty of cash for our lecturers to have a nice espresso made for them between classes. How the hell does that work?'

Addison's eyes shone as she held PLUS 1's hand. 'If my friend doesn't have the same rights I do, the right to dignity, the right to a safe place, the right to be and to identify and be recognized as who they are, none of my rights mean a fucking thing!'

Cheers from students straight, LGBTQ+ and otherwise. As Addison started another song, she noticed a face at the back of the crowd watching intently, a bit older than the students in front of the stage.

After the rally, the guy with the intense eyes introduced himself. 'You should come to one of my lectures,' Poata Raki said, speaking to Addison and PLUS 1 in te reo. He thought that as young, politically active Māori with a voice and an audience, the ideas he talked about might mean something to them.

He was right.

The following week, PLUS 1 and Addison snuck into the back row of one of Raki's classes. He was a shadowy figure at the front of the darkened lecture theatre, his words echoing through the room.

'Colonization is the removal, by sustained and overwhelming acts of brutality and violence, of the right of indigenous peoples to self-rule, and to the governance and protection of their land. The key words? "Brutality" and "violence".'

On the AV screen at the front of the lecture theatre, a

series of slides. Stark, awful historical images. Images of the land wars of the nineteenth century. Burning villages, torched by soldiers in the uniforms of the colonial forces. Dead bodies, men, women, children, the elderly, babies. All Māori.

'The word for land is "whenua",' Raki said. 'But whenua has another meaning. It also means placenta. The loss of land is deep pain. Spiritual pain. Mamae.* Pain passed down from one generation to the next. As raw as the pain a child feels at the loss of a parent.'

The lecture theatre was like pretty much every university lecture theatre. Grey walls, whiteboards, flip-up seats with stain-resistant coverings. Nondescript. Ordinary. But for Addison, this lecture was anything but ordinary. And watching Poata Raki, his voice so measured and calm despite the things he was speaking about, she knew this was no ordinary lecturer. Listening in the back row, she had to remind herself to breathe.

'When Te Tiriti o Waitangi was signed in 1840, I believe the British Crown saw it as a convenient fiction. A stopgap. Our ancestors weren't supposed to survive, that wasn't part of the Crown's plan. And it damn near worked. When the Treaty was signed, there were nearly one hundred thousand Māori, and only a couple of thousand British settlers. Within twenty years, immigrants outnumbered Māori. By 1900, we were thirty-five thousand people and falling fast. A people beaten, raped, murdered. A culture brutalized by war, by introduced diseases, by poverty.

---

* Mamae – profound grief, trauma, spiritual pain

Expected to disappear, like the moa,[*] like the mammoth. But we had the temerity to survive.'

Addison watched Raki's eloquence, his fire, the commitment, the passion.

Looking at him was like looking at someone she wanted to be.

Towards the end of the lecture, a young Pākehā student raised her hand. 'What happened in the past wasn't fair. Nah, it was shitty. Excuse my French.'

PLUS 1 and Addison knew instantly, from the clothing labels she wore, her accent, so like the vast majority of other students, that the young woman had gone to the right school. Not the school either PLUS 1 or Addison had gone to. 'Bet I know what suburb she's from,' PLUS 1 whispered.

The Pākehā student continued. 'But the shoe's on the other foot now, right? All those scholarships only for Māori students. Academic preferences, entry quotas, awards no one else can apply for. That's not fair either.'

'Ms Herrick, isn't it?' Raki approached where the young woman was sitting.

'Yes. Paula.'

'Your roots go back to the high-country farming Herrick family?' Raki was very familiar with the surname, from research on historic treaty claims. 'In the 1860s, I believe, your family bought thousands of hectares of land for a few hundred pounds.'

'I wasn't round then.'

---

[*] Moa – large flightless bird that stood up to four metres tall; became extinct 500 years ago

'I can show you how to find the historical records, if you're interested.'

Raki was neither aggressive nor punitive. This was explanation, not accusation. He told the young woman that for the pittance her ancestor paid the local Māori, the family acquired a massive tract of the best land in the country. But the tribe he bought the land from believed that the payment they received was a rental, for the Pākehā family to share the land with them, to their mutual benefit. 'The idea of individual ownership is a Pākehā idea. Introduced here, like influenza. For Māori, land can only ever be held communally. For the greater good. Land isn't owned, it's cared for. Not possession, but custodianship. Guardianship of the earth and her resources, for the benefit of all, for the future.'

Māori welcomed the idea of sharing with the newcomers from the other side of the planet, Raki continued; it was only fair that newly arrived families like the Herricks could earn money and grow food. By the time tribes discovered that they had in fact signed away their traditional lands, it was too late. Any attempt to undo the mistake was met with legal action, in a foreign system of law they didn't understand. And if they dared press the point further, the next step was guns.

'Two centuries later, here we are. Do you know the average wealth of a Māori citizen today, Ms Herrick?'

She didn't.

'Once, every inch of this land was in Māori guardianship. Now we have an average worth of less than twenty thousand dollars. Less than it costs for a couple of return

business-class air fares to London. The average wealth of
Pākehā? More than a hundred and thirty thousand dollars.'

Listening, Addison gripped the edge of the table.

'Your family can afford to send you to this university.
Your ancestor grew wealthy from acquiring Māori land in
a way that is, plain and simple, fucking fraud. Pardon my
French. Māori who need scholarships to get an education,
if they could reap the benefits of the land that is rightfully
theirs, they'd be wearing the nice clothes you wear. They'd
be taking the business-class trips to London rather than
trying to work out how to feed their family. Maybe you'd
be on the scholarship, Ms Herrick, and if that was the
case, I hope the Māori student sitting in your seat would
be welcoming of the fact that you had been given the
opportunity to be here.'

After the lecture, Raki took a moment with Addison
and PLUS 1, thanking them for coming.

'The things you talk about, matua,* Addison said,
respectful. 'Makes me want to punch the wall.'

'So it should.' Raki smiled. But Addison could see that
there was real pain behind his eyes. 'Māori have limitless capacity for love,' he said. 'And limitless capacity
for trauma and anger. I want to punch walls every day. I
want to see the cities built on our blood bulldozed to the
ground. But I turn that feeling into this . . .'

This being his teaching.

He took PLUS 1 into a hongi.† Then he did the same

---

* Matua – father; also used as a term of respect for older male
† Hongi – the pressing of noses in greeting

with Addison, pressing noses, sharing breath. 'You're doing the same as me,' he said to Addison. 'Turning fury into action. I think we are not so different.' It felt like the greatest compliment she could be given.

The next semester, both Addison and PLUS 1 signed up for Raki's class. But on the first day of teaching the course was cancelled.

He had been suspended.

On Addison's tablet, the video has finished, paused on Raki's face, looking out calmly from the screen. Given what the two friends now know, the image is unsettling. Eerie.

'Sitting in his lecture that day,' PLUS 1 says, perching beside Addison on her bed, 'listening to him, I would have followed that guy to the ends of the earth. I would've done anything he told me to, believed anything he said. But Jesus. Four people, murdered . . .' They carefully, gently adjust Addison's earring, until it's hanging just right. 'The guy is fucking crazy,' they say.

Addison stares at Poata Raki's face on the screen. This person, who seemed to give voice to so many things she believed, things she felt profoundly but had never been able to turn into words. If he now says this is the way to put right the terrible wrongs of the past, what should she even think?

It's a question she has no idea how to answer.

PLUS 1 kisses Addison's forehead. 'No second pills for you again. Never not ever. I was so scared.'

When PLUS 1 is gone, Addison takes out her phone. Scrolls through her contacts list. They'd exchanged numbers after the lecture. 'Any time you want to talk,' Raki said.

She types a text.

Matua I don't understand what's happening

She deletes the text. Types another one.

If you need to talk I'm here

She deletes again.

Are you okay matua?

She thinks about deleting.

She doesn't delete. She presses send.

She watches the phone.

There's no reply.

20

DO NOT BURY ME
IN THE EARTH

Deep in the forest, a strong wind whips through the dense treetops high above. Far below, a figure amongst the trees. He turns, flexing and moving with grace and control, like a t'ai chi grand master. In his hands, a long-handled taiaha. The two-headed spear carved of hard ancient wood, sharpened pounamu inset along the biting edges.

Raki performs a fast, hard swinging stroke that slices clean through a branch, cutting through its three-inch girth as readily as a cucumber sliced by a butcher's knife. He holds the taiaha before him. With great solemnity, he places it on the whāriki, the mat she'd made. The last one she'd woven, before it was too painful for her fingers, impossible for her to focus long enough to do the complex plaiting of the strips of dyed harakeke flax.

He kneels by the whāriki. His fingers trace the coloured thread.

'Promise me,' she'd said to him. Her voice coming in painful bursts, spilling out between the waves of agony fast taking over her every moment, her every breath. 'Promise me. Do not bury me in the earth.'

She was in her early sixties when she passed, still young; she should have had so much to look forward to. The years ahead when he would one day bring a newborn child to her, when she would hold her mokopuna* in her arms. Perhaps she would teach the child to hunt deer, as she did with him. Perhaps she would teach it to weave. There was such a rich storehouse of knowledge built up in her head and heart, so much that she could pass on. But these things he imagined, he knew they would never happen. She did not get to see a grandchild. She did not live that long.

And Raki knows now that he will never hold a child of his own in his arms. *He* will not live that long.

'Swear to me. *Swear it.*' He remembers how hard she fought not to scream, not to give voice to the terrors her body was experiencing. He was trying to be as strong as her. But he wasn't as strong, not nearly as strong; he wept as she gripped his hand. 'Do not let my flesh rot in the ground they stole from us. Promise me. *Promise me.*'

He sees a drop of moisture on the woven whāriki mat: his own tear, fallen unfelt as he was lost in the memory. He wipes away the dampness. Places the two-headed taiaha in the mat. He rolls up the whāriki, straps it to his kitbag.

---

* Mokopuna – grandchild

Sweat pours from his face as he lopes up a long slope. Running hard and silent through the great forest, his kitbag across his shoulders, pushing himself. Ahead of him, a towering kahikatea, fifty metres tall, covered in distinctive red berries, the tree his mother used to call the dinosaur tree because the ancient podocarps have been around since before the Jurassic period. Then he hears something. He drops to a knee beneath the dinosaur tree, silently, smoothly, listening. He hears the sound again. A familiar sound. It's coming from the other side of a rise. He moves to the top of the crest, slowly, inch by inch, staying in the shadows of the undergrowth.

Through a gap in the ferns, he sees the animal he has been hearing.

He silently opens his kitbag. He takes out the other weapon held inside. A rifle with a high-powered sight.

Slowly, slowly, he raises the rifle. The way he was trained in the Territorials, the stock pulled hard against the shoulder, to give a solid anchor, finger tensing around the trigger, not pulling or even squeezing, just a slow, gentle easy tighten.

The stag is completely unaware he is being watched. Blissfully unknowing that a minuscule but deadly pellet of lead is about to enter his body.

Raki pauses. His finger stops tightening.

He thinks of the hearing. The three years he spent, so proud to be lead advocate for Te Tini-o-Tai, his tribe on his mother's side. It was a way to put right the things that had been left undone and unfixed, from the time the tribe's lands were stolen, through to the day as a child he watched his mother dragged away from the protest at the sacred mountain, and all the dark days in between.

He felt the weight of history, as surely as he feels the butt of his weapon digging into his shoulder now, as he argued the case for the tribe. It was a weight he embraced, welcomed. He believed, he *knew*, he would make a difference.

He still remembers the day, during his exhaustive research, when he found the image. The century-and-a-half-old daguerreotype of the tribe's ancestor, hanged by his neck from the tree on the sacred mountain. The image was so devastating, so powerful, so haunting. The faded photo became the touchstone for his arguments to the hearing. It was something tangible and visual he could return to, a visceral, compelling symbol of the decades of violence and theft that remained unaddressed, but that would at last be put right in this hearing and the settlement and compensation that would follow.

He did the best job he was capable of. He gave everything of himself to the process. Believing that at last, justice would be done for his mother's people.

The stag raises its head. Looks around. But Raki can see it's a habitual movement, scanning the surroundings for threats. He knows the animal hasn't heard or seen or smelt him; he's too careful for that. He could take the shot now. But he is composed, calm. Rushing almost inevitably brings about the wrong result.

Patience isn't just a virtue. It's everything.

But the patience the tribe showed in the compensation process came to naught.

When the tribunal released its decision, the monetary figure was a number in the many millions. Certain lands were returned. But for Raki, it wasn't compensation. It was a new insult added to the others. The total amount returned or compensated equated to a figure that represented less than a fiftieth of what was taken. A fiftieth . . .

And what was most devastating – to the tribe, to Raki, to his mother – was that the sacred mountain wasn't returned. It was to be kept as public land, a partnership between the Crown and the tribe. Raki knew what that meant. The government didn't have the courage to tell people they couldn't go and picnic under the tree where his ancestor died. The image he had believed would carry so much weight – the great chief hanged by the neck, surrounded by six mocking soldiers – it meant nothing. The sacred mountain, defiled and disrespected for so long, was once more insulted, treated with disdain and contempt.

After the decision, he packed away the boxes and boxes of genealogical research, the legal case histories, the years of work he and his team had put into the claim. He knew he would never again argue a case in a land compensation tribunal. He knew he could never again believe in or trust the legal process that had betrayed his people for two centuries and continued to do so. And now the image of his executed ancestor became something more than a powerful symbol to be used in legal argument. It became a wrong that remained uncorrected by legal process.

A wrong that should be put right.

In Raki's sights, the stag's head rises once more. But

this movement is different. The wind has shifted. The stag looks towards the thing whose scent the wind has carried to him. For a moment, man and beast stare at one another. Patience isn't just a virtue. It's everything. But there also comes a moment when it is time to act. Raki's finger tightens. *Boom*. There's two hundred metres between him and the stag. The bullet hits the animal between the eyes.

Raki lowers the weapon. He breathes.

Raki had been teaching at the university a little less than three years when his mother took her last breath. The place he found for her was deep in the forest. Far from walking tracks or hunters' routes, far from cycle trails or farmland, a place where her body would be disturbed only by the birds of the trees. For they would have their job to do, as they had done with the dead in the old days. He made her shroud from an unfinished piece of her whāriki. He fixed the rope to a branch in the canopy of a tall rimu tree, and solemnly raised the whāriki sack holding her body high into the air.

The rimu was in flower. Red fruit cups. In southern Africa, for many tribes, red is the colour of mourning. The flowers would attract the birds. They would find the whāriki sack with his mother's remains. The birds, the bugs and the weather would do their work.

There, beneath his mother's body, Raki remembered.

He remembered the mamae, the profound grief and spiritual pain that had haunted his people, generation after generation. The mamae of the confiscation of their land, the execution of their chief, the violence of the police response to peaceful protests generation after generation, decade after decade. He thought of the humiliation of the settlement, a fraction of what had been taken. The final insult of the sacred mountain still not returned.

There, in the shadow of his mother's body, he wept.

He thought of the decades of mamae for so many, for so long, the weight of pain coming together in his broken mother's broken words, her plea: 'Do not let my flesh rot in the ground they stole from us.'

He wept.

The first bird landed on the whāriki sack. It peered into the opening, curious about what lay within. Looking up at his mother's body high in the branches above, Raki thought once more of the image.

The dead chief. The six soldiers, posing beneath the defiled body.

Mamae. Pain passed down through the generations.

As raw as the pain a child feels at the loss of a parent.

It was suddenly so clear to him. He realized in that moment exactly what he had to do.

As he finished the karakia,* he took a long, deep breath. His lungs filled with the pure air of the forest, as a baby's lungs fill with the first breath of life. Looking up to the treetops, he made a quiet promise to his mother.

'When your bones rattle, I will act.'

---

* Karakia – ritual chants, prayers

21

DUTY

A grey, overcast sky hangs over coils of razor wire that run along two towering rows of twenty-metre-high security fences.

Stan's car approaches the front gates of the prison. Two other unmarked cars follow. A set of reinforced gates open and Stan's car moves through. The other two vehicles follow. The gates shut, the detectives show their police IDs to a corrections officer.

Hana watches as the next set of automated gates slide open, and the convoy drives through into the interior parking area.

It's a strange field, genealogy.

Some of the best researchers of historic familial ties

don't even have a degree; many are alarmingly obsessed hobbyists who have honed their skills ferreting their way through the shadows of the online world, hunting out obscure records and long-forgotten microfiches, bouncing around the many databases that have sprung up around the world as people have discovered a passion for looking into the dark corners of their DNA. After Hana found the copy of the daguerreotype in the tunnels under Mount Suffolk, when she faced the unthinkable, when she understood that a series of executions were being enacted because of whakapapa, when she knew that vengeance was being taken following lines of descent across eight generations, she realized that genealogy would be a key weapon in the inquiry, and that she would need to recruit the best and most highly skilled genealogists available. The Church of the Latter-day Saints quickly proved an unexpectedly powerful ally, with its labyrinthine ancestral records used to retrospectively baptize ancestors into the Mormon faith.

With most of the six members of the troop, there was no shortage of descendants. If one of the soldiers had even a relatively small family of say three children, and they produced another three children each, over time the result was a pool of literally thousands of potential victims. And in the nineteenth century, families were on average larger. But the lines of descent from the captain had gone dead. He'd had one child only, possibly a consequence of his greater love for the bottle than for his wife, and the descendants of that sole child were also singularly modest in their efforts at reproduction. The team of genealogists had come up empty-handed. Perhaps it was the negative effect of Darwinism: here was a bloodline that hadn't earned the right to thrive and flourish. On the other hand, there was reason for relief. If there was no descendant, that meant one less murder.

But that morning, the day after Hana was reinstated as lead officer of the inquiry, a call came in to the hotline. The captain of the troop had a descendant after all. His blood had been passed on to one person alive today, only one. There was a reason the genealogists had had no hits from their fervent searching. The sole descendant was a career fraudster who'd covered her tracks with multiple aliases. Her given name was Jonelle Kennedy, but she'd changed it by deed poll twice to escape the heavier debtors who might use a more direct and literal method of getting their pound of flesh than through the benign but mostly useless civil court process.

With knowledge of the woman's birth details, the genealogists quickly confirmed her familial link to the drunkard captain. Hana and Jaye immediately knew they had a problem. Kennedy was in a minimum-security unit. In minimum, the inmates have more freedom, and most worryingly, there's considerably more interaction with the outside world. Tutors come in to teach the subjects the majority of inmates never attended when they were younger; there are apprenticeship schemes with specialist trainers preparing prisoners for the outside world; visitors come and go daily. The police hierarchy decided to transfer the woman to the holding cells in Central Station. The cells are in the depths of the building, behind endless security doors and surrounded by, literally, hundreds of cops. It's pretty much the most secure place in the city.

It's a couple of hours before visiting time at the prison, and the visiting room is empty. When Kennedy is brought in, Hana apologizes for having to cuff her. 'Procedure. Sorry.' The woman takes her time. Looking Hana up and down. Hana has a sense that it's how she operates. A con artist's radar on permanent alert, looking for the way to work past the barriers of the person in front of you, to get something out of them. The habit of a lifetime.

Finally she holds out her hands to be cuffed, giving a disarming smile that Hana knows is intended to be exactly that – disarming.

'No worries, love,' she says. 'I'll forgive you.'

The traffic on the motorway is heavy. The last of the morning rush heading towards the city, though it seems like this morning the tail is lasting even longer than usual. The three unmarked police vehicles move at a crawl, Stan's car sandwiched between the other two.

'Comms, AV Charlie 8, we've got traffic,' Stan says into his handset. 'We'll be delayed another half-hour at least.'

In the front seat, Hana studies the woman's aliases. Jonelle Kennedy became Jillian King. Sometimes Jane Kilmartin. Or Jennifer Kendall. A list of another dozen names in the same vein. Different enough that she'd thrown those pursuing off the scent, similar enough that she wouldn't lose track.

'How long will I be in the holding cells?' asks Kennedy. 'I've kept my nose clean. I've earned the right to decent conditions. Those cells are for battery hens.'

Stan tells her, they can't be sure. But given that she is the only known descendant of her line, it's the safest place for her.

Kennedy shrugs. 'As long as you guys keep your end of the deal.'

'What deal?' Stan asks.

'You're gonna put in a good word for my parole, for co-operating.'

A glance between Hana and Stan. They both know neither of them made this offer, that neither of them would have. Hana turns to look at the woman in the back seat. 'We're moving you for your own protection. There's no trade-off involved.'

The prisoner looks between the two detectives. 'What's this bullshit? The cop who called said there'd be a note on my file for the next parole hearing. A very helpful note.'

Hana can see that if this is another scam Kennedy is running, she's playing a great poker face. Her indignation seems genuine.

'We didn't call you,' Stan says. 'You called us.'

'Yeah,' says Kennedy, 'I called. After the pig called me, last night. Telling me the link you'd found to the soldier. Telling me to phone in to Central Station, say who I am, you'd organize the next steps.'

Hana and Stan both think the same thought at the same time. 'The cop. Was it a woman or a man?' Hana asks, knowing the answer already.

'You go back on the deal, I swear I'll—'

'A woman or a man?'

'A man.'

The detectives both scan the traffic. They're travelling painfully slowly. There are cars either side of them, vehicles in front, vehicles behind. Ahead, an overpass, one of many that cut across the motorway. Any number of places an assassin could strike from. Especially in traffic that is crawling. Hana doesn't need to tell Stan what she is certain of. He is sure of it too. The call to the woman was from Poata Raki. With his experience of investigating genealogical histories and court records for his land rights research, he has as much access and skills as the genealogists Hana is working with. And he had a head start. He found the one descendant of the captain of the troop. And now that descendant is out in the middle of a gridlocked motorway. They're sitting ducks. Except a sitting duck can spread its wings and take flight when it realizes it needs to. Stan and Hana don't have that luxury.

Hana hits the emergency lights, gets on the handset to the other vehicles. 'Take the next exit. Repeat, we're taking the next exit.'

Sensing the severe shift in temperature, the woman in the back seat is suddenly perplexed. 'What? What's going on?'

'Nothing to worry about,' Stan assures her.

'I don't fucking believe you. Don't scam a scammer.'

The police vehicles cut across the lanes of traffic, sirens wailing and lights flashing, and head onto the exit ramp.

Unseen behind them, another car follows.

Off the motorway now, the three police vehicles race through an industrial area. As Stan drives, Hana is on the radio with police comms, working through options. She checks her sidearm. It's discreet, but in the back seat, Kennedy doesn't miss it.

'We've got units on the way plus Eagle,' comms informs them, 'Find a location you can secure and advise us of your position.'

The voice of one of the detectives in the front car comes through. 'Container yard five hundred metres ahead, ten o'clock.'

The vehicles slow. Hana scans the area. Containers stacked high, like the walls of a canyon, with open spaces between the rows for the Eagle helicopter to land. Lots of concealed areas for their vehicles to stay hidden from the road.

'Let's do it,' she says into the handset.

With a squealing of tyres, the three unmarked cars pull off the road, driving fast into the container yard. 'There,' Hana says, indicating a corner protected on three sides. Stan's car pulls into the far end; the other two police vehicles block the opening. As Stan radios their location, Hana pulls out her police-issue Glock, not even trying to hide it from the woman now. 'Don't move,' she tells her.

As the site foreman comes running, the other detectives are readying their firearms, taking positions to defend Stan's vehicle. Hana shows the foreman her badge. 'How many staff here?'

'Just me and the ladies in the office. What are you—'

'Get the others. Go to the tearoom,' she tells the bewildered man. 'Lock the door. Don't come out. *Go.*'

As the foreman hurries back to the office, Stan locks the doors of his car. In the back seat, the handcuffed prisoner can only look around, with no idea what is unfolding. The detectives wait by the other cars. Watching. Silent. Stan speaks very quietly. 'Eagle is fifteen minutes away.'

Then Hana hears something. The sound of a car alarm.

It's coming from nearby. Somewhere within the container yard. Her eyes search in the direction of the noise, but she can't see anything from her position. She knows who it is. She can feel it like a coldness in the marrow of her bones. She readies her Glock.

'Boss?' Stan asks, worried.

She silently signals to him: stay with the woman. Then she heads towards the sound of the alarm.

She moves fast and silent, squeezing between containers, cautiously making her way to an opening between two of the rows, checking the surroundings, heading closer and closer to the car alarm.

She shuffles her way sideways through a particularly tight space. Looking out through the gap . . .

She can see the vehicle. The doors are open, it's empty.

She takes a crouching position in cover. Her eyes urgently search the top of the containers, stacked up to five high. But she can't see anything.

An electronic beep. The car alarm dies. Silence.

Hana's phone vibrates. She pulls it from her pocket. An unknown number. She answers.

'I said we would meet again,' Raki says, in te reo.

She cradles the phone to her ear, her gun raised, held between both hands, the barrel searching the shadows of every opening.

'Where are you, Poata?'

From the other end of the phone, Raki's voice is amused. 'We're on first-name terms now?'

A flicker of movement between two containers on the far side of the space. Hana turns her gun, ready to fire, but . . . a flapping of wings and a bird flies out of the shadows, taking flight.

Hana's eyes hunt. Waiting for a telltale sign. The slightest glimpse, she's ready to fire, to end this. 'Poata – Raki – I don't care, I'll call you whatever you want to be called. I want to talk.' She listens. From the other end of the call, silence. She knows she must keep trying. 'This doesn't have to go worse than it already is. There are ways out. I can help. I want to help.'

A long pause. Finally, Raki speaks. 'You're playing at being the police negotiator. How about you play at being the Māori for once?' When he speaks again, his voice is quiet. Very calm. 'Colonization stole the land from under our people's feet. Ripped away our rights. Relegated us to the underclass, the imprisoned class, the landless class. It happened to your tribe as much as it did to mine. To all Māori. You know what I say is true. And yet you lined up against other Māori. You took the side of the colonizer.'

Again, silence falls.

Then, *BOOM!*, a bullet ricochets off the side of a container, centimetres from Hana's head, barely missing her.

217

She throws herself to the ground, her gun raised, desperately searching, but she is painfully aware that she is now at Raki's mercy. She scrabbles for her phone. Now there's no calm, soothing negotiator talk. Hana is furious.

'Show yourself, Raki, have the courage to show yourself!'

The phone in her hand dies. He has hung up. Then, on the other side of the opening . . .

He steps out from a gap between two containers.

He's perhaps fifty metres away. His rifle is trained on Hana. Her gun is trained on him. A stand-off. He starts to walk towards her. Calmly. Evenly. Taking measured, assured steps. His rifle zeroed between the eyes of his quarry. He speaks, low and calm, as he walks.

'When I was twelve years old, Detective Senior Sergeant, I watched my mother being dragged away. I couldn't do anything about it. I was a child. I could only watch and weep. I want to know why. Why did you do it?'

Hana rises carefully to her feet. Her gun still trained on Raki as he approaches, closer and closer. Twenty metres away, he stops.

'I asked a question. Why did you do it?'

The calmness in his face astonishes her. And she sees something else in his eyes. Someone struggling with profound pain. Deep sorrow.

'Put down your gun,' she says.

'If I do as you ask, will you answer my question?' A long moment. Hana nods. Yes.

To her astonishment, Raki puts down his weapon. Hana swallows. She goes to step forward, to arrest him, but he gestures. Wait.

'I did as you asked. Now it's your turn. Why did you go to that mountain? Why did you turn on your own people? Why did you drag my mother away? Why did you do it?'

Hana's finger stays on the trigger of her gun. But face to face with Raki, knowing that she has the power to arrest him, to kill him if she chooses, with just a squeeze of her trigger . . .

She considers the question.

An image comes to her. The face she saw on the archival footage, slowed down to one-tenth speed. The boy on the mountaintop, reaching out towards the woman the young Hana was dragging away. The screaming boy.

The same boy now in front of her, his weapon on the ground.

Finally, for the first time in eighteen years, she answers the question. A question she has asked herself a thousand times. A question she has never been able to answer. 'I was young. I thought it was my duty to follow orders. I wish I'd had the strength to say no. I didn't.'

Raki is as surprised as she is at the honesty of her words.

But now Hana snaps back to her duty. 'Get on the ground. Put your hands behind your back.'

But Raki doesn't move. He slowly, carefully turns his hand to show her what is in his palm. A hand-held electronic device.

'It's a detonator.'

A tightening in Hana's jaw.

The box of gelignite and detonators, stolen a few weeks earlier.

'Your detective constable is a creature of habit.

Always has a fish burger and fries at Denny's downtown after work. Takes him twenty minutes to finish his meal. Last night was the same as usual. Plenty long enough to wire a stick of gelignite into place under his car in the car park.'

Hana takes another step forward. Her eyes flaring. 'I don't believe you.'

'You should,' Raki says, the detonator in his hand. 'You shoot me, the detonator automatically fires.'

Hana's eyes turn back towards where she's come from. Where the other detectives are, and the handcuffed woman in the car.

'Thank you for answering my question,' Raki says quietly, and he means it. 'I too wish you had had the strength to say no.'

Hana keeps firm hold of her gun, her eyes on the detonator in his hands.

'You have thirty seconds,' he says. 'Tell your officers to get the hell away from the vehicle, Detective Senior Sergeant. Please.'

She doesn't want to believe him. But what if it's true? What if Stan is at that moment at the car, checking if the damn woman is comfortable? The awkward, kind-hearted young cop, getting her a bottle of water?

She makes a decision.

She turns and runs, back towards where the other police are, pulling out her comms radio, screaming instructions at her officers, 'There's explosives under the car, leave the prisoner, get away from the vehicle!'

Hearing her instructions, Stan turns to look at the

woman in the back of his car. Helpless. Locked inside. As the other detectives scatter, taking cover behind vehicles and containers ...

Stan starts running. Towards his car.

As Hana reaches the other cops, she sees that Stan is only twenty yards from the car, running to save Jonelle Kennedy. She cries out, 'Stan, no, stop!'

But her voice is lost, enveloped by a much louder sound.

In the opening between the containers where he was just standing face to face with Hana, Poata Raki hears the explosion. He sees the fireball erupting into the sky.

As black smoke rises, he ejects a bullet from his gun, using the sharp nose of the bullet to inscribe five shapes in the concrete. Five spirals. The familiar koru shape. As he etches, he murmurs under his breath, 'Unuhia, unuhia. Unuhia I te uru tapu nui a Mate ...' A prayer for the wairua* of the person whose life he has just ended. The fifth of the descendants. He finishes the karakia. He glimpses himself in the window of the car. In his eyes, the familiar pain. The terrible torment.

Five times now. Five times he has killed, five times he has taken another's life; each time the action destroys another piece of himself. He looks unblinking at his reflection in the window of the car. Hating himself for what he is doing.

---

*   Wairua – spirit

But knowing at the same time that he must finish what he has started.

Utu is not vengeance, he tells himself. Holding tight to the thing that has driven him this far, that he must cling to so that he can keep going, not falter and fall.

Utu is not retribution. It is duty.

A duty he must see through until the end.

As the Eagle police helicopter approaches the rising plumes of smoke from Stan's ruined car, the pilot sees Raki's vehicle speeding away out of the container yard. 'Should we pursue?'

At Stan's side, Hana is frantically trying to staunch his extensive wounds. The vehicle is still aflame, the other officers using extinguishers from their cars to try and subdue the inferno. For the woman in the back seat, though, it's too late: she was killed instantly.

The pilot repeats, 'Shall we pursue the vehicle?'

Hana screams into her comms radio, 'No! Officer down, officer in critical condition, you need to get this man to hospital, now!'

The helicopter descends towards the scene of carnage below.

And Raki's car disappears into the distance.

22

ON WHICH SIDE LIES EVIL?

The impact of the detonation blew Stan backwards a full three metres, his lower leg taking the brunt of the force of the explosion, his head hitting the concrete surface of the container yard hard as he fell. But even if he hadn't been severely concussed in that moment, his central nervous system would still have taken over, shutting down blood to his brain so that his body's emergency response defences would have full access to the considerable amounts of oxygen they needed to get the grievously injured young man through the crucial golden hour that lay ahead, the sixty minutes that would decide if he would have a long career in the force, grow old and retire to a holiday house by the beach, or if next week a framed photo of Detective Constable Stanley William Riordan would be ceremonially hung on the police officers' association wall, the smiling twenty-three-year-old freckled man-boy memorialized alongside the other cops fallen in the field of duty.

Stan is unconscious; Hana knows he's unconscious. But all the same, running down the emergency room corridors, she won't leave the side of his gurney. As the other detectives fought the flames of the burning vehicle, she made a makeshift tourniquet with her windbreaker for his mutilated leg; she was at his side throughout the rushed ride on Eagle to the hospital, keeping the tourniquet tight, talking to him the whole way, knowing he wasn't hearing her but holding on to the idea that a familiar voice telling him he's going to make it, that he's strong, that he's a fighter, that he's loved might get through and make a difference.

The gurney bypasses the prep room; Stan's wounds are too extensive. Ahead, the doors of one of the emergency theatres are already open, the surgical team scrubbed and ready.

'We have a job to do, Detective. You have to let us do our job.' One of the blue-scrubbed emergency room staff moves Hana from her position at Stan's side, seamlessly taking over the pressure on the area of his wounds.

Hana watches as the theatre doors close in front of her. She drops into a chair.

There's only so long a cardiovascular system can keep operating at maximum adrenaline, and since the unmarked police cars took the off-ramp off the motorway, Hana can't remember either breathing or swallowing. Now that she can take a deep breath, it's nearly dizzying. She grips the arms of the chair she found her way to and looks at the linoleum between her feet.

It surprised her. That moment of clarity, looking Raki in the eye. She'd imagined how it would be, many times; you can't help it when you know the offender you are hunting, when you have read all the profiles, the psych assessments, the accounts from family and friends and colleagues. You build a picture of what it will be like when you are finally in the same room, when you've got that person's face in front of you; how it will play out, how it's going to be.

It's never how you think.

Face to face with Raki, for a moment he wasn't the murderer Hana had been pursuing. He certainly wasn't a crazed killer, a psychopath – the journalist he abducted was right about that. If Hana knows anything about body language, what she saw was a man torn apart by sorrow and pain. But he wasn't mad. He could have killed her easily; a rifle is much more accurate over distance than a revolver, and his Leupold scope made his weapon pinpoint deadly. Hana is quite certain that the bullet that ricocheted off the side of the container a hand's-width away from her head would have ended her life if that was what Raki had intended it to do. He's a killer, she knows, but he made a deliberate decision not to kill her. The journalist believed he was playing by a set of rules. A moral code, as perverse as it might be.

And then there was what he had asked her. The one thing he wanted to know from the person whose job it was to find him, arrest him and put him behind bars for the rest of his natural life: 'Why did you go to that mountain? Why did you turn on your own people? Why did you drag my mother away? Why did you do it?'

Hana had thought that face to face with Poata Raki, she might get the answers to the countless questions that have haunted her about the case. Or perhaps that she would kill him. Or he would kill her. None of those things happened. Instead, he asked her the very questions she has avoided asking herself for eighteen years.

The lino under her feet is a surprising warm lemon colour. A cheerful contrast to the bloodstains covering her shoes and the legs of her pants. As she stares at the blood on her clothes, she realizes that she didn't say goodbye to Stan as they rushed him away. She immediately dismisses the thought.

Why would she say goodbye. There's no reason to say goodbye.

She refuses to believe her friend is going to be a framed photo on the wall. Stan is not going to be one of the fallen.

Addison finally drags herself from her room. Feeling like shit, physically and emotionally. The same way she's felt for forty-eight hours, since the second pink pill and all the painful and embarrassing awfulness that followed. The doctors told her that the aftermath would be like a two-ton truck hit her. Yep. And it's a two-ton truck with big fucking bull bars.

It's been a few hours since PLUS 1 came by with her earring and the deeply confusing news about Poata Raki. She's been left trying to recalibrate so many things, and it's not going well. The things she learned about her mother from the video of her as a young cop dragging away innocent Māori protesters. And the things she now knows about Poata Raki, someone she had seen as a role model, a kind of Māori Nelson Mandela or Martin Luther King, a visionary.

Raki hasn't returned her text. And really, Addison is relieved. She has no idea what she would say next, how the conversation could possibly go: 'So, matua. What've you been up to since I saw you last?'

Though she still doesn't feel even slightly human, one basic human characteristic has kicked in. The need to eat. She cooks a pile of greasy scrambled eggs. Uses a big butcher's knife to dice up avocado and tomato, adding it to the mix. She switches on the TV. A music video is playing. She uses the remote to turn it up loud. Sits down to eat.

Behind her, the door opens. Addison wasn't expecting Hana home. She mutes the telly. She frowns, staring down at her eggs. Not ready to meet her mother's eyes. She's had forty-eight hours of feeling as awful as she's ever felt in her whole life. It scared the hell out of her, and despite the festering fury she feels when she thinks of what her mother did to the protesters on that mountain, seeing Hana hurry into the hospital room was a lifeline. When her mum took her hand, when she stroked her hair, Addison knew everything was going to be all right.

Now Hana's hand rests gently on Addison's shoulder. A gesture of assurance, but it only makes her stiffen. She hates this feeling inside, the roller coaster: how can you love someone so much and despise them twice as much? How do the two things fit? How will they ever fit again?

Then she realizes.

The hand on her shoulder isn't her mother's.

'I didn't reply to your text, but I'm okay,' Poata Raki says. 'Thank you for asking.'

He walks past Addison's chair and sits at the other side of the kitchen table, across from her. He smiles. Warm. Gentle. Exactly as he was when she saw him after his transformative, exhilarating lecture, when they shared a hongi and exchanged contacts. But she can also see, once more, the haunting in his eyes she saw that day, and it's no longer a hint. Now it's consuming him.

She puts down the fork of scrambled egg in her hand. 'My mum is going to be back soon.' It's a lie, of course. She has absolutely no idea when her mother will be home.

Raki can see her tension. Hardly surprising. When he speaks again, it's in te reo. 'If I was here to harm you, I would have done it the moment I walked in the door. That's not why I'm here. Believe me.'

'Then . . . why?' Addison manages to ask, also in te reo.

'When you speak, it's powerful. I saw that myself when you were on stage. Your music, your performances – full of rebellion and revolution. You reach people. Young people. Those who can make a difference. The ones who will change the future.' His eyes are full of the admiration he feels for her. 'You saw my video,' he says. 'You may not agree with my actions. But I think the same things cause both of us pain. I think we believe the same things. We are fighting the same fight. We are not so different.'

For a moment, words come to Addison's mind, shuttled into that place in the cortex, the holding pen, where ideas

228

sit just before the lungs and the tongue turn them into speech. The words she thinks of saying are big: 'You're right. We want the same things.'

But something inside her tells her that if she says those words, if she lets her thoughts take breath, those ideas will become real. And then there's no turning back.

Raki sees her hesitation. 'I'm not the person you think,' he says. 'Every time I take utu for my ancestor, every time I act, it rips out a piece of me. Destroys a part of me.'

He considers his next words. 'Ākuanei ka mate tonu atu ahau. Hei aha, tata pau tōku toiora. Engari mā taku karere e rere tonu atu rā i a koe.'*

He continues, in English, 'The things we could do together.'

Addison swallows. Almost ready to say the words still waiting there in the place between her thoughts and her tongue. She nearly says, 'What do you want me to do?' But once more, instinct stops her.

'Together . . .?' she asks, instead.

'You giving young Māori the message. Me taking my path. Together showing Māori we must take back what is ours. However that is to be done.'

Once more Addison finds herself moved by the strength of Raki's passion, his belief. The feeling of commitment she sees in his every breath, his every word. But then . . .

Behind him, on the television screen, she sees something else. The TV is still playing, on mute. There's a

---

* 'I know I will not live much longer. I will die soon. That's okay. There's so little of me left to die. But my message can carry on. Through you.'

breaking news item. Footage of a smoking wreck in a container yard. An all-caps headline on the chyron scroll: *DETECTIVE CRITICALLY INJURED IN BOMBING.*

The TV is behind Raki's head. He has no idea what Addison is seeing. On the screen, footage of a wounded officer being disembarked onto a gurney at Auckland hospital. For a moment, the camera zooms in close enough for Addison to see the face of the grievously wounded man.

It's her friend. It's Stan.

Other images appear on the screen, footage of the man thought to have caused the explosion. It's the man sitting opposite her right now.

A wave hits her; the image of Stan brings everything into focus, making the theoretical real and actual and awful.

Too late, she realizes Raki has seen the shift in her expression.

He turns towards the television in time to see the end of the breaking news story. When he turns back, Addison is at the kitchen bench. In her hand, the butcher's knife she used to dice the avocado and tomatoes. 'Get out of here, just leave, please, please *go.*'

Raki rises. He moves towards her. Addison holds out the knife, her hand trembling. 'Stay away from me!' she says. 'Please, just go, get out of my house!' But before she knows what's happening . . .

Raki has her by the wrist of the hand holding the knife, his grasp like iron, so tight it hurts. His eyes search hers.

'Two centuries of destruction. The near-genocide of our people. You, me, we are lucky we are even here. In comparison . . . six lives. To wake us from our paralysis.'

To Addison's shock, there are tears in his eyes. His gaze never leaves hers.

'On which side lies evil?' he asks.

It's as if he is searching for something from her, some kind of assurance from someone he has come to respect and admire. But then he sees that she can never give him what he is seeking, and his grasp on her wrist loosens. More gentle now, he pulls her forward, towards him. He draws their faces together, once more in a hongi. Again the profound symbolic gesture of breathing each other's breath.

'You will be a great leader one day,' he tells her, and it's not to persuade or implore; it's the truth, it's what he believes, it's what he knows. 'The things we could do together,' he says once again.

And then he leaves.

Addison's legs, shaking with fear, give way, and she collapses into a chair.

After a moment, she realizes that Raki has left something. On the table, a large manilla envelope. She opens it. Inside, a copy of the now famous daguerreotype. The six soldiers. As he has done with the other five descendants, there is a line drawn from the last soldier to a photo. The photo is of a father and daughter at a concert. The daughter is glowing, alive; she's just been on stage performing, her shaven head shines under the lights, her face wet with sweat. The father's arm is wrapped around her, proud as hell of his girl.

The father and daughter in the photo are Jaye and Addison.

23

THE END OF THE STRUT

You squeeze between the rusty wires of the railing that runs the length of the old bridge.

As you feel the weathered wooden surface of the longest suspension strut beneath the soles of your bare brown feet, the familiar sensation returns in your abdomen. It's somewhere between elation and nausea and you can't quite tell which it is, and actually it's both, thrill and fear tied inseparably together, two sides of the one coin. Below, the blue-green flow of the river. The feeling inside grows as you take a first step along the strut. Then another. Your foot pauses, involuntarily. The fear part in your abdomen winning for a moment over the thrill.

You gather yourself.

You take another step.

Jaye was at the hospital with Hana when the head theatre nurse came out from surgery. Stan was young and strong; he was going to make it. Hana took her first easy breath since that afternoon: thank God. But the news was mixed. His leg had been seriously damaged. A second surgical team was about to take over, it was impossible to know if the leg could be saved. But they'd try like hell.

Then Hana got the call from Addison.

They'd found their daughter locked in the bathroom with the butcher's knife in her hands. When she'd shown them the copy of the daguerreotype that Raki had left behind with a line of descent to Jaye and therefore to Addison, it made absolutely no sense. Jaye and Hana had both had their genealogies researched early on in the investigation; any chance of a link had long since been eliminated.

Jaye phoned his mother. His parents had moved to the Gold Coast a few years earlier, looking for relief from his mother's chronic arthritis in the warmer Australian climate. Didn't hurt that Jaye's dad had been a fanatic long-boarder his whole life, and their apartment was a few hundred metres from a great surf break.

When Jaye said why he was calling, there was a long silence from the other end of the phone. Then his mother told him the thing she'd never thought he'd need to know.

'Your dad. He's not your biological father,' she finally said.

It wasn't easy for her to have to explain, but she was following the news about the series of killings, she knew just how serious the situation was. She told Jaye that she'd fallen pregnant with him when she was a teenager. It was a mistake, an impulsive drunken one-night stand. Someone she had never loved, never even really liked, someone she had no intention of spending her life with. The man Jaye believed was his father was an old friend, a real friend. And he was a good man. After Jaye was born, with Jaye's mother alone and struggling, he asked her to marry him. It wasn't for show. He genuinely loved her. That was forty-three years ago. They'd barely spent a day apart since.

The man Jaye knew as his dad had formally adopted him. There was no mention of adoption on the short birth certificate, the document needed for formal identification. The adoption and the real father's name was recorded only on the long-form certificate, a document Jaye had never had reason to access.

He connected the dots. With Raki's expertise and endless resources with genealogical tracing, he'd discovered the link.

'Love, I'm sorry. If I did the wrong thing, hiding who your real father was . . . '

Hana couldn't hear the words Jaye's mother was saying. But she could see how hard this was hitting him.

'You didn't do anything wrong.' It's no small thing, to discover that you must rethink one of the very fundamental facts of your life, of your identity. It's a seismic shift, the landscape alters. But at the same time, Jaye understood, some things don't change at all. 'I know who my real father is, Mum. The guy who's probably bobbing round out on the water right now, waiting to catch the last wave of the day. Tell Dad I love him.'

He hung up the phone. Hana sat there with him in silence, letting him take in the news.

For Hana, too, the landscape had altered.

The two people she loved most on earth could be the next victims.

Below your feet, the yellowy weed-covered shape in the river, the big old rock.

You consciously will your feet forward. Fear and elation still do battle, all the more so because there's nothing to hold onto any more, it's just you trusting your sense of balance, and if you get giddy or dizzy now, there's no guard-rail, no wire fence to stop you from tumbling out of control towards the brutal hard surface of the rock. There's a story among the kids in the area about a teenager who got drunk and decided to do a midnight jump, slipped off the wooden strut and fell head-first, cracking his skull open on the rock. The river took him, and his body was never found, but if you look in the right spot, you can see where the force of his skull hitting chipped off a bit of the rock.

Another careful step. And another. Below, the rock is behind you now. And now you're at the end of the wooden beam.

You spread your arms wide. Curl your toes over the very end. You lean forward. Slowly. Slowly. Because that's what shows you've really got guts; just walking out to the end and jumping without thinking, that's easy.

Slow is scary.

You keep leaning forward. Approaching the point, the sweet spot. Or maybe it's the awful spot, you can never really decide.

Either way, it's the last moment you have a choice.

After that, everything is out of your hands.

'You need to pack plenty of clothes, love. It could be a while. Who knows if there'll be a washing machine that actually works.'

It's the sort of conversation any mum might have with a seventeen-year-old daughter about to head off camping in the bush or to a drum and bass festival. But Addison isn't going to put up a tent or listen to music. Hana is helping her pack her bag ready to go to a guarded safe house. With Jaye and Addison identified by Raki as descendants of the sixth soldier, there's no choice; father and daughter are being taken together to one of the anonymous locations usually reserved for Crown informants about to enter a witness protection programme. Marissa and her two daughters will be brought to meet them there, the risk of leaving them exposed as potential hostages too great, and Hana will move into a hotel with an armed AOS officer at her side day and night.

Addison packs her favourite pair of Doc Martens, because, priorities. She zips the bag. They stand there surrounded by the carefully drawn pictures on the wall, Addison as a baby, growing up, a child, then a young woman.

Hana takes her hand. 'All I've ever wanted to do is protect you. I didn't protect you today. I wasn't here for you, love. I'm so very sorry.'

Addison folds into her mother's arms. The two of them united in their fear. But in the silence between them, there is something else. A heavy, unspoken thing.

Since Addison saw the video of Hana on Mount Suffolk, since the awful argument, they haven't talked properly. Not face to face, not 'we need to deal with this'. There's been what happened in the emergency room in the hospital, where Addison let Hana stroke her hair. But that feels like a lifetime ago now.

Hana doesn't want her daughter to go without talking. 'The video,' she says. 'I wish you hadn't found out that way. I feel like I've failed you in every way I can.'

With Hana's arms around her, Addison can feel the movements in her mother's chest as she tries hard not to cry. Addison has spent the last few days feeling the same way. Over Hana's shoulder, she looks at one of the drawings on the wall. It's one of the later ones, after Jaye and Hana and Addison became just two, mother and daughter, Jaye gone.

'I love you,' she says. 'You're my mum. I'm never not going to love you.'

She moves out of Hana's embrace. Wanting to see her mother's face.

'I love you. But I hate what you did. You chose to be blue, not brown. That's shit, Mum.'

Hana thinks about the defaults, the things she has always held to about what she did at Mount Suffolk. It was my job.

I had no choice. The police hierarchy. I was bottom of the rung. The answers she has always given herself.

But those answers aren't answers any more.

'I'm sorry,' she says. Which is all she feels she can say.

Jaye comes to the door. The armed officers accompanying them to the safe house are ready to go. Addison hugs her mother tight. Kisses her.

'You've never failed me,' she says. 'But maybe you failed you.'

You're out at the end of the wooden strut. The water flowing far below. No going back; you can't turn around, you can't undo what's done. There's only staying still, marooned where you are, toes curling over the edge.

Or you can take one step forward.

One more movement.

That's all it takes. Then you give yourself over to whatever happens next.

It's out of your hands.

'Why are you stopping?'

Hana doesn't answer. She doesn't know why she's pulled the car over.

She's driven past this exact situation dozens of times before. A marked police car on the side of the road, a shitty cheap car in front where they pulled in when the blue and white lights started flashing, the occupant being talked to by a uniformed cop. The driver is young, maybe Addison's age or a year or two older. And he's Māori.

There's no reason for Hana to stop. She has Jaye and Addison in the car, the armed AOS officers with them, heading to the safe house. A senior detective has no place taking a moment's interest in a run-of-the-mill traffic stop. But Hana stops. She gets out. She goes to the uniformed cop. The cop recognizes her, of course, she has heard about what happened and she tells Hana her thoughts are with Stan, and with her. 'If there's anyone who's going to stop this guy, boss, it's you.'

Hana asks why the driver was pulled over. 'Was he speeding? Went through a stop sign?' The cop says there was no offence. Just a routine check. But the guy isn't licensed, the car doesn't have a current warrant of fitness. She's writing it up now.

In the car, Jaye watches what's going on, perplexed.

Hana glances at the driver. 'Where are you going?' The young man is nervous, intimidated, no idea why there's suddenly someone else there. 'It's okay,' she says. The kid is in a fluoro vest, overalls. 'You're going to work?'

'I just started last week. My first job,' he says. 'Timber factory out west, but there's no buses that go that way. I'm gonna sit my licence, miss, I'll get the warrant for the car. I just have to save up.'

By now Jaye is out of the vehicle.

Hana tells the driver to sit tight. She takes the uniformed cop aside. She tells her that writing this guy up means he'll go to court. He'll have his vehicle impounded, he'll almost certainly lose his job. He'll get a record. 'Is that really the best outcome here?' The uniformed cop is flustered now, especially with Jaye now watching, a detective inspector, for fuck sake.

'Have I done something wrong?' she asks.

'You've done nothing wrong.'

'What do you want me to do?'

Hana knows she can't say what she's going to say next. She says it.

'Tell him to get his licence, get the warrant. Rip up the ticket. Let him get to work.'

The shitty cheap car drives away, the young Māori driver desperately glad he's not going to be late for work in only his second week on the job. The uniformed cop heads off, perplexed at what the hell just happened.

Jaye watches as Hana gets back in the car.

Outside the safe house, Jaye asks the AOS officers to take Addison inside and leave them alone in the car for a moment.

He turns the nub of his left thumb between the forefinger and thumb of his right hand as he quietly tells Hana what she knows already. She had no right or reason to intervene in a legitimate traffic offence, to overrule a cop who was following all the rules, who was doing the job she is supposed to do. If this is ever looked into, it'll be a cut-and-dried case of a very senior detective using her influence inappropriately.

'What's going on?' he asks.

For a moment, unexpectedly, Hana thinks about that wooden strut above the river. Standing out at the end. Slowly leaning forward.

'You've been through so much, Hana. I need to know what's happening. I need to know you're okay.'

She considers Jaye's question.

A man who has killed five times has aimed a high-powered rifle between her eyes. Her daughter has been confronted by him in their home. Her friend and close work colleague almost lost his life when his booby-trapped car exploded. She is terrified that either Addison or Jaye could be the final victim. Yeah, she has been through a lot. There's no training that can prepare any cop on earth to deal with this stuff, no counselling that will truly heal the scars or stop the nightmares or ever make anything normal again.

But there's other stuff burning in Hana. Making her feel like she's at the tipping point. Like she's about to plummet into the unknown.

'Raki. I listen to him speak. And I understand what he's saying. But more than that . . .' She tries to make sense of what she's thinking. 'I know he's telling the truth.'

'He's a murderer, he could have killed you, our daughter—'

'I don't mean the things he's doing are right, Jaye. Christ. His actions are screwed up, they're as wrong as they can be. But what he's talking about, the things that are so utterly fucked with this place and have been for hundreds of years so that now none of us have any idea how they can ever get unfucked again. Those things he's saying. They're true . . .'

Words Hana never thought she would say.

But now that they're said, and now that the things this investigation has churned up inside her have been given voice and sent out into the world, there's a tangible sense of relief. She needs to keep going until she's dug to the bottom of what she's grappling with.

'For eighteen years I denied who I was when I looked in the mirror. I am part of a justice system that suppresses, that represses. Half our prison population are Māori. We're only fourteen per cent of the country's population. You and me and our colleagues add to the number every day. That's our job. That Māori kid back there, just wanting to get to work. We both know that driver's licence violations are the way most young Māori get the first strike on their record. Then they struggle to get a job, they're labelled bad, and eventually it's easier just to give up trying and to *be* bad. I know the stats, you know the stats, we all do. I've just been pretending they're nothing to do with me.'

She trails away.

The end of the wooden strut.

Leaning forward.

Almost ready to fall.

'I pretend justice is colour-blind. It's bullshit. I understand what Raki is saying. What he's fighting for. And why. I dragged the man's mother from the mountain. I took away her mana, her standing, her pride. Because I wasn't strong enough to tell my bosses to go fuck themselves. He looked into my eyes, asked why I did that. I told him the truth. I told him I wished I had the strength to say no. But I didn't.'

She takes a moment to find the right words. 'He has murdered five times. He'll kill again, and it could be you or Addison, unless I stop him. But when he looked me in the eyes, I felt guilty. *I* felt guilty. Know what? I deserve to feel guilty.'

Toes over the edge of the longest strut.

Leaning forward.

The water below.

'Addison told me I made a choice, the choice to be blue, not brown.'

'Addison is a child.'

'No. She's right. She said what I never allowed myself to say. She's right, Jaye, and you don't understand and you can't ever understand because you don't ever have to make that choice.'

Leaning.

Leaning.

Gravity ready to take you.

'I understand what Raki is doing more than I understand my own job.'

Near the car, the waiting AOS officer is restless. Jaye needs to get inside the house. He chooses his next words carefully.

'The things you're dealing with. They're big, really big, I see that, that's very clear. But if you're about to quit the case, tell me now.'

'I'm not walking away. I'm going to stop him,' Hana

says, without a moment's hesitation. 'That's not what this is about.'

Jaye lets go of his thumb.

'I'll stop him, Jaye. Whatever it takes.'

Jaye nods. Good. 'Then afterwards. After all this is over,' he says, very quietly. 'What are you going to do?'

Hana can't answer the question.

Arms spread wide.

Leaning slowly forward.

Inch by inch.

Slowly, slowly.

You find the tipping point.

You stay there a moment. Then another moment.

Then you lean an inch further.

And you are gone.

24

FOOTSTEPS

The cry of the karanga* echoes from the meeting house to where Hana waits at the front gates of the marae. She follows the call, across the forecourt, to where the locals wait for her, knowing she is being greeted with formality and respect. The caller, the kaikaranga, the woman whose job it is to greet visitors, speaks of the land the meeting house is built on, of those who have passed away. She speaks of the history between this arriving visitor and the local tribe now greeting her. About unhealed scars that have never been addressed.

Hana walks on, towards the steps of the beautiful carved meeting house that sits at the foot of the mountain known recently as Mount Suffolk, and for centuries

---

* Karanga – a call ceremonially welcoming visitors onto a marae

before as Maunga Whakairoiro, the mountain of the great
orca that led the tribe's canoe across the oceans.

Inside the meeting house, the elder giving the formal
speech of greeting finishes his words. There are several
dozen of the local tribe here, mostly older, those who
would have been on the mountain eighteen years ago and
who have come to hear what Hana has to say. They join
in a waiata, the song of support for the elder's welcome.
The singing finishes, the locals take their seats. Silence
falls in the meeting house. Only the sound of the wind
creaking the rafters.

Alone before the tangata whenua, the people of this
place, Hana gets to her feet.

'I am no stranger here. Many of you know me. And the
memories you have of me are not fond ones.'

She clears her throat. She can speak without a hint of
nerves to scores of reporters, to her extensive investigative
team, to television cameras and the thousands of viewers
they take their images to. But in front of this group of
quiet, respectful locals, her voice trembles. 'I cannot undo
what happened to your ancestor. I cannot undo the theft
of your land, a crime that has never been put right, to this
day. Nor can I undo what I was a part of nearly twenty
years ago.'

The kuia, the older woman, is not in the whites of her
lawn bowling uniform today. She has dressed formally, as
befits the occasion. Hana addresses her directly, in te reo.
'Last time I was here, you talked of the men in uniform
who came to your maunga one hundred and sixty years
ago. And I came too, in a different uniform, but with no

more friendly intent. You said you remembered what I did, and my colleagues who were with me. You should remember. As I remember. It is a memory that fills me with shame.'

Among those gathered, there are murmurs. The locals are glad to hear Hana's words, and the genuine emotions behind them.

'Apologies are only words,' she continues. 'Words cannot right the wrongs that have happened to your people for centuries. Nor the wrongs I committed on your maunga. But you have my apology.'

The kuia can tell that Hana's words are not empty, she recognizes the shame and the pain in Hana's eyes. She nods her head gently, a barely visible movement. But Hana sees it; she sees the woman's silent recognition of what Hana is doing, of the courage it took her to come here.

Hana goes on, her voice stronger now. 'You have my apology. And you have my promise. The man I am trying to find is committing great crimes in the name of your tupuna. I do not believe your ancestor would agree with his actions. I believe he would condemn them, as I know you do. This man is one of your own. But he has lost his way. I will not rest until I stop him. I want to find him before he hurts others, or before we have to hurt him.'

She stands, head bowed.

She expects nothing of this occasion. She doesn't expect forgiveness. If her apology goes unacknowledged, as the pleas of this tribe to leave them peacefully to their protest went unacknowledged years earlier, there is a justice in that. She has no right to look for that which she did not herself give.

Movement. The kuia stands, supporting herself on her walking stick, her grandson at her side. She gestures to Hana: come. Hana crosses the floor towards her.

The kuia takes Hana's arm. She presses her nose against Hana's nose. She holds Hana for a long moment. Then she kisses her on the cheek.

One by one the other members of the tribe do the same.

In the wharekai, the kuia and the others share a cup of tea with Hana, a way to seal the process that has just taken place. For all those gathered, what is happening – the things Raki is doing in the name of an ancestor of their tribe – is devastating. 'He is an extraordinary person,' one of the elders says, grave and troubled. 'He fought so long and so hard for us. But the battles he waged for this tribe left a darkness in his wairua, in his spirit. As wars do so often to those who fight them. And now, this.'

As her grandson pours more tea, the kuia asks if Hana has a copy of the recording Raki made. Hana opens the video on her phone screen. The locals watch Raki's message again. All around, tears flow.

'If we could talk to him,' an old woman says. 'If he would only come here, look us in the face. He is not the same man who stood alongside us in the land claim process. A shadow has fallen over him. If he came back to us, we would help him return to who he is.'

As the video ends, the kuia asks Hana to play part of it again, one of the places where Raki spoke in te reo. She says, 'The translation of this phrase, in the newspapers and on TV. They did not really understand. They translated it as "I am following the path of my ancestor, the great chief." But that's not what he's saying.'

Around her, nods of agreement. 'He is very precise in his language,' one of the men says. 'Tuakana did not take a path of violence or utu. He was a man of peace. Poata is not saying he's following the path of the chief. The chief never took that path.'

'Footsteps. That is what he is saying,' says the kuia. '"I am walking in the footsteps of my ancestor, the great chief."'

It's dark as Hana heads out from the hospital. She avoids polite conversation with Gillian, the armed AOS officer who has been assigned to be alongside her with the threat of Raki growing ever greater. It's a melancholy feeling, someone other than Stan driving her back to Central. The last thing she wants to do is make small talk.

In the hospital, she wasn't allowed to see Stan. 'The second operation was nine hours,' the registrar on overnight shift in intensive care told her. 'He's been back in for two smaller operations. He's still under sedation. We're going to bring him around in the morning.'

'His leg?' Hana asked.

The registrar paused. The kind of pause even those

249

most experienced at this kind of thing make when there's particularly bad news to pass on. 'We did everything we could to save his leg. The damage was just too severe.'

If Hana is being honest, on that awful helicopter ride where she was continually reassuring Stan he was going to be all right, she didn't actually believe the words she was saying. She was rehearsing in her head what she would do if he went into full cardiac arrest while they were still in the air; she knew the routines, she knew the Eagle carried oxygen and a defibrillator, but she also knew full well that with the amount of blood he'd lost and the severity of the wound, if he went downhill, he'd go downhill fast. Anything she did would be putting her finger in a hole in a dyke. Running down the corridors of the emergency room, keeping the desperate pressure on the tourniquet, she was amazed he had even lasted that long. She's been ready for bad news for the last day. She knows things could be a lot worse. Stan will survive. He's not going to be a framed photo on the wall.

But he's lost a leg.

His life will never be remotely the same again.

Before she was taken to the safe house, Addison wrapped up the copy of *Where the Wild Things Are* and asked Hana to take it to hospital for Stan. 'Tell him the little freak hopes it reminds him of me.'

Hana left the book with the nursing staff.

'Across here, D Senior.' Gillian takes a short cut across a stretch of lawn to where her vehicle is parked. There's dew on the grass, and her shoes leave imprints on the wet lawn. She unlocks the car, turns back.

Hana is standing still, staring down at the grass.

'Boss?'

Hana kneels. Running her fingers over the footprints. From years on the job, she can tell at a glance that the young officer wears size six, six and a half at most, and has a slight pronation issue with her left foot – the markings on the left side don't fall evenly. But that's not what she is thinking about right now.

The AOS officer tentatively approaches where Hana is crouched on the lawn. She knows that the boss has had a hellish forty-eight hours, and now she is worried that she is about to unravel right here in front of her, on her haunches on a damp lawn in the middle of the night.

'Are you okay? D Senior?'

Hana's eyes rise from the imprints on the grass. If she knew the young AOS officer better, Hana might hug her. '"I am walking in the footsteps of my ancestor, the great chief",' she says.

The accurate translation of Poata Raki's phrase.

Now she knows how to find him.

25

THE CAVE

Above the mountain range stretching away inland towards the east, a first faint hint of yellow glows in the sky. It is still an hour before the sun rises. Fifty kilometres south of the Auckland motorway system, the roads are narrow, one lane north, one lane south. The rural highway heads towards the coast, cutting through the deep forest of this sprawling tract of more than eighty thousand square kilometres of national park reserve. There's a lot of land in this country to get lost in.

A lot of places to hide.

There are no street lights along this particular section of highway. But even in the pre-dawn darkness, the road is lit up like a concert stage, with flashing red and blue. A seemingly endless row of police vehicles, a handful of dark armed offenders SUVs, army Unimogs, a large converted container truck used as a mobile police command base.

The vehicles drive nearly bumper to bumper in an eerie quiet, their sirens silent. Heading steadily deeper into the darkness of the bush.

A few hours earlier, just after midnight, Hana was back at the carved meeting house at the foot of Mount Suffolk. She apologized profusely to the kuia for waking her. The older woman was bleary-eyed, impatient. Wrapping a blanket around her shoulders, her grandson told Hana that she couldn't keep her long, that she had to be fast in what she wanted to ask.

'Your ancestor, Hahona Tuakana. You said that when he burned the buildings the settlers erected on your tribe's land, he went to a forest,' Hana said quickly, knowing she was on borrowed time. 'You said he hid there, a secret base from where he waged his war of disobedience, have I got that right?'

The kuia nodded, yes.

'Do you know where, exactly?'

'To the south. Not the exact place. But somewhere near the Hīwawā river.'

Hana remembered what Grant Wirapa had said about the locked room Raki had taken him to, how he could hear the distant sound of a river.

'I don't know why this can't wait until morning,' the grandson complained.

'"I am walking in the footsteps of my ancestor, the great chief",' Hana said, quite certain now. 'Poata wasn't being metaphoric when he chose those words. He was speaking literally. His feet are walking the same ground Hahona Tuakana walked. The same forest. The same land. That's where he's hiding. The place where your ancestor sought refuge when he was pursued.'

The kuia's face was solemn as she looked out to where the sun would be rising in a few hours' time. She drew her cardigan around herself.

'I pray that when you find him, blood is not spilled,' she said quietly. 'His. Or anyone else's.'

By mid morning, the base camp has been established in a parking area beside a conservation hut several kilometres upstream from the main highway. Search-and-rescue specialists have divided dozens of square kilometres of dense forest bordering the river into large grids, with pairs of officers assigned to thoroughly comb their designated area. The goal is to complete the sweep of the initial grids by early afternoon, with the second zone further upstream being searched through the rest of the day.

Hana is paired with a local uniformed cop, Vince, an older guy with an extensive knowledge of the local area. They make their way through rough terrain to the top of a rise, emerging from dense bush to a vantage point. In the distance, the sun reflects off the river, which is flowing a muddy brown after recent rains. Hana spots another pair of officers in the distance, heading quickly across a clearing, weapons drawn, moving efficiently from point to point, getting out of open terrain as fast as possible.

At the final briefing earlier that morning, before the first sweep, firearms, ammunition and bulletproof vests were distributed to each officer. The AOS commander read the fire orders, the legal requirements before the use of firearms. Everything took place in hushed tones. A manhunt doesn't want to broadcast its presence. But the quietness also reflected the solemnity most were feeling about their duty. With the instructions and grid maps issued, the hand-held radio network checked and rechecked, there was a silent moment before everyone dispersed. The several dozen men and women stood still, their breath coming in puffs of steam. The sound of the river flowing nearby. In the canopy all around, the morning chorus of native birds. The sun arcing down through the tall trees, just starting to bring warmth into the shadows of the forest.

Hana looked around the faces. She knew what was going through each person's mind. The same thing she herself was thinking. Nobody welcomes a day when you go to work knowing your job might be to end a life.

The search team headed into the forest.

'You've had a gun pointed at your head. Let the others do the groundwork today, Hana. It's not even your job.'

A few hours before, in the middle of the night, a difficult conversation. In the safe house where Jaye and

Addison are being guarded with Marissa and her daughters, Jaye sat at the dining room table, talking quietly on his phone so as not to wake the others. He had stayed in contact hour by hour with the investigation and with Hana, remotely monitoring and overseeing everything, and he was the first person Hana called when she had put together the pieces and decided to request a go-ahead from the commissioner for an urgent armed manhunt.

'This has got too close to our family already. Christ, Hana. For our sake. Stay on the command truck.' Jaye hadn't consciously intended to use that phrase: 'For our sake.'

But he meant it.

Since relocating to the safe house, Marissa had been sleeping badly, getting up to look in on her girls every hour of the night, despite the 24/7 presence of an armed officer. She tucked in her daughters for the fourth or fifth time that night, then opened Addison's door a crack. Addison had fallen asleep with Netflix playing on her tablet, as usual. Hearing Jaye's voice in the dining room, Marissa quietly approached, not wanting to interrupt.

'Christ, Hana. For our sake. Stay on the command truck.'

The cold pool of light from the single bulb hanging above the cheap Formica table illuminated his face. Unseen in the shadows of the doorway, Marissa watched silently.

'Even if I made it an order, you wouldn't stay on the truck. You wouldn't, would you?'

She could see the deep worry Jaye was feeling. And

there was something else she saw in his face as he talked to Hana.

Something that made her want to cry.

'Be careful,' Jaye said. 'Please.'

He hung up and sat there at the table, head bowed, the phone clutched in his hand, surrounded by shadows.

Marissa watched him for a few moments.

Then she turned, still silent, still unseen, and went back to their bed.

The sun is getting lower in the sky as Hana and the local cop make their way through dense bush towards the far quadrant of their second grid of the day. In the distance, two officers searching beside the river disappear into the cover of dense flax and the treeline beyond. In Hana's earpiece, the constant crackle of the round of checks and reports. From base, the command unit gives instructions that there's only another hour of light left. While the AOS officers in the search team have thermal and night-vision apparatus, there isn't sufficient equipment to safely continue after nightfall.

'Any groups who have not completed their grids are instructed to start returning to base in ten minutes at the latest.'

Hana passes a tall tree, well over a hundred feet. A kahikatea. The ancient podocarp affectionately known by many as the dinosaur tree. 'D Senior.' Vince keeps his voice low. He's found something. Hana hurries to his side.

He's kneeling by an animal carcass. The remains of what used to be a wild stag, the head and disembowelled guts. She looks carefully at the rotting head. There's a bullet wound plumb between the eyes.

She asks Vince for his bush knife. Doing her best to ignore the smell of decaying flesh, she digs into the wound, looking for the bullet. She finds the piece of lead, showing it to the cop. 'You're a hunter, Vince. This is from a .270, right?'

He nods. Yes.

In the next grid to Hana's, two figures pick their way along the crest of a steep ridge. A junior detective, Bethell, and her partner, Davison, an AOS officer. As they finish the last few hundred metres of their search grid, Hana's message comes over their radios. 'Search group Lima, we have a dead stag, north-western quadrant of our second grid, shot by a .270 bullet. The same calibre weapon the suspect used in the confrontation in the container yard.'

Davison and Bethell exchange a look. This area is remote as hell, somewhere deer hunters wouldn't be routinely expected. The air is dead for a long minute. Decisions being made in the command post. Command comes back on the line. 'All search groups return to base. We're too close to sundown. Repeat, return to base, all search groups.'

It's frustrating as hell. At the very moment when they

could be on the verge of narrowing the search area, getting specific, maybe closing on their target, they have to bail. Davison starts back in the direction of the base camp. The junior detective pauses for a moment, looking down the long slope below her. A glint catches her eye – the lowering sun reflecting off something.

'Look, down there,' she says to her partner, keeping her voice low.

Davison hurries back to join her at the edge of the ridge. They take out their binoculars, focusing on the shiny surface below.

It's a solar panel.

The panel is fixed discreetly in the branches of a tree, where it would usually be all but invisible. Except for the rare moments when the setting sun might hit it at just the right angle. As Bethell radios in their position and reports the discovery, the AOS officer takes a step forward, trying to track with his binoculars where the electric cable from the solar panel goes to. He takes another half-step . . .

And without warning the edge of the ridge gives out under his feet. He flails at foliage, grabbing a thin branch, but it comes away in his hand. His junior partner watches helpless as he tumbles forty metres down the steep slope, landing heavily at the bottom, a stone's throw from the solar panel.

Davison groans. He knows his leg is broken, twisted at a nauseating angle; it's all he can do not to cry out in pain, but he can't make any more noise. He prays that the sound of his chaotic fall hasn't already given him away. He looks around, urgent. His weapon has fallen from his hands, and is halfway up the incline, a mission to reach at the best of times, impossible with his shattered leg.

At the top of the slope, Bethell urgently radios to all officers their GPS co-ordinates, requesting assistance as she picks her way down, moving as fast as she can without falling as her partner did. Forty metres below, Davison drags himself painfully into cover behind a tree. He looks towards the solar panel. Most of the electric cabling leading from it is hidden underneath earth and moss, but he catches a glimpse of cabling disappearing into an opening in the rocky wall of the slope.

The opening of a cave.

Hana and Vince are the closest grid to where Davison is lying, his leg badly broken. Hana leads the way, sprinting through the fast-growing shadows of the forest, following the GPS co-ordinates, heading for the base of the slope. Vince trips over tree roots, his weapon flying.

Hana pauses long enough to haul him to his feet before she starts running again, unholstering her Glock as she goes.

Scrambling down towards her injured partner, Bethell retrieves Davison's weapon halfway down the slope, reaching his side just as Hana and Vince arrive. Hana holds a finger to her lips. With hand gestures, Davison indicates the cable leading to the cave.

Hana carefully approaches the opening in the rock. The other cops have their weapons drawn, covering her. Vince readies his torch. In complete silence, Hana nods and the torch flicks on.

In front of her, set a few metres back from the opening, a reinforced wooden door carefully built into the contours of the cave. The three cops approach slowly, silently. Hana looks at the others, an unspoken question: are you ready?

She shoulders the door, and it flies open, unlocked. She scans the room beyond, gun drawn, calling out, 'Armed police!', Bethell and Vince taking positions behind. The room is empty. Hana can see another door further back; she shoves it open with her gun raised and ready, but this room too is empty. Assured that the hidden structure is deserted, she takes the torch, using it to illuminate the dark corners of the first, larger room.

This room is a workshop: tools, a workbench. Low-wattage electric lamps run off the solar panel, hacksaws and welding equipment. Cooking utensils, supplies of food and water. The torch beam picks out something on the wall. The daguerreotype of the six soldiers and the executed chief.

'D Senior.'

Vince has found something under the table. A box. Hana shines the torch on the label on the side. *DANGEROUS. BLASTING GELIGNITE.* The top has been prised open. She cautiously points the torch inside.

The box is empty.

An hour later. It's completely dark in the forest. The area at the foot of the slope is alive with activity. Portable lighting equipment is being set up, SOCO officers and their forensics testing gear are ferried in by quad bikes to examine Raki's hiding place.

'He went in a hurry. Left behind food and water supplies.' Hana is on the phone to Jaye.

'He's out in the open now,' Jaye says. 'He's vulnerable. He's not calling the shots any more.'

Hana looks out into the darkness of the forest. What Jaye is saying is true. Raki doesn't have a hiding place now, he's on the run. At last the cops have what feels like an advantage. An advantage to be pressed. But she's not celebrating. Not yet.

The opposite.

Raki has his gun. A plan. And enough explosives to blow up a square mile of central Auckland.

26

THE RATTLING OF BONES

In the dream, his mother is walking away from him.

She's climbing a long hillside. Raki is a hundred metres behind her, maybe more. He can't see her face, she's too far away. But he knows it's her.

'Māmā,' he cries. He hasn't used the name since childhood, but now it seems the right thing, the only thing to call her. 'Māmā, wait!'

But his mother doesn't stop. There's a strong wind whipping down the hillside; it seems to Raki like every step he takes to try and catch up to his mother is a battle against a chilling blast that only wants to push him back down the hill and away from her.

He calls out to her again, asking her to slow down, to stop, to wait for him. Perhaps the wind is blowing his words back at him, for if she could hear his voice crying out for her, begging her to stop, if she heard that, then surely she would turn, surely she would take him in her arms and hold him?

He calls out again, the wind whipping his face.

But his mother keeps walking.

Isolated rolling farmland. There are no cliffs or forest here; it's a very different landscape to where the manhunt uncovered Raki's hideout. This is the middle of rugged back-country farming land, no roads, no residences. Hidden in a thick copse of mānuka,* the 4WD vehicle that Raki stole after the confrontation at the container yard. Broken branches cover its roof, concealing the vehicle from the air.

In the dream, the wind gets stronger still, harsh in his face, burning his eyes.

Walking up the slope is like walking on oil. The harder he tries to reach his mother, the less his bare feet seem able to find any kind of purchase. He keeps calling, louder still. Desperate now. But ahead, his mother keeps walking.

He redoubles his efforts. Shaken, confused. Why is she not stopping?

Leaning into the wind, he forces himself up the

---

* Mānuka – tea tree

seemingly endless slope. Sheer determination, refusing to falter. The steeper the slope, the stronger the wind, the harder he pushes himself. It is his mission now, to get to his mother, his sole purpose, the only thing in the world that matters any more.

He seems to be making ground. He keeps calling, getting closer. But still his mother doesn't stop. He's close enough to see her more clearly now, but he realizes her hands are covering her face.

Closer, closer, now only a few steps behind, and though the wind has grown to a tempest blowing straight and hard into him, threatening to knock him off his feet and send him tumbling back down the endless slope, he is relentless.

It is all that matters now.

To see his mother. To hold her. For her to hold him.

The previous morning Raki was high up on a ridge when he saw in the distance a pair of what were almost certainly armed police working their way down the banks of the Hīwawā river. He scanned his binoculars across the landscape, seeing many other officers. He waited long enough to count dozens of heavily armed police, searching methodically and meticulously through the bush. Once again, DSS Westerman had earned his respect. But he had no time to work through the mystery of how she could possibly have found him.

He hurried back to the cave. He took the things he

could carry, the things he knew he would need in order to finish what he had begun.

And he took the whāriki sack. He would not leave that.

'Māmā, stop!' he cries in his dream.

But still she doesn't slow.

He is closer, much closer, but the effort it has cost him to get this far has taken its toll. Struggling up the unrelenting slope, fighting against the cruel smash of the wind, he is exhausted, heart pounding, throat burning, eyes raw, and though he is only a dozen steps behind his mother, so near, there is very little left inside for him to call upon to drive himself forward the final few steps.

But he knows he must. He cannot falter now. If he gives in to the exhaustion he is feeling, even for a moment, all is lost.

'Māmā!'

With a final burst of will, he forces himself forward, his hand reaching out, closer and closer to his mother, and at last, his hand finds the sleeve of her rainbow-coloured cardigan.

His fingers grasp.

He won't let go, he can't let go, his world depends upon it.

She stops.

He tries to turn her towards him, but she stays facing up the endless slope. Instead, he moves around, fighting once more against the wind, until he is in front of her. 'Show me your face, Māmā.'

Her hands are covering her eyes.

'Why won't you show me your face?'

In the 4WD, hidden in the mānuka copse, Raki is awake, jolted from his troubled sleep by the vividness of the dream. He's exhausted. After having to flee so unexpectedly from his hideout, he drove for hours and hundreds of kilometres through hidden back-country roads and fire breaks, difficult and demanding driving, putting a vast swathe of land between him and the cave that he was quite certain had by now been discovered.

He'd found this place amongst the concealing mānuka trees, a place he believed was many miles from any settlement or homestead, and had parked for the night, but despite his exhaustion, he'd struggled to rest, finally falling asleep in the pre-dawn hours, only to find himself thrown once again into the uneasy dream he's had so many times now.

The dream of his mother.

He pulls himself out from under the thin jacket that he used to keep himself warm overnight and looks out at the sun cresting the distant mountain range. A calm day, so different to the tempest of his dreams.

It was another still and calm day months earlier when he went, as he did whenever he could, to the tall rimu tree to shake the rope. The sun was setting, shafts of evening light breaking through the treetops and the towering ferns. In the distance, the gentle sound of the flowing river. The last of the red fruit cups were still in the high branches, almost as if the tree was saying: it is enough, time to finish with the red; this forest has had its fill of the colour of mourning.

He took hold of the rope that ran from its tethering at the base of a nearby tree and up to the highest branches of the rimu. A bird emerged from the open mouth of the sack and took flight, flapping lazily away through the surrounding forest. He pulled the rope. High above, the sack moved. From within . . .

A sound like the gentle clacking of pebbles below the surface of a fast-moving creek. The sound he had been expecting. The sound of rattling.

His legs were suddenly weak, threatening to buckle beneath his weight. He had been waiting for this sound, anticipating it and the certainty it would bring, but now that he had heard it, he had to fight an avalanche of emotions. He took a moment to breathe. To pray. His tears fell.

Then he unleashed the rope from where it was double-knotted to the adjacent tree trunk. He lowered the sack until it was within reach, then took hold of it in both arms and laid it carefully, so carefully, on the deep moss of the forest floor.

It had been raining the night before, and he scooped a handful of rainwater from a bowl formed by the thick roots of the rimu and sprinkled it into the opening of the sack, a blessing. Then he cut a section of the rope, using it to bind the sack closed. Picking it up with great tenderness and respect, he spoke to his mother's bones in his arms.

'Tāria te wā. Tāria te tau.'*

Now, as he looks out at the blueness of the sky beyond the mānuka branches, he is suddenly aware of his hunger. He hasn't eaten in more than a day. The meat from the stag he shot had run out, and he'd had to leave behind most of his supplies when he fled the cave. Now that he has let the thought into his head, he realizes the hunger is gnawing at him. For the things he needs to do, he needs fuel. He needs energy.

He moves through low scrub with his rifle, in pursuit of a rabbit he spotted on a nearby hill. As he takes the long way around the slope, keeping out of sight and scent of where the animal is grazing, he thinks again of the dream.

It always ends the same way.

He catches up with his mother. He stops her, his hand on her arm. He moves around so he can see her, but her hands are covering her face. He reaches out, gently taking her hands in his.

He feels her hands are wet. He moves them away from her face.

'Why are you crying?'

Each time the same.

Her face covered in tears as she looks at her son. Weeping.

He emerges to a vantage point above and behind the rabbit. But a rabbit at this time of year can be way more nervy than a deer, and this one senses the presence of

---

* 'We have waited. Now the time has arrived.'

danger. It starts to run. Raki breaks cover, his weapon to his shoulder.

His mother's face, covered in tears.

He fingers the trigger, the rabbit in full flight.

Why does she come in the dream? Is there something she's trying to say to him? A message?

He has the animal plumb in his sights. Controlling his heartbeat. His eye unblinking.

Why is she crying?

He pushes down the thought, focused instead on the trigger, gently squeezing, ready for the jolt in his shoulder, about to fire when ...

'Hey! Bro!'

He freezes. The rabbit bolts away, sprinting headlong into a dense stand of forest.

Two boys emerge from scrubby bush on the far side of the hill. Raki can see that both are Māori. They look like brothers. One is in his teens. The other younger, perhaps nine years old. The younger carries a dead rabbit. The older holds the rifle he used to shoot it.

'This is our family's farm, bro,' says the brother holding the rabbit. Though he's the younger, he's the feistier one. 'Can't walk round like you own the place.'

The moment he heard voices, Raki made sure his head was down. He keeps his face to the ground, calling out with careful lightness as he turns and heads towards where the 4WD is hidden in the stand of mānuka.

'Aroha mai.* My bad. I'll go.'

---

* Aroha mai – I'm sorry

'Sweet as, bro. He Māori koe,'* the younger one calls after him. 'Not like it's some Pākehā stealing our kai.'†

Head still down, Raki increases his pace. When he glances back, he sees the brothers' eyes are on him every step of the way. He walks faster. But the silence behind him is screaming a warning. Over his shoulder he hears low whispering. He knows what is being said. He took a moment too long to lower his head. His face has been on every screen and every newspaper in the country for days now; the two boys saw enough to know who was trying to illegally poach rabbits on their family land.

His grip on his gun tightens, every nerve heightened, almost feeling through his skin what is happening behind him. Imagining the older brother raising his rifle, aiming at him exactly as he himself had just targeted the rabbit in his sights, Raki waits for the sound he knows is about to come, so completely inevitable now. Finally he hears it, the rifle's hammer being engaged, and even as the sound of the low *click* reaches him . . .

He is already throwing himself down and sideways, the bullet ripping into his leg before he has even heard the report. He rolls across the grass as he rehearsed in his mind in the moments prior, ignoring the injury to his leg, coming straight up to his feet, hauling his gun scope back to his eye.

In his sights, he sees the rifle in the hands of the older brother, the younger boy paralysed with fear as his

---

* He Māori koe – you're a Māori
† Kai – food

sibling grabs for a bullet from his pocket to reload. He knows he has no time to think this through, no time to hesitate. Gun to his shoulder, he runs straight at the boys, screaming as he goes, trying to multiply the pressure on the older brother, and it's working, the boy's hands shaking so badly he's struggling to lodge the fresh bullet into its chamber. As he charges, his finger again squeezes the trigger, just as with the rabbit.

A flash comes to his mind. A memory from years before, driving with his mother, seeing a pūkeko* that had been recently hit by a car, dead on the side of the road. Beside it was its long-legged, blue-feathered mate, standing above the body, unable to move, unable to walk away, even with the danger of the vehicles that were roaring past so close.

The sight of the grieving bird made the young Raki want to weep. As their car passed, he looked back to see a truck behind them strike the poor bird, its body disintegrating in an explosion of blue feathers.

On the hillside, the memory of the pūkeko is gone as fast as it arrived. As he sprints at the boys, he hears as if from somewhere outside himself the guttural bellow coming from his lungs, sees the older Māori boy struggling, terrified, to reload his weapon, the younger brother frozen, silent. His finger squeezes; even at full sprint his sight is cleanly lined up on the older boy. There is no way he will miss.

In the dream, why is his mother crying?

He feels the last millimetre of give in the trigger, the

---

* Pūkeko – swamp hen

microsecond before the firing pin hits the primer, sending the tiny piece of lead erupting down the barrel and across the fifty metres between him and his target. Both boys are screaming now, Raki ready to fire, ready to do what he must do, ready to end the older brother's life then turn the gun on the younger and do the same, just as the grieving pūkeko on the side of the road died side by side with his mate. His finger keeps squeezing, and at the very last possible moment . . .

He jolts the barrel skyward.

Boom! The bullet launches, sailing ten metres above the older brother's head. Raki stops dead. Engaging the next bullet before he has taken a breath.

The echo of the gunshot bounces around the surrounding hills.

The older brother drops his rifle.

The two boys turn and run.

Raki watches until they have disappeared into the same stand of trees that the rabbit fled into. He glances down at the wound in his thigh. It's bleeding badly.

He picks up the boys' gun and hobbles towards where his vehicle is hidden in the stand of mānuka.

Hana sits beside Stan's bed. His parents have been with him since he was taken off sedation, and they're grabbing the chance while Hana is there to go back to the motel to shower and eat. Stan is conscious but hazy from medication. His remaining leg is in traction. He's struggling with the news he has received, but he's trying his hardest not to show it.

'On the plus side, I'll be eligible for the Paralympics. Might be my best shot at representing the country.'

Hana reaches out and holds his hand, as he did for her after she was suspended. She's not going to tell him he doesn't have to be brave, it's okay to cry. Being there with him is enough. She feels his hand tightening around hers.

'You . . . you're close? Right? He's out in the open, you're gonna get him . . .'

Her phone goes. She glances at him. 'Answer it,' he says. In truth, he's exhausted; he's happy not to have to talk.

Hana sees it's a private number, something that now puts her internal alarm on high alert. She answers.

'Detective Senior Sergeant Westerman.'

A long silence from the other end of the line.

'Detective Westerman.'

She recognizes the voice.

Stan sees the look on her face and he knows instantly. Hana moves away from the bed, but it's too late, his face is red with fury. 'You evil prick! You evil fucking bastard! Fuck you, Raki, you evil fucking monster!' As he screams, Hana hurries from the room, a nurse running to Stan's bedside to try and calm him.

She finds a quiet place in a corridor. She takes a moment. Steadies herself.

'Raki. I'm here.'

'There is honour in what I am doing. Honour.'

Listening to these words, Hana tries to stay controlled. It doesn't go well. 'You planted a fucking bomb, you piece of shit.' Instantly she regrets the words. But it's done. No turning back. Move forward. Do your job. Find a way to talk him around. Find where he is. Bring him in.

'Your officer who lost his leg. Was that him just then?' Raki asks.

From the other end of the phone, Hana can hear that something has changed in his voice. His words are shaky. Like he is short of breath. Ready to break.

'I'm at the hospital with him,' she says, consciously keeping her voice even.

'I'm sorry he was hurt. That wasn't my intention.'

She listens to the laboured breathing from the other end of the phone. 'Where are you, Poata?' she says, battling against every instinct in her body to tell him that she wishes she could have the moment back when her gun was trained on him and she didn't fire. But she is thinking straight enough to know she can't. 'Tell me where you are. You have my word, if you co-operate, we can end this without you getting hurt. We can stop this together. We can stop it now. It's time to end this.'

She listens. There's no reply.

Raki's phone has disconnected.

27

HŪMĀRIE,
AROHA, MANAAKI

A sea of raised candles, the flickering flames protected in clear plastic cups. The marchers walk slowly up Queen Street, heading towards Aotea Square in the heart of central Auckland.

There are tens of thousands of people. Young, old. But they walk in complete silence. No one speaking, no chanting, it's not that kind of march. Occasionally there is the sound of crying. Perhaps someone overcome by the power of the sea of candles, by the gentle rhythm of the footsteps, by the rawness of the emotion everyone is feeling. Perhaps a relative of one of the five victims who have died.

The police tried to stop the protest, fearing a mass gathering at such a tinderbox moment. But the marchers came anyway, coming together at sunset; they weren't going to be stopped. A quickly built agreement formed on social media that there would be only three words on the banners and flags that they would carry.

'Hūmārie', the lyrical word for goodwill and peace.

The equally beautiful word for love, 'aroha'.

'Manaaki', kindness and compassion.

Flapping above the candles, held aloft in upraised hands, these three words repeated thousands of times over, lit by the flames, flickering in the darkness.

The same scenes all over the country. Mass gatherings, Māori side by side with Pākehā side by side with members of the more than two hundred ethnicities and religions who now call New Zealand home, one of the most diverse populations on earth. People from lower socioeconomic areas, from wealthy suburbs, marching in small towns, in big cities. Candlelit vigils across the country, a mass outpouring in response to what has happened. Rejecting the bloodshed. Rejecting killing. Calling for an end to violence.

Hūmārie. Aroha. Manaaki.

'He was going to kill Maika.'

Himiona is the younger of the two Māori boys who were rabbit hunting when they stumbled across Raki, Maika the older brother who held the gun. They'd been way up at the back of their family's farm, heading out early to hunt rabbits, and after the awful confrontation, it had taken them several terrifying hours to make their way back to the homestead.

When the report came in from the local cop that two boys had chanced upon Raki and a shot was fired, for a moment Hana's heart sank. Another death? The local cop assured her that both boys were unharmed; shaken as hell but all right. The cop stayed with the family, keeping the only weapon from the rural police station at hand, while a police chopper flew Hana from Auckland to the family's farmhouse.

'He was ready to kill my brother. Then me. I could see it.'

When Hana arrived, the family were still on a knife edge. The boys' mum had quietly explained that Hana wouldn't get much out of Maika. Not a talker, a quiet, self-contained boy. Himiona was the perceptive one, the one who never missed a thing, confident and wise beyond his years, and never shy about saying what he thought.

'He was gonna kill the both of us. He'd made the decision. Woulda done it. But something changed.'

'What do you think happened?' Hana asks. 'What changed?'

Himiona looks at his older brother, but as his mother predicted, Maika sits silently. The big, broad-shouldered father is beside his older son, holding his hand, a touching display of unmasked love.

'I dunno. A switch flipped,' Himiona continues. 'Like he realized something. He raised his barrel. Shot over our heads. That's the only reason we're here.'

At last Maika speaks.

'I'm sorry, miss.'

'What for?'

'I've been shooting since I was big enough to hold a gun. I tried to kill him, but he moved so fast and . . .' Maika is crying now, overwhelmed, unable to hold it in any longer. The father's arm goes around his shoulder. 'I'm sorry, miss. I wanted to stop him.'

Back at the helicopter, Hana gets on the radio to Jaye. The farmland is more than a hundred kilometres from the cave that was Raki's hiding place. He'd put a hell of a lot of space between himself and the teams searching for him; he'd found a place he thought he'd be safe. Except for the chance arrival of the boys.

'They weren't hurt.' Jaye's voice crackles through the radio. 'One thing to be grateful for.'

As the chopper carries Hana back to the city, her eyes search the vast expanse of forest below. The two boys were never part of Raki's plan, she is sure of that. It was sheer bad luck they came across him. But what the younger brother said worries her, hugely. His absolute certainty that Raki meant to kill them. The code Raki set himself, seeking only the blood of those with a line-of-descent connection to the six soldiers. Is that changing? Have the posts suddenly shifted? Are things now about to escalate?

She remembers how Raki sounded on the phone earlier that day, the shakiness in his voice. He was injured, she knows now, a bullet in his leg. But she heard more than just physical pain, and she didn't know what that meant.

Sometimes a wounded animal on the run will curl up in a dark space between two rocks and give up. Other times, it will make the decision to defend itself with everything it has, to lash out tooth and claw at anything and everything, to fight to the death.

For Hana, any certainty has disappeared.
Raki is unpredictable. Unknowable.
All the rules are gone.

The hours since the confrontation with the two young boys had been dark and awful. He'd taken a circuitous route along tracks and through farmland, as fast as he dared, putting as many hours as possible between him and the place where the two young rabbit hunters came across him, trying to staunch the wound in his leg as he drove, the pain intense and made worse by the rough terrain.

When it became too much, he found an area of dense bush. He had a well-stocked first-aid kit that he'd thrown in the 4WD, the kind of kit they'd had in his time in the Territorials. On the ground beside his vehicle, he sterilized a hunting knife, breathing deeply, trying to settle his mind.

Then he cut, digging into the torn, damaged meat of his thigh.

It was a nightmare.

He swabbed away the flowing blood with rags, cutting deeper still into muscle and fat, nearly passing out more than once. The tip of his blade touched metal at last, and he steadied himself, gritted his teeth and forced his little finger into the wound, fast so as not to prolong the awfulness, but still he was unable to suppress a raw cry of anguish. After a few seconds that felt like hours, he pulled out the piece of lead.

He sat hyperventilating, the bullet in his hand, trying not

to faint. He'd lost blood, a lot of blood; the soil around him was stained red. All he wanted to do was give in to the debilitating pain, but he knew that if he lost consciousness now, there was a better than even chance he would bleed out. He washed antiseptic through the wound, but he'd had to cut deep, and every splash of the liquid became a new wave of agony. When the antiseptic bottle was empty, he took a needle and surgical thread from the first-aid kit, stitching together the flesh as best he could, covering the wound with gauze that was already liquid red the moment he put it in place. He bound the wound with several rolls of bandage, as tight as he could bear, in the hope of arresting the flow. Then, at last, he could stop. Give in to his exhaustion.

He subsided on the ground, the soil wet and red, and lay there unmoving.

A few hours later, when the helicopter passed only a couple of kilometres away, carrying Detective Senior Sergeant Hana Westerman back from the farmhouse where she had interviewed the two young brothers, Raki was still unconscious, his body forcing itself to remain shut down, to snatch the few brief hours of respite that might provide some kind of recovery. From the air, Hana's eyes searched the vast tracts of land below, but the 4WD was well hidden by the tall forest canopy.

Lying by his vehicle on the red-soaked earth, Raki never heard the chopper blades. He was dreaming again of his mother, following her up the steep slope, the strong wind blasting his face as he called her name.

The police helicopter carried on to the city.

When Raki woke again, it was dark.

The safe house isn't much to look at. But it's not in competition with the waterfront five-star-plus hotels. The usual clientele in this well-worn apartment are mostly concerned with surviving long enough to get new ID and be relocated to a town at the farthest end of the country, or better still, Australia. They don't care if the wallpaper is peeling and the view from the windows is the grey concrete rear wall of a ten-pin bowling alley.

'At least I've got my own room,' Addison said when they arrived. Which Jaye had to admit was about the most positive take on the place it was possible to have.

In the time they've been in protective isolation, Jaye and Marissa have done their best to keep Addison, and Marissa's girls, Sammie and Vita, away from the news. There's only one story now, the killings, and it's impossible to turn on a screen without seeing Raki's face. Jaye has tried to get Addison interested in the trending shows on Netflix, tried to get her to play her music for the recently graduated constable who has been assigned as their minder. But it's wasted effort. Addison is refreshing her news feed every minute. On her screen, reports about the marches happening around the country. She watches the silent processions, the flapping banners. Jaye notices her fingers twisting the bottom of her sleeve. He recognizes the thing his daughter has done since she was two years old, the thing she does when she wants to cry but she doesn't want anyone to see she is crying.

'Hey, Phil,' he says to the young constable. 'You like PlayStation, right?'

The young guy has been on his absolute best behaviour, very aware he's on show to a detective inspector. He's been fastidiously checking doors and windows, making sure to call in regular updates to his senior officer, even washing the dishes the moment someone has a cup of tea. It's been a bit over the top, if Jaye is being honest.

'No, boss.'

'C'mon, you're nineteen years old. Xbox then. Did you bring it with you?'

The young guy looks confused: is this a test? Jaye can see the answer is yes.

'It's okay. You're doing a good job, Phil, brilliant, very thorough. But I think we can all relax a bit. No one knows where we are. Go get your Xbox.'

With the constable in his room, Jaye sits by Addison. He watches the footage with her. He reaches out and takes the twisted end of her sleeve from between her fingers. Her eyes stay on the screen. Not wanting to look at her dad and risk losing it. 'I'm such a fuck-up,' she says, watching the marchers. Jaye takes her hand. Which is enough to start Addison actually crying.

There's something she hasn't been able to say to anyone since Raki was in the house with her. 'When I was with him, Dad. When he was talking to me. Looking me in the eye. Saying him and me were the same. Saying we wanted the same thing. For a second, I . . . Fuck.'

She almost said, in that moment, 'You're right. We want

the same things. What do you want me to do?' And now it fills her with a sick aching guilt.

'For a moment I believed what he was saying,' she says. 'Then I saw Stan being lifted off the helicopter. And I realized that Poata Raki isn't a visionary. He's a murderer.' She wipes her eyes. Looks back at the footage on her phone. 'I wish I could be there. With those people. All of us together. Standing up.'

Jaye takes the phone out of her hand. Turns the screen off.

'Make pizza with me?'

Addison grins suddenly. Making pizza is the thing she and her dad do together. But then her smile fades. 'Is Mum going to be okay?' she asks.

'Yes,' Jaye says, immediately, with absolute certainty.

But the certainty is only for his daughter's sake.

In truth, he has no idea what's going to happen.

And he's scared as hell.

The news feed of the marches is playing on another screen. Raki watches the footage on his phone. His 4WD is on a rough fire break cut through pine forest in the hills high above the southernmost entrance to Auckland's motorway system. Far below, traffic is backed up for kilometres. After the discovery of the cave deep in the forest by the Hīwawā river, when it was realized that Raki had fled with his weapons and a frightening amount of gelignite, roadblocks were quickly established all around the arteries leading into the city. Every car, every truck and bus is being checked. In the darkness, the roadblocks are lit up like a concert stage.

The few hours of sleep have helped. But Raki feels an aching weakness from the lack of food and the loss of blood. There is nothing he can do about either. He looks up from the footage of the marches to the roadblocks far below and considers all that has happened. His meticulous planning, the painstaking research to find the descendants, the care with which he planned each killing, making sure the deaths were as swift and painless as humanly possible. Seeking recompense only from those who carry a burden of debt for the actions of their forbears whose blood flowed through their veins.

Then, so close to the end, seeing the police coming through the forest. Having to unexpectedly take flight, and in haste taking refuge in what turned out to be the wrong place. Giving in to hunger, and in his uncharacteristic lack of caution being found by the boys with the gun.

Better the blood of the innocent than no blood at all.

That was what he had said, what he believed, what made him able to live with the things he was doing. But this was different. Two boys hunting rabbits. Brothers who carried no collective guilt in their bloodlines.

And the worst thing.

The feeling of his hand on the trigger. Ready to shoot them. In his mind, committed to shooting them. Feeling that thing inside him, feeling what he was capable of, knowing he would pull the trigger and kill those two boys.

His eyes turn to look at himself in the rear-view mirror of the 4WD.

Has he stepped off his path? Has he lost his way, fallen

to a place from which there is no chance of return? He'd called Westerman, telling her, 'There is honour in what I am doing.' He'd said those words not so much as a way to lash out at her, the woman who had acted against his mother with no honour, but in truth as a way to desperately assure himself that what he was saying was true.

He looks again at his phone. The silent processions. The flags and banners and hand-painted cards.

Aroha. Hūmārie. Manaaki.

In his classes he'd talked so many times about these fundamental, core aspects of what it means to be Māori. He had written about these principles in his submissions of claim for the tribe, about how the colonizers had come to this land without conception of or respect for these basic codes and tenets of social interaction for Māori, of how one should live with one's neighbour. How those who arrived here on their tall ships were driven by very different things, things like self-aggrandizement and profit, values that flew in the face of how te ao Māori – the Māori world view and way of living – was ordered.

The three beautiful words, lit by the flames of tens of thousands of candles.

When he committed to his path, Raki had held an image in his head. Young Māori across the country rising up, hearing his words and his message, looking at their lives and the lives of their families and their friends and their forebears and understanding that they were being told a truth they had been denied for generations. He believed that the spark he would light with the flint of his actions would ignite an unstoppable revolution.

But the messages the marchers are holding high are very different.

Aroha. Manaaki. Hūmārie.

On the newsfeed on his phone, Raki sees someone walk slowly out onto the stage to address the Auckland crowd. He knows her. It's the kuia of the Te Tini-o-Tai tribe, standing in front of tens of thousands of marchers holding their candles and banners. But when she speaks, it is to only one person. Someone she knows and loves.

'Come back to us,' she says to Raki, in te reo. 'You are our blood, Poata. You are one of us, you are ours. You have chosen a path. You think you are enacting utu. But in your pain, you have gone down a completely different path. Utu is the seeking of balance. You are following the way of rānaki – perpetuating violence, keeping vengeance alive. With rānaki there will never be balance or peace. Only the opposite. More violence. More pain. More darkness.' On stage, the kuia weeps. 'Stop what you are doing. Return to us. Return to who you are. We love you.'

Raki turns off his phone, unable to watch more.

The kuia, the woman he respects so much, weeping.

His mother, in his dream, crying.

When she comes to him in his dreams, are his mother's tears for a son who has lost his way, who is caught in the storm, no star to guide him? Has he made a mistake, as the kuia says, and in doing so made himself as lowly and irredeemable as those six soldiers whose actions so many years ago began all of this?

He thinks of that first time. Walking down the corridor of the dilapidated building. He had found where the man lived, the descendant of the first soldier, the man who had killed his own child. In the decaying, graffiti-laden corridor of the Palace, Raki stopped ten metres from the man's door. The world was shifting under his feet, like he was standing atop a volcanic eruption. He turned around. Ready to walk away from the things he had decided to do.

But in the corridor, he remembered the pledge he had made to his mother's lifeless body, suspended in the treetops. He remembered the old image he'd found, six soldiers standing proudly in front of the body of his mother's ancestor, hanging by the neck from the branch of a tree on his sacred mountain. He remembered the two centuries of despair, theft, oppression, murder, disenfran-chisement that lay between those two bodies suspended from those two trees.

Holding onto these images, the tumult beneath his feet became still. He found again the determination in his puku, in his gut, in the very seat of his being.

He turned. He walked back down the corridor towards the last flat on the second floor.

He opened the door.

After that, there was no going back.

Now, there is no going back.

He looks a moment longer at his eyes in the rearview mirror. He turns the mirror away. He looks past the roadblocks at the entrance to the motorway, far below. In the distance the faint glow of the night-time lights of Auckland.

Blood seeps from the wound in his leg.

28

TELL ME WHAT I
HAVE TO DO

Chicken and pineapple pizza for Marissa, Sammie and Jaye. Vegetarian for Addison and Vita, who is even more soft-hearted about animals than her mother and hasn't eaten anything that once had a face since a kid at primary school explained to her where the ham in her sandwich actually came from and Marissa had to leave work and pick her up from school because she hadn't stopped crying for an hour. Addison and Jaye also made two meat lovers, one for the young cop Phil, and another for his replacement when his shift ends at midnight.

As Marissa read with her girls, she watched Addison and Jaye cooking together just like it was normal times.

But it wasn't normal times.

After dinner, Jaye persuades Phil to get over his shyness

and bring out his Xbox. Addison finds an adventure game that's okay for Vita and Sammie and she organizes a bit of a tournament. Since Marissa and Jaye got together, she has been good with the younger girls, the little sisters she never had. She orchestrates the competition so that after count-backs and a careful adjustment for Vita's age, the two girls are dead-equal winners.

'Funny how that always happens,' Sammie observes. But she's not grumpy. She loves her big sister with the beautiful bald head, and most of the time she can tolerate her younger one.

Much later, after Phil has been replaced, Jaye is still in contact with the eighth floor, monitoring the investigation. It's well after midnight when he climbs into bed, quietly, so as not to wake Marissa.

But she is already awake.

It's a clear Auckland night, a big moon hanging over the city. In the cold blue moonlight, he can see her looking out through a gap in the curtains. 'Can't sleep?' he asks.

The house is silent. The suburb is some distance from the central city, a quiet, nondescript residential neighbourhood. Outside, the low thrum of a delivery truck idling as it delivers the next morning's milk to a nearby convenience store.

'The night Addison was in hospital,' Marissa says. 'After you and Hana took her home. You said you had a drink together when she was asleep. You cried together.' Her voice is emotionless. Her eyes unblinking. Even before she speaks again, Jaye knows what she is about to say.

'Something else happened. Something you never said. I know it did. Don't insult me by pretending otherwise. Allow me that dignity.'

On the street outside, *beep-beep-beep* as the delivery truck reverses. It pulls away, the sound of the engine growing quieter and quieter as it drives off to the next delivery. Then everything is silent once more.

'More than anything on earth, I want to walk out the front door of this shitty fucking dump of a house, take Vita and Sammie, get the hell away,' Marissa says. 'I can't. I won't. For the safety of all of us, I will lie in this bed with you. But when this is over . . .'

She doesn't finish the sentence. She doesn't need to.

Jaye reaches out to try and hold her hand.

She turns away.

The blue of the moonlight falling on the bed makes the white sheet look like an expanse of ocean, separating the two of them.

'I'm sorry,' Jaye says.

Marissa makes no reply.

Auckland is a harbour city. Commuter ferries and tourist boats leave from a big wharf complex in the middle of the downtown area and head out across a network of routes to destinations around the harbour, and further afield to the dozens of idyllic islands scattered across the surrounding gulf. That morning, groups of tourists file aboard the *Harbour Queen*, a big tourist ferry, for the first departure of the day, a popular and well-patronized cruise around the inner harbour.

Up on the bridge, Debbie Kavanagh, the skipper, prepares her vessel to depart.

The ropes are unmoored and hauled aboard, Kavanagh shifts the engines into reverse thrust, backing the boat out from the dock where it was berthed overnight. As she turns the ferry out towards the deeper water in the middle of the harbour, she remembers the night before, being in Aotea Square among the candles and the solemn silence.

Standing with tens of thousands of other people, a silent expression of unity from so many of her fellow citizens, she was brought to tears. She had watched the video the offender had posted, as had everyone. She had listened to the things he said with deeply conflicted emotions. She understood the abuses and travesties he was identifying. This country had so much to pride itself on, but it also had so much that was and remained just plain wrong, historically and ongoing, problems that desperately needed fixing. But she abhorred the way Raki had chosen. Holding her candle high in the sea of thousands of others, she prayed that somehow the sheer unified will of those gathered in the name of love, peace and compassion could change the course of events. That no more lives would be lost.

Moving into the deeper channel, the ferry picks up speed. As the boat approaches the maximum knots allowed in the inner harbour, Kavanagh's phone goes.

'This is Kavanagh.'

The call has been connected through to her from the

head offices of the ferry company, an outside number asking to be patched through. As she settles her vessel into a steady fifteen knots, Kavanagh notices the group of Japanese tourists gathered below her window. The ferry is heading towards where Rangitoto Island rises from the middle of the harbour, and the group are taking photos of each other with the perfect black volcanic cone behind. One of them, in a wheelchair, is smoking. Kavanagh hopes her crew will notice and deal with it.

'Captain Kavanagh speaking,' she repeats, wondering if the connection has been lost.

'Turn off your engines.'

'I'm sorry? Who is this?'

'Shut down your engines. Please do as I say.'

The skipper's hand tightens involuntarily on her phone. The words themselves are enough to cause concern, a peculiar request made in a forceful, commanding tone. But it isn't just the order that is alarming. Kavanagh is good with voices. She has heard this man before, and she knows exactly where she's heard him.

It's the voice of the man on the video. Poata Raki.

'There's a group of tourists just below your bridge. They're taking photos of each other.'

The tourist in the wheelchair finishes his cigarette and stubs it out against his wheel.

'The guy in the wheelchair just finished his cigarette,' Raki says on the other end of the line.

And now Kavanagh knows that the most wanted man in the country is somewhere in sight of the vessel. He is watching her boat.

'Shut down your engines. I'm not going to ask again.'

Her hand goes back to the handle of the throttle.

The throb of the large ferry engines quietens and dies.

The CCTV monitoring room is on the third floor of Central Police Station. Hana watches the feeds from the extensive network of cameras across inner-city Auckland that play on a bank of monitors. All leave has been cancelled for police personnel across the country. Uniformed cops maintain a high-profile presence on the streets of Auckland, and in every city and town within a day's drive of the area where Raki was last known to be. Most of Hana's team are on the streets; gun safes in stations and cars around the country have been emptied. Every sworn officer, either plain clothes or in uniform, is openly carrying a weapon.

Hana and a team of police staff scan the feeds on the dozens of screens in the monitoring room. On a weekday in central Auckland, there are thousands of workers and students on the streets. Looking at the sea of constantly moving people, Hana knows the odds of finding the one face she needs to find aren't great.

Her phone goes. It's the kuia's grandson. He passes the phone to his grandmother. 'You should know,' the old woman tells Hana solemnly. 'Today is the anniversary.'

'Of what?' Hana asks.

'The day our ancestor Hahona Tuakana was executed on the maunga.'

'Keep your engines idling, turn your bow against the tide, keep the vessel exactly where you are, please.'

With the boat holding its position well out in the middle of the harbour, more than a kilometre from either of the nearest shores, Raki tells the skipper to hand the vessel over to the first mate and get down to the bottom level.

She hurries down the stairs from the bridge to the main deck, her phone clutched to her ear, ignoring the perplexed looks from passengers and staff members who have no idea why the boat has come to a halt just fifteen minutes into its trip. Taking three steps at a time, she continues down the next set of stairs from the main level.

'I'm on the lower deck,' she says into her phone.

'The women's toilets, at the stern.'

The skipper pulls open the heavy metal door of the female bathrooms. An older woman is washing her hands at the sink. Kavanagh hurries her out, closing the door behind her. 'I'm here.'

'The middle cubicle.'

There's an *Out of Order* sign on the door of the cubicle.

'Don't open the door.'

The skipper swallows. Oh God. In her mind, she runs over the passenger list she was given as they pulled away from the dock: sixty-three passengers onboard, as well as eleven crew. 'What do I do now?' she asks into the phone, as calmly as she can.

'Look under the door,' Raki tells her. 'Take a photo

on your phone. Then go back to the bridge and contact the police.'

Kavanagh wipes away the cold mist of sweat she suddenly feels on her forehead. She gets down on her knees, her phone in her hand.

She looks under the cubicle door.

Much earlier that day, just after three in the morning, Raki paddled silently through the dark waters of the harbour.

He'd driven a route he had used a number of times now, a circuitous pathway along back roads and through abandoned farmland, bypassing the roadblocks that surrounded the Auckland isthmus on all sides. Back in the city, well after midnight, he'd made his way to one of the tiny tree-lined beaches along the inner-city coastline, finding his way to a place where he knew locals kept their kayaks locked up above the high-tide line. He chose one big enough to hold the waterproof rucksack he needed to take, cut the chains and hauled it down to the water.

It was a still night, luckily. Normally the three kilometres or so he had to paddle would be no problem for someone of his strength and fitness. But with the lack of food and the loss of blood and the aching pain of his wound, his tanks were near empty, running now on adrenaline and the strength of his willpower, and nothing else.

He paddled the kayak into the berth where the ferry moored overnight, pulling up between the vessel and the dock. He sat there for a moment, his pulse racing much higher than he would have expected, his body drenched with sweat. The wound on his leg was seeping blood again. His body warning him that an infection had already started.

A warning he didn't have the luxury of paying heed to.

He hauled himself and the rucksack up onto the dock, lashing the kayak to one of the bollards the ferry was moored to. Above him, the gangway that gave pedestrians access to the boat was raised and locked in place, a precaution taken to prevent water movement damaging the structure. He was expecting this, he had planned for it. What he hadn't planned for was a bullet wound in his leg.

He hurled the kitbag across the two-metre gap between the dock and the ferry, over the handrail of the boat. He looked at his watch. Two and a half hours until dawn, then the first tea cruise would leave mid morning. He had to keep going.

He took a few paces back, to the other side of the dock. He gritted his teeth, anticipating the intensity of the pain he was about to feel in his wounded leg. But he couldn't let the thought of the agony slow him or make him falter. He had ten paces to get up to a fast enough sprint, then he would spring hard like a basketball player rising for a dunk, throw himself across the gap between the dock and the boat, find a grip on the boat's railings, take the whole weight of his body without losing hold of the slippery metal rails. If he stumbled, if he wasn't going fast enough before he leapt, if he lost his grip, if he fell into the water, or worse still, if he hit his head against the edge of the dock as he tumbled, he was sure he wouldn't have enough left for a second chance.

He tensed every muscle. Readying himself. Blood pressure escalating. He felt the wound leaking. He ignored the feeling. If he could scream, maybe that would help with the pain that was about to engulf him.

But he couldn't scream.

He ran. Jumped.

His body hit the side of the ferry, hard, his wounded leg slamming against the hull, an agonizing impact. His hands just managed to grasp the lowest of the metal railings. But the effort and pain left him suddenly foggy, faint. One hand slipped from the railing, the other fast losing purchase. Somehow he found the strength to get both hands back on the bars, but the fog in his head was descending, his body saying: you've done too much now, time to shut down, time to redirect the remaining oxygen to where it's needed most, the fragile brain and central nervous system.

With all he had left, he managed to haul himself up, pull himself over the top rail, tumbling across, sprawling face-first onto the hard wooden deck. He lay there unmoving, breathing long and deep. When he had rested as long as he dared, he tightened the tourniquet above the wound in his thigh and got unsteadily to his feet.

He found the kitbag where it had landed.

Then he forced open the doors of the boat and found the stairs to the lower deck.

A dozen police boats race out across the inner harbour to where the tourist ferry is sitting stationary, well offshore, as Raki had demanded. Hana is in the lead vessel, her binoculars trained on the ferry.

The urgent call from the skipper had been put through to the CCTV monitoring room. 'We've moved all the passengers towards the bow of the boat, as far as possible from the bathrooms,' Kavanagh explained. She sent Hana the photo she'd taken under the door of the cubicle. Five brown tubes labelled with explosives warnings, wiring, some kind of electronic detonation device. 'He told me not to open the door. I think it could be wired,' she said. 'He's watching us. He's got his eyes on my boat. What do I do?'

Hana ran the scenarios in her head. Send the ferry towards the terminal after the explicit order not to, with the very real possibility that Raki had a way to remotely detonate the explosives, as he had in the container yard. Or follow his instructions, leaving several dozen people floating helpless in the middle of the harbour, with five sticks of gelignite on the boat. There was no good choice for Hana here. Just the responsibility of being the one who must choose the least bad option.

'Do as he asked. Hold your position.'

The police boats pull up alongside the tourist vessel, arriving at the same time as coastguard boats from their nearby base. Between the various emergency vessels, there will be space enough to take all the passengers and crew. But Hana knows that getting several dozen alarmed tourists off the boat isn't going to happen quickly; the skipper warned that the majority of them were elderly. As a news helicopter hovers overhead, she helps lift the terrified disabled Japanese man down onto the police boat, his wheelchair passed down behind. As she settles the man, reassuring him, her eyes turn back to the tourist ferry.

It's her worst scenario.

Her biggest fear in the last day, since Raki came so close to killing the two young Māori brothers, has been that he is about to cross an awful line. But to endanger or actually kill so many? Dozens of people who have not even the slightest connection to the six soldiers?

Kavanagh is the last off the ferry. The skipper hurries down the disembarkation ladder onto the deck of the police boat. As the other vessels pull away from the abandoned tourist boat, Hana's hand stays on the ladder. Everything she knows about the man she is pursuing tells her this isn't how Raki thinks, this isn't how he operates.

None of this makes sense.

She turns to the policeman at the wheel of the vessel. 'Get these people ashore.'

'D Senior?'

'Go. That's an order.'

And she scales the ladder up to the deck of the boat.

Addison is in her room in the safe house when her phone beeps. It's an email with a video attachment. She opens the video. The footage is from inside a cubicle in a bathroom somewhere. The camera moves across five sticks of gelignite, wired to an electronic detonator. She doesn't understand what she's looking at. Then her phone rings.

'Turn on your news feed.' She recognizes the voice. 'Do it.'

Hands shaking, she opens a news app. The first story is a breaking news item, an urgent police operation out on the harbour. There's chopper footage from a few minutes earlier, of police and coastguard vessels approaching a motionless ferry.

'There are seventy people on that boat. They will all die unless you do exactly as I say.'

Addison looks again at the video of the explosives. She remembers what happened to the prisoner who was being relocated, the explosion that maimed Stan. She remembers the night before, watching the protests calling for peace and unity and an end to the killings, and wishing she could do something about the terrible things that were happening. She remembers standing in her mother's house, a knife in her hand as she faced the man on the other end of this call. She thinks of the seventy people on the boat.

'Tell me what I have to do.'

Hana makes her way down the length of the ferry, past the belongings hastily abandoned on the seats, past the café and bar left open and untended. She hurries downstairs, to the toilets at the rear of the boat. She finds the cubicle, the *Out of Order* sign on the door.

There's a porthole in the bathroom, through which she can see that the police boats and coastguard vessels have all retreated at speed, getting the rescued passengers and crew well away from the ferry.

She faces the cubicle.

She turns the handle.

The door swings open.

There's no explosion.

On the floor of the cubicle, the five tan-coloured sticks of gelignite, taped together into a single package. Wiring leads from the caps of each of the sticks to the electronic detonator device she saw on the photo sent by the skipper.

She takes several deep breaths, doing her level best to get her heart rate somewhere near normal. She doesn't want her hands shaking for what she is about to do. She kneels on the floor in front of the sticks of gelignite. She reaches out, slowly, slowly.

Hana has handled gelignite as part of the anti-terrorist training all senior cops are given to get experience with identifying the most common forms of explosives they may one day encounter. She knows well the surprisingly solid weight of a cylinder of compressed nitroglycerine and nitrocellulose. She knows how the cardboard tubes are made much heavier by the concentrated gel than their size would ever suggest.

Her fingers close around the carefully constructed bomb. Very, very gently, she lifts the package. The weight in her hand is barely more than that of five empty toilet rolls.

The five tubes weigh virtually nothing.

She cautiously removes the cap of one of the gelignite sticks. There's nothing inside. The cardboard tube has been completely emptied of explosive gel.

Back out on the deck, she looks towards the city. The gelignite was a decoy, a facade. But why? A way to turn the attention of those pursuing him in the wrong direction? Look here, don't look there? But what is it that Raki is drawing their attention away from? And where was he watching from when he was talking to the skipper?

With no one at the bridge, the disabled ferry circles slowly, at the mercy of the currents of the harbour. As it rotates, on the opposite side of the harbour a landmark comes into view. A distinctive volcanic cone. The peak known for a thousand years as the mountain of the guardian orca, Maunga Whakairoiro. More recently, Mount Suffolk.

Look here. Don't look there.

Hana's phone rings. It's Jaye.

'Addison is gone.'

29

THE SACRED MOUNTAIN

She wishes now she'd actually got round to doing those final three lessons.

Jaye and Marissa bought Addison a course of five driving lessons for her seventeenth birthday a few months earlier. Addison thought it was a good idea at the time, but after the first couple of lessons, she kind of lost enthusiasm. Maybe it was living in the central city, where you can pretty much walk anywhere or grab a scooter or get a five-buck Uber ride; maybe it was all the complicated rigmarole involved in actually becoming a fully licensed driver – six months learner's licence then six months restricted before you could properly drive. Maybe it was the whole idea of driving a carbon-burning car in a rapidly overheating world. Anyway. She got as far as lesson two. Still, she knows enough to drive the young cop's car. Thank God it's automatic, not manual shift. But as she drives painfully carefully, her hands gripping the steering wheel, continuously reminding herself which pedal is the brake and which the throttle or whatever the stupid name is, she really wishes she'd done those last three lessons.

It was too easy getting out of the apartment. The young cop, Phil, was boiling water to make a cup of bad instant coffee when Addison came out from her room after the phone call. Marissa was with the girls, helping them with the schoolwork their teachers had organized for them online. Addison could hear her dad talking on the phone in the bedroom, his door closed. She couldn't hear what he was saying, but the tone of his voice told her the conversation was very probably about what was happening out in the harbour at that moment, the tourist ferry with the dozens of helpless people onboard. The sense of urgency she could hear in his muffled words only confirmed to her what Raki had said. This was a bad situation that was about to get a whole lot worse.

'You all right?' Phil asked.

Addison nodded, knowing she was looking shaky after the phone conversation she'd just had.

'I'm just a bit tired,' she told the young cop, one eye on his car keys sitting on the table. 'Might have a shower and a lie-down.'

As Phil finished making his coffee, she discreetly pocketed the keys. Went into the bathroom, locked the door, turned on the shower. Then she opened the bathroom window. A safe house is about concealment, anonymity, keeping those inside hidden and away from the outside world. But it's not a prison; there's nothing stopping them from leaving if they get the urge.

Before clambering out the window, she took a moment to text PLUS 1.

Love you babe. Always

PLUS 1 immediately sent back an orange heart emoji. Addison smiled. Wanting to cry. She tapped out a reply.

If either of us were the kind of person who fell in love itd be dangerous

Outside, on the street, she beeped the remote. The flashing hazard lights of a shiny boy-racer car told her which car was Phil's. She knew it would be at least twenty minutes before the diligent young cop or Marissa realized she'd been in the shower a surprisingly long time.

Now, approaching the road leading up to the mountain, she indicates to turn, except she makes the rear windscreen wipers go instead. She manages to find the correct lever and makes the turn. She heads past the carved meeting house and up the steep, narrow road. The gnarly, twisted branches of the pūriri tree come into sight. She pulls into the car park in the borrowed car. She turns off the ignition. She looks at her hands on the steering wheel, the knuckles white. And that's not just because she's a nervous driver.

There's a figure standing in the shadows of the ancient tree. Waiting. Addison knows who it is.

A line of police vehicles heads over the Harbour Bridge, lights flashing. Hana looks across the string of north-shore suburbs towards the volcanic cone in the distance, the same view as when she was in the convoy eighteen years ago, heading to the same destination.

After Phil raised the alarm that Addison had disappeared, a police car was dispatched to pick up Jaye. There was no way he was staying in the safe house with his daughter out there somewhere. His car is three vehicles behind Hana's as they crest the top of the bridge.

As she answered Jaye's frantic phone call, Hana was staring at Maunga Whakairoiro. The place at the centre of the concentric rings of the spider web, a spider web whose first strand was woven one hundred and sixty years ago with the posing and taking of a macabre daguerreotype, the strands added to and radiating out over the years with the shameful history of confiscations, with the violence against those who were only claiming what was rightfully theirs, with the sacred land never returned, the knots of the web becoming hopelessly complex and twisted and messy, until a young, inexperienced Māori cop dragged a woman in a rainbow-coloured cardigan from the mountain and a terrified boy watched and wept.

Looking at the mountain as the abandoned tourist boat drifted in the tide, Hana understood that every thread of the web led back to that one place. That was the reason for the decoy of the five empty tubes of gelignite. Maunga Whakairoiro, the place where all this started, with the execution of the revered chief. The place where Hana knows now that Raki will finish the mission he has taken upon himself, his campaign of utu.

As the row of police cars speed on towards the mountain, Hana phones Addison again and again, praying that her daughter's inexplicable disappearance will not lead, like everything else, back to the centre of the same spider web.

On the passenger seat of Phil's car, Addison's phone rings unheard, multiple missed calls from Hana and Jaye.

Walking towards where Raki waits for her, Addison tries to ready herself, to be composed and calm – or at least have the appearance of calmness – but it's a jolt when she gets close enough to see him properly. He is badly injured, a dark bloody stain seeping through the thigh of his trousers, walking with difficulty, alarmingly pale from loss of blood.

And in his eyes, something has changed. The burning passion that Addison saw when he stood in front of his class, the intensity that took her breath away every time they met, that fire seems to have faded. 'You look so tired, matua,' Addison says, but even as she says it, she knows that isn't really the right word. What she sees in Poata Raki's face is something far deeper. A weariness of the spirit more than the body.

'I didn't know if you would come,' he says in te reo, his voice weak.

'How could I not come,' she says, and it's not a question. When she knew about the people on the boat, that seventy lives would be lost if she didn't do as Raki asked of her, for Addison there was no choice to be made. She didn't know what would happen at the maunga, and she still doesn't. But she had to do whatever she could to stop those people dying.

Two things lie at the base of the great pūriri tree. A rolled-up woven mat. And the sack, made of a similar whāriki design, the sack that holds the bones of Raki's mother. He kneels and unrolls the mat, taking out the taiaha with the two sharpened pounamu heads. He stands, and Addison looks at the spear in his hands. She remembers the daguerreotype Raki left on the kitchen table, the line from the last soldier to the photo of her and Jaye. She knows the things this weapon with its eleven-centimetre striking blades has done.

Addison came to the maunga so that seventy people on the boat would not be killed. She didn't come there to die.

The half dozen police cars drive nearly bumper to bumper, setting off speed trap cameras across the lower north shore as they race towards the maunga. There's no possibility of stealth, no hiding their intent, lights flashing to clear the busy city roads.

In the second car, Hana fits reinforced Kevlar plates into her body armour vest. For a moment her mind goes to a day in weapons training, a live-fire session. It was an obstacle course exercise, kicking in a reinforced door, scaling a three-metre wall, leaping to the ground on the other side with nothing to soften the fall, immediately back to your feet to confront a target, two polystyrene figures; a mock hostage situation, a kidnapper holding a gun to the head of a victim. The situation was a clear and immediate threat to life, no room for a shot to the arm or the leg to disable without mortal injury.

Heart racing, adrenaline pumping, lungs burning, you had to control all your natural bodily reactions as you lined up your weapon on the offender. A perfectly still hand. An unblinking eye. One option only. One shot and it had to be a headshot. Incapacitate offender. Bring him down.

As the maunga comes into view, Hana press-checks her Glock.

One round in the chamber, ready to go.

'You had the chance to kill me. You didn't. I don't believe that's what you want, matua.' Addison is fighting to stop her voice from breaking with the fear she is feeling. 'Give me the taiaha. Give it to me. Then let the people on the boat go. I'll call my mother, I'll drive you to the police station, I'll tell her you're unarmed, they won't hurt you if you're in the car with me, I'll make Mum promise.'

'I think your mother knows where I am,' Raki says. And now Addison becomes aware of the sound of sirens, the chorus of police vehicles closing at great speed through the neighbouring suburban streets.

Raki holds the taiaha in his hand with reverence. He bows his head, speaking low and quiet. 'Ka tūāumutia e au te mata o taku rākau – kāore e ora i a au.' Addison hasn't heard the karakia before, but she understands the meaning.

Poata Raki is sanctifying his taiaha, making it ready to do its job.

To take a life.

The police vehicles sweep off the main road, past the carved buildings of the Te Tini-o-Tai marae. The lead car has the heavily reinforced bull bars used to shunt stranded vehicles that have chosen the unhappiest place in Auckland to run out of gas: in the middle of the harbour bridge. As it approaches the locked gate blocking access to the maunga the car accelerates, the bull bars hit the barrier at eighty kilometres an hour, the gate explodes, metal bars flying into the air and across the road.

As the convoy climbs the hill, for a moment Hana catches a glimpse of the ancient tree. She sees the two figures beneath. And she sees what Raki is holding in his hands. Then the cars crest another rise, and the tree is lost from sight. 'They're there,' Hana speaks into the radio on her vest. She keeps her voice steady and unemotional, though it's a nearly impossible task.

'The offender has a weapon.'

The karakia finished, Raki's eyes rise to meet Addison's. 'The people on the boat are safe.' For the first time Addison looks towards the harbour, she sees the tourist ferry far below, surrounded by police vessels, officers moving around the deck of the boat. Knowing the tourists aren't in danger shifts things for her. She is still terrified, of course she is, but she's no longer responsible for several dozen lives. Her mind works fast, desperate to find a way out of this. For her, and for the man for whom she held so much respect, and despite all that has happened, still does.

'We will face the police together,' Addison says in te reo, as the sirens draw closer. 'Blood does not need to be spilled here today. Lay down the taiaha, matua. *Please.*'

Raki's grip on the carved shaft of the spear stays firm. 'When I first consecrated these cutting edges, when the weapon first did its work, it was all so clear to me. How the path ahead would unfold. Māori would hear the truth of my words,' Raki says. 'At last our people would rise up, in anger at the mamae, the pain that has weighed us low for so long. The people rose up. They marched. They spoke out. But they did so to tell me to stop.' Addison can see the flame returning to his eyes. Readying to act. Preparing to use the taiaha.

Hearing the sirens die, Raki glances towards the police cars as they pull into the car park. Addison sees a fleeting opportunity, she moves fast, shoving him with all her strength. He stumbles backwards, but before she can take even two steps towards the safety of the vehicles, his hand is on her arm, his fingers clamping on her wrist with an iron grip, energy surging anew within him. She feels the taiaha, held in his other hand, now resting against her sternum. After holding resolute for so long, Addison starts to sob. She had hoped there would be a peaceful end to the day. That she would walk away from the maunga. That Poata Raki would walk away with her.

Feeling the cold, sharpened pounamu of the taiaha blade against her now, that hope dies.

Hana is first out of the cars. Jaye hurries to her side, his gun drawn, a dozen more armed police behind. There's a hundred metres between the car park and the two figures beneath the tree. Hana orders the others to stay by the vehicles. She starts towards the tree. She feels someone a step or two behind her, and without having to look, she knows who it is. 'Jaye,' she says, her voice firm, 'Stay with the others. I have to do this.'

It fights every impulse in Jaye's body, every instinct. But in Hana's voice, he hears her absolute certainty. Better than anyone, Hana understands Poata Raki. How he thinks, how he will react, what he is likely to do. Jaye falls back.

Hana moves slowly across the hillside. Her weapon raised. Just as in the live-fire exercise where the carved polystyrene figure of the victim was between her and the offender, Addison is between Hana and Raki, blocking any chance of a clean unobstructed shot. Hana focuses, steadying her breathing. A perfectly still hand. An unblinking eye. Practised so many times, drilled into her in training so it becomes second nature. But now, it isn't a polystyrene figure in front of her.

This is her daughter.

Beneath the tree, Raki sees Hana inching her way

MICHAEL BENNETT

forward. For a moment his eyes meet hers over Addison's shoulder. Both become very still, each knowing as they hold the other's gaze that years earlier they were both here, on this same sacred land, that something was set in motion that day, something that will come to an end today, eighteen years later, but neither knowing yet exactly how that circle will be made complete.

Hana silently wills Raki to move just two inches away from Addison's shoulder, even an inch would be enough. But Raki shifts his weight in the opposite direction. Hidden once more behind Addison. Hana starts to move forward again.

'Tell your mother to stay where she is,' Raki says. Addison fights a new wave of panic. She wants nothing more than to be in Hana's arms. But the grip on her arm is firm and unyielding. '*Tell* her.'

Addison turns and screams at Hana, 'MUM! STOP!'

Hana stops dead. In her earpiece, a flurry of communications. On the downtown side of the harbour, Eagle is lifting into the air. Two of the best snipers in the New Zealand police force are on board. The chopper will look for a position where they can take a clean shot that won't endanger Addison. But Hana knows the helicopter base is a minute away, across the harbour. She has seen the taiaha, pressed against her daughter's torso. Addison might not have a minute.

Hana breathes once, deeply, fighting the hyperventilation. She takes a tiny step forward. Another imperceptible step. Another. Trying to get herself to a better position. Trying to find a clear shot.

'You are one who speaks the truth,' Raki says to Addison. 'Tell me what you believe. Was I wrong?' Addison has never been more afraid in her life, but to live, she believes now, she must give Raki the answer to his question. And although she doesn't know what the consequences will be, she isn't going to lie.

'The people rose up,' she says in te reo, tears falling. 'But they rose up for peace, for love, for the things that are so much bigger than anger, so much stronger than violence. That is the right path, matua. It is the *only* path.'

Raki takes in Addison's words. He thinks of what the kuia said, in front of the flickering candles in Aotea Square, the same message as Addison's. He thinks of his mother coming to him in his dreams, weeping. In her tears, an unspoken message to him. The same message. A stillness comes over him. Certain now of what he must do.

From where she is, less than fifty metres from Addison, Hana can see Eagle coming across the harbour. Still half a minute away. Her eyes shift to the two figures under the tree. She sees Raki's hand. She sees the tell-tale flex of his tendons as they tighten on the taiaha.

Hana starts to run.

Even as Hana is sprinting, screaming at Raki to drop his weapon, he draws the taiaha's cutting edge away from Addison. 'I was right,' he says to her, with admiration and tenderness. 'You will be a great leader one day.' Then he takes the opposite head of the two-headed spear, pressing it into the soft tissue beneath his own ribcage, one of the most vulnerable regions of the human torso, his solar plexus.

He pulls the taiaha into his body, hard.

It lodges deep inside his abdomen.

'I take to myself the burden of your ancestor's sin,' Raki says to Addison, his voice fading, his blood already flowing down the shaft of the taiaha and falling onto the grass beneath his feet. 'I pay the final debt. Mine is the sixth death. The last. The death that ends this.'

Hana reaches the screaming Addison, dragging her away, her gun clean on Raki now, but there is no reason to shoot. For a moment Raki stands tall, his eyes fixed on the branches of the tree from which his ancestor was hanged two centuries earlier. Then his eyes fall, looking towards Hana. But he is no longer seeing anything.

With the last of his strength, Raki throws himself forward.

All his weight falls on the weapon.

The biting tongue, inlaid with sharpened pounamu to make the cutting edge the more deadly, goes clean through his torso and out the other side.

His body subsides, falling among the dead leaves from the pūriri, coming to rest beside the whāriki sack that holds his mother's bones.

In the car park, there is the hubbub that comes in the aftermath of a violent encounter where police weapons have been drawn and serious injury incurred. Eagle hovers above, the snipers' weapons trained on the man lying unmoving on the ground beneath the tree. The armed officers around the vehicles remain on alert, adrenaline still flowing, weapons still primed and at the ready. Addison is with Jaye in the back seat of a police car. Safely out of sight of the tree, but certain to never forget what happened there, she weeps. Jaye stays with his daughter, with no intention of letting her out of his arms.

Later, in the hours that will follow, the kuia will climb the maunga, steadying herself on the arm of her grandson. Others of the tribe will walk at her side. A low wailing will rise from many voices, a keening, echoing out across the slopes. To mourn, to weep; an outpouring of grief and pain. For the terrible things that happened so long ago in this place. The terrible things that happened here eighteen years before. The terrible things that are coming to an end now, in the long shadow of the ancient pūriri.

Kneeling at Raki's side, her gun in her hand, Hana carefully feels for his pulse. From the trajectory with which the biting tongue of the taiaha entered and exited, Hana knows the spearhead and shaft travelled fast and unforgivingly through the area of the highest concentration of vital organs and major arteries, doing cataclysmic damage. Raki's breathing and his heart rate are erratic, but he is hanging on, and Hana can see, beneath his closed eyelids, his eyes move frantically. Seeing what? When the end waits close and ready, do we turn our eyes back, towards the peaks and valleys we've traversed, the pathways we trod, grappling in those last moments to find order, to arrange, to make sense of the journey? Or do we look in the other direction? Towards the faint glow of light far out to sea, beyond the distant rocky headland at the northernmost tip of the motu*, the jumping-off point, our eyes seeking a glimpse of that which awaits, of the passage beyond, and of who will greet us there?

An ambulance climbs the hill at speed, siren screaming. But Hana knows there is nothing any hospital or doctor can do for Raki. She holsters her Glock. She lays her hand on Raki's trembling arm. She speaks gently in te reo. 'Go now,' Hana says. The words are not a command, but said with quiet compassion. 'It is time. You can go.'

The flickering beneath Raki's eyelids slows. A last shallow breath.

He becomes still.

His mother is walking up the long hillside. A strong wind is whipping down the slope into his face as he calls to her: 'Māmā!' His voice fights against the wind as he uses the name he hasn't used for so long. 'Māmā, wait!'

Leaning into the wind, he forces himself on towards her. Closer, closer, now only a few steps behind, he calls again. 'Māmā!' he cries, reaching out, his fingers finding the sleeve of her rainbow-coloured cardigan.

She pauses. Her fingers take his. The wind falls. Just a light breeze now. The sun emerges. Warm on both their faces.

They walk onwards, up the slope, hands clasped.

Together.

---

*   Motu – island

30

WATER

In the pre-dawn light, Hana and Addison are waist deep in the ocean. Water drips from Hana's cupped hands, spilling down onto Addison's face. Cleansing. A ritual of healing and renewal, from mother to daughter.

Addison's fingers circle in the water.

Water. The element that sustains, nourishes, gives life. The water that a millennium ago carried Māori the ten thousand kilometres across the ocean from the ancestral home of Hawaiiki, here to Aotearoa.[*]

Water that purifies. That renews.

A few weeks earlier, after Raki's body was taken from the ambulance, after the autopsy was completed, the kuia

---

[*] Aotearoa – New Zealand (literally 'the land of the long white cloud')

came to the hospital to bless him, to say karakia over his body. For whatever he had done, Poata Raki was still one of their iwi, he was someone who had committed his life to fighting for Māori, for his tribe, who had battled in the courts and in the classrooms and in the protest lines against the pain and damage and trauma wrought by two brutal centuries of colonization, but who at a certain point had become submerged and overwhelmed by that very same pain and damage and trauma, defeated by the grief of seeing his mother die in his arms with all her hope and belief shattered and gone, defeated by his inability to return the stolen land of his tribe, defeated by a legal system that was expert and accomplished in its cold, grim determination to never truly undo the wrongs of the past. And in his torment, he committed to a different fight. An awful path. A path that would cost six lives, the last his own.

On which side lies evil? The broken man? Or the two centuries of trauma and oppression and injustice that broke him?

Hana stayed at his side until the rites were completed and the kuia had said a final prayer over her. Then she went and washed Raki's blood from her hands.

Water.

Afterwards, she returned to the eighth floor of Central Station. She embraced her team, she had a beer or two with them, she listened as Jaye thanked every officer for their dedication, their commitment, the hours they had put in, the risks they had taken and the brilliant work they had done in what would undoubtedly be one of the most

difficult jobs any of them would face in their careers. And
with emotion and humility, he paid respect to the finest
police officer he had ever had the honour of working with.
Detective Senior Sergeant Hana Westerman.

The applause and cheering lasted a full two minutes.

Hana declined to speak.

She finished her drink. She went and opened her computer. She started typing.

A huge spread of takeaways was delivered, more beers
were brought in, bottles of whisky opened. Things were
unravelling a bit, getting loose, as they do in a job where
every day when you pull on your socks and work shoes
you can't put your hand on your heart and swear in the
mirror that you know you'll be coming home that night.

Hana finished what she was writing. She printed the
document. She logged out of her computer. She went into
Jaye's office. She put her letter of resignation on his desk,
where he would find it the next morning.

She took the elevator down from the eighth floor and
she walked out the front door of Central Station for the
last time.

You lean forward.

To the tipping point.

You keep leaning.

And you're gone.

Water, beneath Addison's hand.

'He believed vengeance would end the mamae. But it

only brought more pain.' She looks at the trace of the circling she has made, the shape sitting there in the water for a moment, then gone. 'Nā te ahi ka tahuna he ahi anō. Violence only brings more violence,' she says. 'Pain brings more pain. Māori must continue to fight. We were born brown and screaming. We must stand together and fight. Until the scars of two hundred years are truly healed. Until things truly change. Not by making new wounds. Not by blood. We will fight with words. With love. With light. And we will win.'

Water. As the sun rises, water drains from Hana's hands, over Addison's face. Then Addison cups her hands in the water and cleanses Hana's face.

Side by side, daughter and mother watch the sun edge its way slowly, slowly above the distant horizon.

Nothing more is said.

Nothing more needs to be said.

Addendum

HANA WESTERMAN'S TĀMAKI MAKAURAU

Better the Blood is set in Tāmaki Makaurau (Auckland), Aotearoa (New Zealand), today. Auckland is a city of just over 1.5 million people, the population of Budapest or Philadelphia, but spread over a massive geographical area of almost the same land footprint as Los Angeles. It is consistently ranked as one of the world's top ten best cities to live in, a place of natural beauty, great cafés, restaurants and theatres, thriving filmmaking, arts and music communities, the home stadium of the greatest rugby team ever known. Auckland is ringed by fifty beautiful volcanic peaks, perched between two harbours full of idyllic islands. A genuinely multicultural city in the south of the Pacific Ocean, with over thirty different languages regularly spoken.

But beneath the Tourism New Zealand billboards, beyond the Instagram-ready gulf views, blood is soaked deep into the volcanic soil of this place, from a recent past that is far less idyllic. Aotearoa/New Zealand is a paradise with an awful and bloody colonial history. In the nineteenth century, an unstoppable flood of British settlers sailed to the farthest point of the globe, a place to which they had no legitimate claim, backed by the might of the greatest military force on the planet, the British Army.

One of my daughters is a poet and she writes:

> *When my cousins visit from England*
> *I show them how the pavements of Auckland*
> *streets look red when you remember*
> *what's buried beneath them*
> *I remind them how the bones were bleached*
> *by gunpowder*
> *this is New Zealand and it's dead.*

The wounds of colonization remain raw and unhealed. The past is not the past and we cannot let it be.

The author respectfully acknowledges the iwi of Ngā Mana Whenua o Tāmaki Makaurau, the tribes of Auckland – Te Rūnanga o Ngāti Whātua, Ngāi Tai ki Tāmaki, Ngāti Maru, Ngāti Pāoa, Ngāti Tamaoho, Ngāti Tamaterā, Ngāti Te Ata, Ngāti Whanaunga, Ngāti Whātua o Kaipara, Ngāti Whātua Ōrākei, Te

Ākitai Waiohua, Te Kawerau ā Maki, Te Patukirikiri. The iwi of this book, Te Tini-o-Tai, and their ancestral mountain, Maunga Whakairoiro, are entirely invented, and while the historic injustices and the later peaceful protest movements seeking restoration of traditional lands depicted in the book are recognizable to many iwi in Tāmaki Makaurau and across the country, the events and characters portrayed in the narrative are fictional and are not intended to portray actual tribes, their lands or their histories.

ACKNOWLEDGEMENTS

Writing is a solitary occupation. For the most part that is self-evident, there's room for just ten fingers on a laptop, but I have been privileged to have had many generous people at the margins of my keyboard.

The characters and narrative of *Better the Blood* were developed with Jane Holland. My foundation stone, solid ground in stormy seas – partners in life, partners in love, now partners in crime. X.

Better the Blood explores the unhealed brutalities for Māori of the colonial experience, challenging cultural terrain, and I humbly acknowledge the safe hands of the pou matua of this book, Ngamaru Raerino (Ngāti Awa, Ngāti Rangiwewehi), for his profound knowledge and guidance in the realms of te ao Māori, te reo Māori and tikanga. I am eternally grateful to Tim Worrall (Ngāi Tūhoe) not only for his deep and insightful cultural guidance on the manuscript, but also as a brilliant writer who unselfishly and with love and generosity lifts up his fellow creators.

Tim also created the origin story of the fictional iwi (tribe) at the heart of this novel. Ngamaru and Tim – ngā mihi nui, ngā mihi aroha ki a kōrua.

I have never had more gratitude for Guinness than for the pints I shared with my agent Craig Sisterson in a London pub a couple of years back, when I pitched him the idea for the scary novel I was thinking about writing. Craig has played a huge role in my career as an author, and he found a home for this book with one of the great publishing houses, Simon & Schuster.

My editor Katherine Armstrong's belief in the manuscript from the moment she read it was both humbling and affirming. Her laser instincts, insights, guidance and probing, unflinching challenges gave the book wings.

I give aroha and thanks to many friends who gave advice or suggestions or support or love or big dollops of each – Alan Sharp, Cian Elyse White, Tajim Mohammed-Kapa, Detective Constable Turi McLeod-Bennett, Jacquelin Perske, Carthew Neal, Taika Waititi, Phoebe Eclair-Powell, Senior Constable Debra Brewer, Dr Tiopira McDowell, Ainsley Gardiner MNZM, Jessica (Coco Solid) Hansell, Morgan Waru, Nacoya Anderson, Miriama McDowell, Hemi Kelly, Amie Mills, Benedict Reid, Nic Finlayson, Matthew Saville, Keely Meechan, Tim McKinnel.

Ngā mihi to Sian Wilson for her haunting cover design, and to Māhina Bennett for the original Māori illustration used on the cover and throughout the book. Ngā mihi to project editor Louise Davies and copy editor Jane Selley for an incredibly enjoyable and fruitful process. Ngā mihi to Matariki Bennett for creating Addison's rap, 'Brown and Screaming', and for the extract from her poem 'Guns and Bad Stuff'. And a huge shout out to the incredible Simon & Schuster rights team.

The writing of this book was made possible by the generous support of Creative New Zealand, the Arts Council of New Zealand Toi Aotearoa. In particular, ngā mihi to Simonne Likio and to Richard Knowles.

My dad left me with a lifelong passion for fighting the important fights. My mum gave me an awe for the beauty and the power of words. Without their precious gifts, I would never have become a writer.

ABOUT THE AUTHOR

Michael Bennett (Ngāti Pikiao, Ngāti Whakaue) is an award-winning screenwriter, director and author. His first book, a non-fiction novel telling the true story of New Zealand's worst miscarriage of justice, *In Dark Places*, won Best Non- Fiction Book at the 2017 Ngaio Marsh Awards. Michael's second book, *Helen and the Go-Go Ninjas* is a time-travel graphic novel co-authored with Ant Sang.

Michael's short films and feature films have won awards internationally, and have screened at numerous international festivals including Cannes, Toronto, Berlin, Locarno, New York, London, and Melbourne. Michael is the 2020 recipient of the Te Aupounamu Māori Screen Excellence Award, in recognition of members of the Māori filmmaking community who have made high level contributions to screen storytelling.

He lives in Auckland, Aotearoa (New Zealand) with his partner Jane, and children Tīhema, Māhina and Matariki.